Rich Mr. Fixx

Rich Mr. Fixx
#1 Crystal Clear

Mystical Adventure Superhero Series

Bray Zephens

Fresh Ink Group
Guntersville

Rich Mr. Fixx
#1 Crystal Clear

Fresh Ink Group
An Imprint of:
The Fresh Ink Group, LLC
23 Lake Breeze Dr.
Guntersville, AL 35976
Email: info@FreshInkGroup.com
FreshInkGroup.com

Edition 1.0 2003
Edition 2.0 2026

Cover design by Stephen Geez / FIG
Book design by Amit Dey / FIG
Associate publisher Beem Weeks / FIG

Cataloging-in-Publication Recommendations:
FIC031070 FICTION / Thrillers / Supernatural
FIC063000 FICTION / Superheroes
FIC030000 FICTION / Thrillers / Suspense

ISBN-13: 978-1-958922-71-2 Papercover
ISBN-13: 978-1-958922-72-9 Hardcover
ISBN-13: 978-1-958922-73-6 Ebooks

For my grandson

Zane Gannon Wright,

Award-winning

Percussionist/
Music Prodigy

& extraordinary young man

ABOUT THE *RICH MR. FIXX* SERIES

W HEN I CREATED THESE characters in the early 1990s, I was inspired by pulp serials and novels such as Doc Savage dating back to the 1930s. Any similarities to characters from DC or Marvel's constantly expanding multiverses are purely coincidental. Shawn D'Fixx and his mystical adventures are my tribute to the rich tradition of tales about people transcending normal human limitations in their quest to help others and make the world a better place.

Revisiting these stories reminds me of the indelible role played by my friend and first managing director of The Fresh Ink Group, the late Ann Estelle Stewart of Roanoke, Texas. I will always think of her as my own real-life superhero.

CHAPTER 1

A WHIFF PERMEATED THE GENTLE Costa Rica breeze, a fragrance redolent of the sweetest nectar. Wally and Chuck caught the scent, recognizing the exquisite allure of nature's most succulent blossoms, the objects of manly men's deepest desires, the fruits of a quest that brought them all the way to this tropical paradise . . .

Love pockets—the hot-babe variety.

"They're out there waiting for us," Wally announced from the bathroom. "I can smell 'em."

"I know all you can think about right now is diving into some sweet tail," Chuck admonished, studying his outfit in the dresser mirror, "but we need to be extra careful."

"I'm taking precautions." Wally dabbed at several bleeders, pimples he'd nicked while shaving his beefy jowls.

"I don't mean just hermetically sealing your weenie," Chuck called back.

Wally lumbered out in time to catch his lanky business partner adjusting the fabric over his crotch, as if the right pair of pants could make a gangly colt hang like a stallion. "What are you talking about?" He counted out sheaves of cash to secrete here and there around his body.

"Thieves, kidnappers, hot-headed boyfriends—"

Wally snorted. "You worry too much," he scoffed, now stuffing his passport, visitor's papers, and several credit cards into a cheap wallet, packing the rest of his stash in a satchel for the resort manager to lock in the safe. Wally Flaunt-yer-wad knew Fraidy Chuck was right, and he'd planned ahead this time. "I'm carryin' only so much cash, and these cards has got limits of just two-grand."

Chuck revved up his electric razor, shaving again for the umpteenth time, apparently determined to take every last layer of skin off a chin that couldn't work up a beard to save its life. "How did you get such a low limit? Banks always beg me to accept their diamond-club platinum cards with all the bells and whistles."

Wally stood behind Chuck, watching himself in the mirror as he rubbed oil into his hair, running a comb through the bushy curls. "They're secured, so can't nobody up the limit without my say-so." Wally sniffed his pits, then decided no amount of deodorant would help once he stepped into that sweltering rainforest humidity.

"Then after we pay for the crystals, I'll leave mine in the safe. Here," he said, leaning too close, "do I need more aftershave?"

"Go sniff your own ass." Wally belched, then checked his watch, pronouncing, "She's expecting us now."

They studied themselves in the mirror. Both thirty-four years old, Wally needed to drop a hundred pounds, and Chuck could stand to pick up thirty or forty. Wally's bad complexion still cultivated bumper crops of acne as surely as Chuck's retreating hairline prepared for imminent surrender. Wealthy from the software house they founded together, both had frittered away fortunes buying their way out of failed marriages. They'd grown tired of trying to seduce heifers too dumb to boot up a screen-saver but smart enough to memorize the community-property laws in all fifty states—and most of the U.S. territories.

Even hookers had gotten too risky, snapping cellphone pics and keeping client histories on flash drives in case some prosecutor offers to cut a deal.

"We didn't have to come all the way to Costa Rica," Chuck said, adding more aftershave anyway, "—not just to find some tail."

"Look, it worked for Farkus, so maybe there really is a way to unlock the secret of making babes come after *us* for a change. Hell, we can afford to try it out, so why not?"

Chuck grinned licentiously, a gesture seconded by Wally.

They hurried down the plank walkway, sand crabs skittering this way and that. Lush trees and flowering shrubs swayed gently in the Caribbean breeze, the setting sun refracting in hues of purple and orange through wisps of cloud passing over the sprawling resort.

"*Please,* I must caution you," the manager, a Costa Rican woman, explained, "stay near the resorts of this cove. South to Limón is not as safe for the tourist. Our shuttle takes you." She gestured to the gleaming van out front as she walked them to a private office. "You call anytime, and shuttle man comes to bring you back."

Closing the door, she offered chairs and rum punch, then slid documents across the table. "For each of you, your credit account is charged ten-thousand U.S. dollar fee for tonight, plus fifty-thousand holder in case you do not return the crystals. Please sign here saying you had orientation this morning, and here for credit card."

"This map of the resorts," Chuck started, fishing the photocopy from his pocket. "These are *all* safe?"

"Oh yes, this cove is safe for tourists if you do not go with local girls." She removed a jewel-encrusted, hand-carved case and opened it reverently. "With these crystals, *many* women cannot resist you, so choose the ladies you like. Tourists from America are the best. Local girls may know wearing the crystal means you have money, and they will take you where some men can rob you. Tourists, they have their own money, and just want to have fun."

"And they're probably cleaner, too," Chuck mumbled.

"Like *you'll* be wearing less than three layers of latex," Wally snorted.

At a gesture from their host, each man removed his watch, then stared in fascination as she applied a fixative and tweezed tiny shards of crystal to the backs, careful not to touch them with her hands.

"This helps the crystals channel power to your bodies," she explained, dabbing a sparkling white paste to their wrists. "Do not remove your watches or the power may be broken," she warned.

Both men put them on . . . *and felt it!*

Almost immediately, Wally could sense the power welling up inside, the heat of passion, that heart-pounding frenzy of unabashed sexual prowess, his aphrodisiac pheromones siren-calling the evening's tail. Chuck nearly fell out of his chair.

The woman began breathing hard, gazing longingly at her customers, forcing herself to snap the reverie by whispering with hot breath, "Please, this is not easy for me if you stay longer. Remember, be here to return the crystals by nine, and we will talk about more and better."

All hands and gentle caresses, she let them out, signaling the driver to take these magnificent men any place they preferred to unleash their sexual maelstrom on the luckiest of unwary souls.

It would be The Pink Parrot, an open-air bar with a steel-drum band and nightly drink specials, just up the road.

Wally strutted in, ready to boff every babe in the room, while Chuck paused at the entranceway, his eyes roving, sizing up prospects a bit more selectively. Maybe Chuck had the right idea; some looked too old, too fat, too ugly, not alone—why settle when you have *this* kind of advantage?

Never had Wally felt more confident, the power cascading over him in waves, the eyes of so many women watching their every move. They selected seats near the bar.

Almost immediately, two *phenomenal* young ladies entered and surveyed the room. Gawd, they couldn't be much older than college-age, white girls, probably from the states, with innocent eyes and pouty nipples, tight jeans like topographical maps of paradise.

Wally caught a whiff. Chucky held his breath.

"Dibs on the blonde," Wally whispered, selective after all.

"Man, they're puckered up—and I don't mean their mouths."

The babes stood there transfixed, staring unabashedly at the two sexiest programmer dweebs anywhere in the Caribbean.

Wally stood, gallantly offering a chair, Chuck awkwardly following suit.

It turns out the ladies had just graduated from college. Their friends all went to Europe—been there, done that. They wanted to try someplace exotic, heard Costa Rica had it all. They could hardly talk for the ripples of passion obviously washing over them.

Wally booted up the old hard-drive, Chuck blatantly ready to log on.

The babes each had a very nice room down the beach, and they both liked the idea of a little privacy with the guys. The brunette had it for Chuck, so off they went. Wally followed the blonde and found himself flopped on a king-size bed while she poured wine.

"Say, Lilly, you ain't got no boyfriend back in Texas?"

"It's *Lyla*," she corrected, sitting beside him with two goblets. "Lyla DeCivvio. Um, actually yes. I'm engaged, but I quit wearing the ring because I'm gonna break it off." She started twiddling the coarse brown chest-curls peeking out the front of his collar.

He downed the rest of his drink in one gulp.

"Actually, I've never—" She looked down, embarrassed, then up to search his face, her deep hazel eyes glistening. "I was saving myself, you know—I'd never felt it was right . . ." She was breathing hard. "I've never felt like this before."

"That's all right, sweetie. I can teach you. I'll be *real* gentle-like," he vowed, his hand groping under her stretch-top until its bounty spilled forth.

He kissed and fondled and slobbered and prodded until he could hold it no more. She yielded to his every desire, swept away by her passions, writhing under the raw macho power of the man called Wally.

By the second go-round, she cried out that she loved him. He lost his inhibitions enough to start making those grunting, braying sounds his ex-wife hated. He even did that move where he wiggles his fat butt back and forth in a frenzy. She loved it!—joining in until both collapsed, spent and fulfilled.

Wally prided himself on being able to go all night—and he could, five minutes at a time.

He wound up, like always, lying on his back, snoring like a banshee, a protective hand holding his crotch even in sleep.

Lyla cuddled close, exhausted, her dreams of a real man finally fulfilled.

A HUGE SWEATY BUTT smiled at Lyla when Wally finally rolled over onto his side.

She got up quietly, studied him a moment, then eased into the bathroom and scrubbed herself thoroughly. She peeked out to check on him. Good, snoozing like a dog. She went to the bar and retrieved a tiny vial from behind a canister, hiding it in her purse.

Creeping back to the bed, she fished under the mattress until she found the broken capsule of fake blood that had been her virginity. She buried it in the trash, checked the pockets of his pants on the floor, then crawled back in beside him.

She carefully reached over and tilted his watch, peering underneath to make sure he'd not lost his crystal, then pulled the sheet over his fat ass so she wouldn't have to look at it.

Might as well try to get some sleep before he awoke.

Sure bet, old Wonder Wally would be wantin' one more.

AFTER SEVERAL WRONG turns, Shawn D'Fixx eventually found the employee lunchroom at the back of the lab complex, then set about preparing to feed his newest pet.

"Shawn! Quit playin' with your lizard, and come watch this! He's shooting lasers in it and everything!"

"I'll be there in a minute. Hey, Marcie, does his color look okay to you?"

She snorted and flounced over for a cursory inspection of the seventeen-inch iguana perched unconcernedly on the commissary countertop. "I don't know," she said, shrugging. "He looks fine to me." She cast Shawn a playful look of mock derision, then ran fingers through her flowing orange-red tresses and sighed before suddenly smiling and reaching out to muss the hair he'd just combed. Beating a hasty retreat, she hurried off to watch the tech perform more tests.

"You feel all right, Scallywag?" he asked, leaning closer to the lizard, one hand absently rubbing his own hair.

Ding! Lunchtime!

Shawn carefully removed a tub of macaroni and cheese from the microwave, then flipped up the ring and tried to peel back the lid. He wound up getting sauce all over his sleeve. He tried to wipe it off with napkins, smearing it and making it worse. He ran water on the mess, but accidentally soaked a good portion of his crew shirt.

At least it wasn't permanently stained.

The food still too hot, he went to the restroom and stood in front of the hand-dryer until his shirt quit clinging. He studied himself in the mirror and tried to comb his unruly brown hair, noticing a new cowlick off to the side. He'd swear that thing moved every day—and sometimes multiplied at night. Time for a cut, he decided, yet another in his quest for a style that still looks good after the next wash. He squared his shoulders, drew his gaunt frame up authorita-tively, decided he looked like a wet goof, and headed out. He stepped into the hallway in time to be run over by ninety pounds of unbridled enthusiasm with freckles and red hair.

"Shawn! University just called and said they're *millions* of years old—maybe even *sixty-five* million, but it'll take weeks for some kinda carbon test. Are you gonna come look at this laser?"

"Um, in a minute. I left—" He gestured toward the commissary. "You think they'll mind if I use some of those coffee-stir deals to—?"

"Shawn, you *own* this company."

"Oh."

Off she went, shaking her head.

He found his iguana waiting patiently. Using a plastic coffee-stir from the condiment counter, he fished out a cheesy macaroni elbow, examined it closely, then gingerly touched it with his tongue. Good, not too hot.

Like a fierce pirate, he growled, "Here ya go, you Scallywag," proffer-ing the tasty treat.

The iguana eyed it with delight. Well, he *eyed* it anyway; then he snatched it with his mouth, chomped several times, and swallowed.

Shawn guffawed, then peered around to make sure nobody could hear. He fed another piece, then another, then ate one himself and fed several more. There they sat, a twenty-some-year-old gazillionaire and his lizard, snarfing mac like it was manna from the gods.

"Shawn! He's doing spectro-analysis. This is *so* cool!"

Marcie waited impatiently in the doorway. She wouldn't leave until he followed, so he ate the last pieces, then carefully rinsed the tub and coffee-stir before depositing them in the trash. Scallywag arrayed across his shoulders, he trotted dutifully down the hall.

"This is remarkable," the tech breathed, absorbed in reading several scopes and a frenzy of colored lines emerging from a plotter. "It's amethyst, sort of, but it's shot through with trace gasses and metals. Look, see here?" He pointed at a spike in the line across one screen. "Nickel. *Nickel!*"

Marcie looked blank, Shawn feigning interest.

"That's what suggested meteorite. How an impact translates into crystalline structures, I can't explain. You'd need a geoscientist."

"Wow," Marcie breathed, rapt.

"If you'll document all this for us," Shawn started, "we'll be on our way."

The tech hesitated. "This analysis was hastily authorized—I'm not even sure by whom—but there may be some cost to docu—"

"Oh, don't worry about that," Marcie assured him. "We're doing this for Foster."

"*Foster B. Garbus?*"

"Yeah. Use this as a chance to impress him with your thoroughness. In fact, have all your findings shipped to him ASAP—" She made a card appear, handing it over. "Mark it *per McNair.*" Marcie McNaught had given him one of her favorite aliases.

"Yes. *Yes!* I'll get on this *right* away. Um, you know, I have a lot of ideas how we could—"

Shawn interrupted, "And he *likes* it when members of the team contribute—but he's a busy man, so you need to put it all down clearly on *one* page. Include it when you ship your findings."

"Send that crystal along with the info," Marcie instructed.

The tech fidgeted excitedly at the mention of Mr. Garbus, at suddenly learning he had direct access to the man who could open new doors to opportunity. Everybody knew of Foster B, wealthy young tycoon with fingers in everything on multiple continents. Truth be told, Foster *was* wealthy, and he did invest far and wide, but his greatest role was playing front man for Shawn D'Fixx's vast holdings in an empire that rivaled anybody's anywhere.

"Um, what was that about the laser?" Shawn wondered, impressed by this room full of fancy equipment. Maybe there'd be a good light show or something. What was this place for, anyway? He'd have to ask Foster why he owned this sprawling complex of research facilities.

The tech led them to another room where he carefully clamped the small, purple-tinged crystal into a device, then trained a pinpoint beam of light on it. He kept adjusting the angle until the light broke into refractions splayed around the room. Then he went to the laser and began making adjustments. The light sharpened, narrowed, and began shifting through a spectrum of colors until it burned bright white.

All at once, the hair on Shawn's neck stood up. Scallywag quickly climbed over his shoulder and down his collar, hiding against his master's belly where shirt tucked into pants.

The refractions from the crystal created a spectacular display, every color of the rainbow.   Marcie gaped, the tech clearly amazed. Shawn looked around awkwardly, trying to fathom why they were staring at him. He examined his outstretched arm, but could detect nothing unusual.

"You see it?" Marcie breathed.

The tech nodded. "It's like—like he's bending the light around him or something. I've never—"

"Don't you *see* it, Shawn?"

"See what?" He squirmed uncomfortably. This wasn't fun.

"It's your aura—your rainbow aura. It's, well, it's *dancing!*"

"I don't see any aura," the tech added, "but the light is doing something *really* odd."

Shawn couldn't hide how much this bothered him.

"Turn it off," Marcie instructed. "Now."

The tech complied, still puzzled. "What—?"

"Just get those reports sent right away," she interrupted, a protective hand hooked in the crook of Shawn's arm. She hustled her friend and his lizard out before the tech could discuss it any further.

Neither said anything until they climbed into the van. Shawn carefully put his iguana in the back where it had water, heating pad, and a newspaper potty.

"Come on, Marcie, I play *Rich Mr. Fixx* and you pretend I have mystical powers—that's our schtick—but we don't make fun of each other in front of strangers." He tried not to look annoyed, but it wasn't working. Sometimes he wished he'd never told her about his big brother's deathbed vision that Shawn would be the one to someday "harness the power of the mystic rainbow and hold back the waters," to ascend to his rightful place as the world's "Mr. Fixx," a prophecy long whispered from one generation of D'Fixxes to the next. He didn't expect her to be the one person who believed it true, or that she would devote herself to helping him fulfill this rather ridiculous notion of destiny.

She started the engine and picked up the signal-encrypted cellphone, then paused. "Shawn, you know I'm as big a tease as the next girl, but I swear you made the colors dance."

"Even if you do see something others can't, it doesn't mean I'm somehow *different*. Maybe you're just tuned into me because we're such good friends."

"But I saw your mystical rainbow even before I got to know you."

Shawn snorted and grinned. "Whatever burns your incense, Marcie."

"Sure, call me your spaced-out new-age spiritual companion traveler of the ages, but these crystals are the first thing I've ever seen affect it." She tapped the phone to call Kinte.

"Whatever . . ." Shawn rolled his eyes.

"I think I might finally have discovered a way to unlock your powers," she pronounced, "and these *crystals* are the key."

"I TOLD HER TO MEET US at The Gaseous Giant here in Houston," Marcie reported, "because it's—you know."

"I appreciate your forethought, Ms. McNaught," Kinte responded, seated at his console in the main control center of the Monterey Compound, speakerphone to cellular. At more than six-and-a-half feet and fifty-some years old, the still *very*-trim Jamaican dwarfed the equipment before him. His boxing days at Cambridge may be distant past, but don't let the gray hair fool you.

"She's bein' a good girl for you, old man," Foster B. Garbus jibed. He sat at a nearby console scanning a stream of reports. The same age as his old boarding-school roomie, Shawn, Foster looked movie-star handsome with chiseled features, wavy blondish hair just long enough to bother bankers back east, and an underwear-model bod that kept him on all the celebrity-mag "most" lists and more than a few private lists, too.

Both had their own obscenely elaborate offices elsewhere in the complex overlooking cliffs and crashing waves on the Pacific, but Kinte Bilal tended to make foundation contacts here for quicker access to aides and assistants, preferring real faces over impersonal screens. Foster just liked hanging around Kinte, and he wanted to be on hand when Marcie and Shawn checked in.

"Is that you, Foster?" Marcie called. "Hey, Shawn wants to know why he owns the research complex here—and what it's used for."

"Tell him it is ostensibly for developing petroleum-reclamation technology, but that's just a small part. It and a dozen others he owns around the country are secretly studying spectral energy-transfer methodologies—staying ahead of the competition, as it were."

"Like solar energy?"

"Yeah, ways to convert and store the power of light."

Kinte listened patiently, the big Jamaican stroking his salt-n-pepper goatee.

"Anyway, Kinte, we're gonna be there about eight. I'd appreciate it if you'd arrange easy access for Joelle Bulagrét. I told her just give her name."

"Yes, that was wise," Kinte praised. "I understand long lines form outside that establishment."

"Come on, Kinte," Foster teased, "you just like having an identifiable target to plan your little security circus around."

Ignoring the jibe, Kinte asked, "Shall I have the jet pick you up after your meeting?"

"Shawn! Quit playin' with your lizard!" She'd pulled the phone from her mouth, but could still be heard over the speaker.

Foster quipped, "I used to have to tell him that *all* the time back at school."

"You wanna stay here tonight or go home?" she was asking. Then into the phone, "He's worrying something might not be right about his lizard."

"Just like boarding school." Foster chuckled, but he hushed when Kinte turned and gave him that look.

Affectionately called "The Arranger" by Shawn, the big man was trying to get his charges to come home, and Foster wasn't helping. "I can arrange to have a veterinary reptologist here—" he started.

"Ain't nothin' wrong with his critter," she interrupted. "We're gonna stay here, maybe stick around The Gaseous Giant later on, shake our fannies a little. We'll go straight to the Galveston house for the night and come home tomorrow."

"I will send the jet tonight and have a car there in the morning."

"We'll drive ourselves to the airport. Just have the van taken back to the house after we board."

"As you wish, Ms. McNaught."

"Do us good-good service and there'll be a fiver in it for ya," she joked. Not that he ever laughed at the good-natured taunting—or that he had less than a hundred-million of his own fivers, thank you very much. Even with a staff of hundreds, he still took it upon himself to make arrangements for Shawn, Marcie, or Foster whenever they traveled.

Or when they stayed at home.

He'd never forgiven himself for letting Shawn's big brother die of a rare spinal cancer at barely sixteen, not that every possible treatment hadn't been tried. Adopting Jeremy and Shawn, his dead partner's young sons, was the least he could do for his best friend, but then losing one of them was almost more than he could bear. He became obsessively determined to protect little Shawn and the boy's childhood friend, Foster, eventually adding college-pal Marcie to the mix, all three of whom he regarded with great affection, whether he ever actually said it or not.

"I will pay you ten," Kinte countered, "if you convince him to come home tonight."

"Not a chance, old man." She laughed. She always appreciated his droll sense of humor so often lost on Shawn.

Foster cut in, "Hey Marcie—*I'll* pay a hundred for verifiable proof you got him to dance at the club."

"Make it a thou and I'll get him to dance with his lizard."

"If you mean the iguana, you're on!"

Kinte shot that look at Foster again. "Surely, Mr. D'Fixx will not take his reptile to your meeting—"

"Can't rightly say, Mr. Arranger, but you know Shawn."

"Hey, Marcie, who're you meeting?" Foster had shifted into business mode. "Is it that woman who contacted you about magic rocks to sell in your Herbs & Oils stores?"

"They're *crystals*—gemstones formed sixty-five million years ago when the big meteorite hit, the one they think filled the atmosphere with debris and cooled the planet enough to kill all the big dinosaurs."

"Where's she get 'em?"

"She hasn't said. She claims they channel psychic energy, depending on the psi of the holder."

"Shiny glass for space-heads, huh?" Foster chuckled.

"Actually, Foster B—*no*." Marcie sounded indignant. "The lab confirmed they really are millions of years old, and filled with gasses and metals and stuff consistent with a meteorite crash." She explained what happened with the laser and Shawn's aura. Foster looked interested, but showed no reaction to her aura assertions.

"I would be curious," Kinte said, "to learn more about the background of your crystal vendor.

Foster agreed. "If these are something authentic—oh, not to say they channel power—but if they're real meteorite crystals, something you believe in and think might further brand and boost sales at your stores, then we should go after the source."

"I wouldn't sell them if I didn't believe in 'em, Foster—you know that."

"That's why we need control. You can't afford to spend a lot promoting them, then come up short or inconsistent in your supply—or unable to manage the cost."

"I sure don't wanna create the demand only to have competitors better stocked."

"You don't know *anything* I can run down yet? Shipping address, company name? Delivery methods? Anything?"

"Nothing. She left the samples and a note here at my Houston store, then called to set up tonight's meeting while I was picking them up. She insisted it be an international bank draft for cash in U.S. funds."

Foster pondered a moment. "It's a blind trail then. She doesn't want to be found out or infiltrated or taken over. Hmmm . . . Well, get what you can, and I'll take it from there. I'll have your payment waiting at the club."

Having waited patiently, Kinte admonished, "Please, you and Mr. D'Fixx, be cautious tonight—and check in with me immediately afterward."

"Don't I always, ol' man?"

"You are better about it than Mr. D'Fixx, yes."

The call terminated, Kinte set about finalizing security arrangements at The Gaseous Giant.

"Kinte," Foster suggested, "why don't you have that woman followed when she leaves the club? I got a feeling Shawn and Marcie won't learn anything I can use."

"It has already been arranged."

Foster smiled. "Of course it has—and somebody else following the follower, too. I can set up their meeting at The Giant if you still have a lot of Mr. Fixx foundations to contact," he offered.

"Thank you, no—I have but three remaining. They can wait for more pressing matters—" Kinte sighed. "Like arranging VIP admittance to a dance club for a *lizard*."

HOOKER, WHORE, SLUT, PROSTITUTE . . . more than a career, it defined her very identity. Chaleeshia Poeky had been working the streets of Houston five years now, since she was fourteen years old. The beautiful young African-American had nice clothes, a place to live, and the protection of her not-too-brutal "manager." She paid a woman in the barrio to look after her two-year-old son while she hustled, saving every penny in desperate hope of someday escaping the streets. Resisting pressure to do drugs, eluding the common diseases, she wanted a better life for her boy so much that she risked her manager's retribution and joined FuturePlan, a new community outreach center opened by some obscure foundation.

She'd learned about it right after her older sister was found brutally murdered, throat cut, body dumped in Miller Park late one night. After police questioned Chaleeshia, a friendly yet mysterious white woman had shown up claiming to be a friend of her sister's, sad but determined to help her avoid the same fate. She'd driven her to FuturePlan that same day and promised to keep track of her progress.

But now Chaleeshia wanted to quit the program and reach for the stars. Walking from her rental flat near Highway 10 in the barrio, she crossed under the freeway before Houston Zoo and the park so she wouldn't have to pass where her sister—

She shook the image from her mind, wondering if she'd ever understand what happened, what those last minutes had been like, who could have done such a thing.

She headed north on Main Street, still a dozen or so blocks from her destination. Waiting to cross intersections, she would ignore cars slowing to assess her charms, seedy men propositioning her services. The world had taught her detachment—just get the job done and move on, use her cut to pay rent, buy food and clothes for her son . . .

There, two blocks behind Main Street, stood FuturePlan, a converted bankrupt supermarket. Miss Vivian had given her a chance there, the only place in Houston she felt safe.

"Chaleeshia!" the director, Mr. Suggly, greeted her. "You're not scheduled today—what brings you here?" A plump, gray-haired man with lots of wrinkles, he supervised the program for getting young prostitute mothers off the streets and trained for good jobs.

"I'll be dropping out from the program," she explained, twisting her keys nervously. "I just wanted to come tell Miss Vivian myself. I got a good chance for something better, and I don't want her thinkin' I'm goin' back on the streets."

He studied her for a moment. "What is this new opportunity?" he asked suspiciously.

"I can't say," she cautioned. "If I do, I won't be able to get in."

"How did you learn about this?" he prodded.

She hardened her resolve and shook her head. "Please don't ask."

"Isn't there *anything* you'll tell me about it? How about telling Miss Vivian? What are you going to say to her?"

"Please, I don't have much time. I'm just going to say this is best for me, but that I can't say no more."

Leading her toward the upstairs-rear office of the building they shared with several other programs and a job-training center, he whispered one last time, "You know you can trust me. If you want to say anything about it, let me know in private, and it'll be just between us."

She shook her head, determination steeled in her face. "I can't tell nobody."

"Well," he allowed, "I trust your judgment. Good luck, Chaleeshia."

VIVIAN PODRASSKY checked her watch, then glanced toward the equipment console behind her desk, anticipating another contact from Mr. Bilal. She studied her reflection in the glass of a framed recruitment poster. A gaunt woman in her forties, she wore comfortable but dowdy-looking clothes. She wished she'd gotten around to shopping for something nicer, but her responsibilities as Region 84 coordinator always kept her at the office too late, or too tired to go out. She straightened some loose strands of wispy, yellow-white hair, then hurried to her top desk drawer for a quick bite of tuna fish dusted with sugar before the call, part of her ritual to control the effects of hypoglycemia.

Mr. Suggly entered with Chaleeshia Poeky, the young woman fidgeting nervously. Suggly's expression suggested disappointment.

"Please sit, Chaleeshia," she urged.

"I really can't stay," she apologized. "I just wanted to tell you myself why I have to leave the program."

"Oh no!"

"But it's good. I have a chance for a new career, except I have to move away from Houston. I swear it's legal and all, but I can't say no more about it."

Vivian tried to hide her frustration. She understood better than anyone how attrition of half or more from these kinds of outreach efforts is common, but she'd developed a good sense for judging who might persist and succeed, and she hadn't expected to lose Chaleeshia. "Other trainees have left for what sounds like the same opportunity. If it's honorable and safe, I applaud your initiative, but I don't understand why it has to be kept secret from me. Maybe I could screen applicants, refer good candidates— I mean, I'm here to help."

"Please, Miss Vivian. She don't want lots of girls trying to get in, so I promised, and if I break my word, I'll get cut out. I just come to thank you for all you done, and to promise I'll do good."

Noting Chaleeshia had mentioned a "her," Vivian wanted to keep her talking and see if more would slip. "Where did you meet her?"

Chaleeshia shook her head, fidgeting again.

"Well," Vivian suggested, "maybe you could ask her to contact me, just to see how I might assist."

The director nodded at Chaleeshia, encouraging her to consider that option.

"Well, okay," the young woman allowed. "I got to go now, but I promise I'll come back someday, and you'll be proud of me." With that, she fled the room and hurried down the stairs.

"She'll be okay," the director assured Podrassky, turning to leave.

She sighed, then closed the door and started toward her desk just as a *beep* from the console signaled an incoming communiqué. She quickly seated herself, straightened her hair, and activated the equipment. "Good afternoon, Mr. Bilal!" she greeted, pleased to see the man in charge of the entire organization was still taking a personal interest in her program. "How are you?"

"I am well. I trust you are the same?" They could see each other on flat view-screens, microwave relayed and satellite transmitted, encoded and decoded for security. The big Jamaican looked handsome as usual.

"Well, I'm a bit befuddled—but let's cover your agenda; then I'll explain, if you're interested."

"I have reviewed your reports and approved all of your applications for the week. I continue to be impressed by how much you accomplish, by your effectiveness with local resources, and by your savvy about the target population."

Vivian Podrassky blushed. A spinster who'd long since decided she would never attract a man worthy of her passion for serving others, one accepting of her idiosyncrasies, she was a lonely woman surrounded by people she cared for, feeling so often like nobody would truly love her. Mr. Bilal shared her commitment, a kindred soul who understood and appreciated her like no other. She'd thought about him so many nights . . .

"Please explain why you are befuddled," he prodded.

"Just a few minutes ago, we lost another one—that's number three."

"To this enigmatic opportunity offered to local ladies of the evening?" For some reason, he always seemed loath to use the words "prostitute" or "sex worker."

"Yes. Chaleeshia Poeky, younger sister of the, um, the one who was found murdered a few months ago."

"Also a mother?"

"All three each had a very young child."

"I understand why you were suspicious with the first, concerned after the second. I agree a third establishes a very alarming pattern. Have you approached the local police?"

She snorted, absently reaching for a chunk of tuna, then remembered she always made it a point not to eat during conferences with Mr. Bilal or his assistant, that young Mr. D'Fixx. "Not officially. I mentioned it to a detective I know. Obviously, they can't spend time on something that doesn't appear to be illegal. He did let on there's a pattern that concerns them even more. So far two of the major, um—" She tried to find a better word for pimp. "Two of the most powerful ladies' *managers* in this area have disappeared in the last few months. One was found with his throat cut in the water off Freeport. He says there's a bloody struggle going on over who's to control the sex trade in a large part of the barrio—and it's getting racial. The one found in the water was black, possible retribution for the one still missing, a Mexican. The first two girls who left for this new opportunity were, um, *affiliated* with the Mexican. Chaleeshia had worked for the black man."

"Maybe with their managers suddenly gone, those women recognized an opportunity simply to move away before being recruited by a newcomer."

"I'd like to think so, but I thought whoever was moving in on the missing Mexican might be behind it. Then Chaleeshia got involved, too. Now I think it must be bigger than that."

Kinte paused a moment, waiting to see if she had more to say.

Vivan Podrassky struggled not to let her frustration show. She worked hard at proving herself an ideal region coordinator, a meticulous administrator, a motivator, not afraid of wading in where she wanted change, a soul who truly cared about those she helped.

"How would you like to proceed?" he asked.

She glanced up, her reverie broken. "I'm not sure, Mr. Bilal. I need to investigate more, consider my options."

"I will provide reasonable support when you decide. Do not hesitate to contact me sooner than our regular conference next week."

"Thank you, Mr. Bilal. I appreciate that. You know, I think I even counted on it."

The transmission over, she stared at the blank screen a full five minutes, lost in her world—or lost in the one just outside FuturePlan's door. Finally, she shook her head and moved back to her desk, flipping through her card file. She had a call to make.

"Hello? Yes, it's me. You wanted to be kept apprised of Miss Poeky's progress. I'm sorry to say she came in today and resigned from the program, citing an opportunity to move away and start a new life. I wish I knew more, but it's all very secret."

She answered several questions by explaining the same things she'd told Kinte. "Yes, I sometimes have to accept that I will lose people, but I'm worried most about the children. I promise to keep you informed, and if there is any way you can help, I will let you know."

She hung up and studied the card for a minute. This Carly Geiss was an enigma. She'd shown up with Chaleeshia right after the elder Poeky was murdered, offering to pay whatever would assure her a slot in the program. Vivian Podrassky hadn't accepted any money—Mr. Bilal would not approve—but she had promised to keep Miss Geiss updated on Chaleeshia's progress.

Of all the people who need help, Chaleeshia had people who cared and limitless resources to back her up.

Whatever lured her away must have been very attractive.

THERE IT LOOMED, VIBRANT AND BRIGHT, a huge multi-hued gaseous planet with a medieval giant standing atop it sideways and grinning sheepishly, slightly bent at the waist, small bursts of steam blowing intermittently from his butt.

Pffft. Pffft. Pffft.

Long lines, a raucous crowd, cars stopping to spew bodies and be valeted away, everybody looked excited with anticipation.

Pffft. Pffft. Pffft.

They pulled up in their van with Marcie at the wheel, suddenly surrounded by large, earnest men. She stepped out, smartly dressed in a shimmering frock that sparkled and refracted varying colors in the light. Shawn climbed down from the other side, tan slacks, button-down denim, iguana perched on his shoulders.

Pffffffffffff-BOOM!

The crowd went wild as sparks flew out the giant's butt, cheering for the randomly timed *big* fart, a regular show in itself.

Vegas ain't got nothin' on this.

They were led past the crowd, directly into the club. Shawn heard several whispers—"guests of Mr. Garbus"—and saw people snap-to.

The place was packed, the crowd noisy, the atmosphere some kind of space-stellar motif. Planets floated here and there against a backdrop of stars with eerie, misty lighting. Sparkling tails followed comets flying around the rooms, all dancing to the synth-pop strains of Holst's *The Planets* whenever the featured band took breaks from pounding in the central theatre.

Yes, Marcie understood they had a room waiting, but since the other guest hadn't arrived yet—they were an hour early—just back off a little, thank you very much. Wanna check the place out.

Pretty cool, actually.

"This place is *stompin'* for a weeknight," Shawn whispered, staying very close to his friend, a bit awkward in the madding crowd.

"That's why we're making so much money," she whispered back. Well, it was sort of a shout in his ear, but it had the same effect amid this cacophony.

"We *own* this place?"

She gave him that look of fond exasperation reserved solely for him. "Gawd, you need to keep up. You own fifty percent, and me and Foster each got a quarter. Kinte didn't want in. We got fifty-some of these across the U.S. and a dozen in five countries. Foster says the biz-plan calls for two hundred in the next eighteen months."

"Whose idea was the farting giant?"

She just smiled.

The security detail had backed off a little, but they were hovering, trying not to appear too obtrusive. Shawn's lizard attracted some attention, mostly from guys, though. One emaciated nymphet tried to pet Scallywag, but he scurried down the front of Shawn's shirt, then poked his head out to look around. A goon hustled the vixen away.

Shawn and Marcie found themselves standing adjacent to a chairless high-table, a buxom waitress in elfin costume with Saturn rings around her head wondering what they might be drinking.

Whisper whisper: "Foster B—" Whisper whisper.

Anything they wanted. Drinks, food; they didn't normally serve snacks in this room, but she'd personally run next door—

Marcie liked a Belgian beer, Shawn a clear soda with chunks of fruit in it. Oh, and did they have any macaroni and cheese for Scallywag? They didn't, but—whisper whisper—it could certainly be arranged.

Marcie suggested there wasn't time. Just the beer and soda.

And don't forget the fruit.

Scallywag climbed out onto Shawn's shoulders again, apparently scanning the room for scrumptious lizard tail. Shawn noticed Marcie sizing up guests of various gender, so he looked around to see if anybody caught his eye.

Wow, actually there were some beautiful young ladies there—though most had dressed a bit spacey. Theme and all.

Most were matched with guys, though. The rest hung with girlfriends, eyeing the fellers, lots of babes, a few dogs—not that looks mattered a whole lot to Shawn.

Hello! Man, she's *beautiful.* Long, chestnut hair, shiny hazel eyes with flecks of gold—a bold, sexy look, confident yet demure, and a bodacious pair of—

"She's got money, too," Marcie whispered.

"Um, how can you tell?" He absently tried to straighten his hair, a wayward cowlick taunting him mercilessly.

"I just can," she pronounced, chugging her beer and burping.

A young couple with spiked, colored hair eyed Marcie from across the room, attention she seemed to enjoy.

Shawn kept gazing at that woman with the chestnut hair and stunning—

Damn!—it looked like she'd joined a small group. Rats. Two men and two other women mingled intimately, drinking, laughing, playing seductively with each other. He watched for a minute, deciding the others were paired off—but not her! Yet she seemed to be the life of the party, touching and teasing, each sip of her drink a sensual caress of the straw with those glistening lips, sidestepping clandestine gropes with a seductive smile . . .

The band started again, pounding and vibrating the room. She began swaying back and forth, testing at first, easing into the rhythm, closing her eyes and tilting her head back as if to feel it surround her then pass through her, giving in a little, then more, and then completely, sweeping into the crashing waves and riding out with the tide. Others watched, many also swaying, caught up in her raw sensual power.

She turned this way, now that way, brushing aside a lock of one man's hair, her finger tracing down another's arm, breathing harder, chest heaving, taking charge.

She laughed, moving through the crowd, surprising the unwary with fingernail flicks popping their buttons—buttons flying all directions. Soon everybody was swaying with her, following this exotic seductress wherever she would take them.

A button landed in Shawn's drink.

A glance right at him from the beautiful woman . . . then she turned again, eyes closed.

Shawn sat there in awe, amazed how she stirred passions without a care.

One of the men tried to kiss the beautiful woman, but found himself deftly danced into the arms of another before he knew what happened. All eyes watched her move through a world she owned. Her subjects bowed before her, most too afraid to touch but still drawn in, submitting as much as they dared, letting her show them how.

And still she danced, everywhere but to Shawn, the shy gazillionaire now standing with his mouth wide open.

She was driving him nuts.

And now . . . she stood alone, the music fading away.

Marcie leaned over to say something, Shawn intently watching the woman with big hazel eyes and silky chestnut hair pausing to speak with a different group.

"Go for it, Shawnee," Marcie whispered.

"She's talking to those people—"

She was leaving. Damn.

"Go talk to her—"

"Excuse me, Miss McNair," one of the goons interrupted, "but your guest has arrived."

Marcie sighed. The woman had gone, leaving Shawn disappointed. The lizard hadn't found any tail, either.

Time to get down to biz.

They were led to one of the smaller, private banquet rooms. Their guest already had a drink; Marcie and Shawn begged off another. A small device was left for them to activate if they wanted for anything. *Anything*—you name it.

"I may want somebody killed later," Marcie joked. Goon didn't laugh. Apparently, that wouldn't be too tall an order.

Just press that button.

Marcie shooed everybody out and introduced herself and Shawn.

"And I'm Joelle. Joelle Bulagrét."

A striking woman, she looked about Marcie's age—guess mid-twenties if you want to escape with your gotchies intact—high cheekbones, dark hair, Hispanic.

"If I may," she said politely, reaching out to stroke Scallywag's head, then down the side of his belly. For once, the lizard didn't hide. He seemed to like it, shifting his weight toward her hand, closing his eyes.

Shawn found himself pondering other ways she might apply this talent.

"We have these where I am from. They are pests, though some people eat the tail. But certain people, they see these are special animals and make pets of them."

She smiled, now standing very close. Several strokes caused the back of her hand to brush Shawn seductively—on purpose, he felt sure.

"I'm interested in your proposal," Marcie began.

"I believed you would be."

They sat around a small table, Scallywag climbing down to sit in front of their guest.

"Tell me about the crystals," Marcie prompted.

"It is only theory, based on ancient legend but supported with science. As I say in the note I left with the sample crystal at your store, a big-big meteorite crashed sixty-five million years ago. The impact, it helped to create the Gulf of Mexico and the Caribbean Sea, pushing up land to become Central America."

"This is the dinosaur killer?" Shawn asked.

She shrugged. "I have heard such sayings, but this story goes back ten thousand years at least. I'm not sure the people knew of dinosaurs."

"So where do the crystals come in?" Marcie wondered.

"This meteorite was almost big as the moon. It burned so hot it *evaporated*, turning into the gasses. As the Pacific sea rushed back through giant cracks, it cooled very fast, and where gasses built up in the rock, magnificent crystal caverns formed, many far below the surface. The Tsala peoples, ancestors to the Guatusos and Bribri and Cabécar, they found one such cavern pushed up by volcano earthquake. They learned the secret power of the crystals and passed this knowledge down to each new generation."

"And how do *you* know about it?" Shawn asked.

"There are but a few of us Tsala left, spread around the world. I went back to find my heritage and learned this. I wish to share what I know with others."

"For the right price," Marcie rejoined.

Joelle smiled. "For the *fair* price."

"And what does my three-fifty-K buy?"

"Four cases, packed. We estimate about seventy-thousand shards total."

"Five bucks a pop," Shawn announced. And he didn't even need a calculator.

"And you can get easy fifty or a hundred when people learn of their powers. I cannot bargain the price, but I promise it will not go higher as long as you buy four cases every two months, and you will be the *only* customer. I will contact you each week to see if you want extra shipments."

"Well, we'd need to work out a lot of ifs, ands, or buts in the contract—" Marcie started.

"I am so sorry. There is to be no contract. We agree and live by our word. You must pay each time with a bank draft for cash, U.S. funds. I have studied you carefully before deciding to take this chance on you. You have hundreds of stores, plus other companies that can sell them, plus you can do mail-order and internet distribution to other countries, advertise on television and in magazines, sell through other marketplaces, maybe even make deals with psychic phone lines for a percentage. If you do not buy four cases every second month, I may deal with your competition."

"All authentic, no substitutions?"

Joelle smiled again. "You are a smart lady. I hope you had the crystal analyzed, learned it is unique. We cannot afford to have fraud if we are to make good money for a long time. There is more crystal than we could ever sell."

"What do you know about the power?"

Joelle chuckled. "It is like all things psychic. It is only as powerful as the buyer believes. Your lawyers will tell you how to advertise without guarantees. I do not have to believe ancient superstitions to recognize how we can make money."

Shawn brightened. "So you admit there's nothing actually powerful about them?"

She gave him the get-real look.

"The one we tested was," Marcie said quietly. "It affected Shawn."

Bulagrét seemed amused, maybe curious. She reached into her purse for a glistening, faceted jewel the size of a jawbreaker. She fingered it, tossed it up and caught it several times, shrugged, then handed it over to Marcie.

Shawn watched his friend carefully. A calm seemed to spread over her features, a serenity he didn't often witness. She offered it to him.

He didn't want to touch it, still spooked from what happened at the lab. The lizard watched him expectantly.

He took it in his hand. The noise from the next room died down, everybody quieter. He felt queasy, must be freaking, shouldn't be making this into something it wasn't.

Marcie gazed at him in awe, rapt, fascinated. So did Joelle Bulagrét, but more like surprised. Shawn quickly set the hot potato on the table.

"May I?" Marcie breathed.

Bulagrét nodded. Marcie made it disappear.

"I have the cases in my car if you are ready."

A press of the button, and suddenly four goons appeared with a locking satchel and impressive bank draft. Satisfied with the payment, Bulagrét led the entourage outside. Shawn didn't like the idea of taking the gems to the Galveston house or carrying them on the jet—didn't want to be around them at all, actually—so Marcie told the boss goon to safeguard them until Kinte could arrange shipment to Monterey.

Bulagrét thanked everybody and climbed into the driver's seat. The shipment as expected, Marcie and Shawn walked around to the window to say good-bye . . . but there was nobody inside.

Bulagrét had disappeared.

One of Houston's highest-rated security and investigation details would be hard-pressed to explain to Mr. Bilal how they lost her so fast.

Marcie wanted to go back inside and mingle, maybe indulge in a bit of shake-yer-fanny. Shawn reluctantly agreed, stopping by the van first to leave Scallywag on his heating pad.

They had barely stepped through the door when all eyes turned to watch. Just as quickly, everybody resumed their activities—but lots of women kept looking at Shawn, smiling, winking, touching their lips or boldly fingering their breasts. Several approached, asking where his lizard went, encouraging him to dance, offering to buy him a drink. Marcie chatted with a group of pierced punkers, keeping an eye on her friend, looking pleased that he relaxed a bit and came out of his shell.

He liked that nobody there knew him, or knew how rich he was, or even seemed to care.

He did pass up one highly suggestive invitation to go out to the car. She wanted to see his lizard.

He felt pretty sure she wanted more than a look.

CHAPTER 2

"**B**ITCH SAYS WE GOTTA WAIT till tonight," he growled. Wally was too used to employees jumping-to—how high? and all that. He figured paying the bill meant she worked for him. "Harmonic convergences or some shit—won't work if we power it up again too soon."

"We could just give up the fifty-grand deposits and *keep* 'em after tonight," Chuck reminded him.

Wally whistled to the waitress. He wanted another drink, dammit. A tiny lizard scurried across the stone ledge separating the open-air lounge from a white beach dotted by glistening, oiled bodies.

"Won't know if they're the *right* crystals, though. Remember that speech about each person's pissy—"

"*Psi*," Chuck corrected.

"Each guy's pissy is different, has to be matched to the crystal that channels him best. You think *last night* was hot, wait'll we get matched up right. Then the power's supposed to be limitless."

"That's how she gets away with the price goin' up an extra thou each night. She gets us hooked, then proves it gets better and better."

The drinks arrived. Wally let Chuck sign the tab.

"So why let her keep the fifty-K for a so-so crystal when we can match the perfect one and buy it outright for two hundred?" Chuck asked.

"Two-fifty," Wally corrected. "It's only four-hundred thousand for the pair if we *both* buy in."

Chuck grinned. "I know *you'll* be in. You been walkin' funny all day!"

Wally grinned back. "Made her howl all night!"

"Why don't you wanna get with them same two women tonight? I told mine I'd call—"

"Forget 'em, Chucky. Hell, they coulda been planted on us. No playin' sucker. If these crystals really work, we need to test 'em right. Different place tonight—see if we get the same reaction."

"Or a better one," Chucky offered hopefully, though that would be a tall order.

Wally snorted a *Yeah, right!* He knew Chuck had never even imagined doing *that* well. If his babe had been even the least bit patient or understanding . . .

They commandeered covered loungers for an afternoon nap in the shade, Wally wanting to rest up before another night of acrobatics. He knew the best Chuck would do is drowse fitfully, that he wouldn't be able to take his mind off the woman he'd been with, that by now he'd probably already convinced himself he'd fallen in love. What a dweeb . . . Wally rolled over and started snoring in no time.

Later, after dinner, they followed the same routine. The manager lady offered them rum punches, had them sit and sign, removed the ornate case of crystals from the safe . . . This time she pressed close against their bodies, one at a time, feeling the residual power from the night before, reading their psi, capturing the essence that would help her narrow the selection of crystals.

She carefully tweezed through the case, pausing and closing her eyes, going over to Wally again so she could press her breasts against his back while she felt his head, finally selecting two of the most powerful babe magnets in the box.

She applied the crystalline paste to their wrists, affixed the shards, grew entranced by their overwhelming spell, and begged them to leave and enjoy while she could still win the struggle to maintain her dignity.

It would be The Wet Orchid, a karaoke lounge rife with fat and sunburnt charter tourists.

"Ain't nobody in here I'd even *wanna* boff," Wally bitched. He was about to suggest they walk around, check out the area—when *they* came in. The foursome of babes turned out to be three divorcées and a widow from Tampa, each with enough alimony or insurance money to grow bored with working. All in their thirties and still quite hot, they'd given up finding some not-too-young fun in that sea of old-timers back home, so they bought the seven-day package to paradise, continental breakfast included.

A paltry four-thousand apiece to rent crystals for the night was all it took for Wally and Chuck each to get his first taste of *ménage a trois*.

Wally found himself with two women in one of the gals' rooms, drinking beers while their overwhelming passion for him slowly overcame their awkwardness, their modesty, their inhibitions about doing it, you know, with another woman—something neither had ever tried. Slow and tentative at first, they quickly embraced the novelty of the experience.

Wally kept it relaxed and fun, teaching them how to open new horizons, explore their basest sensuality, get down and dirty. He was in rare form, a teacher and mentor, encouraging them to cut loose.

One even broke out some studded leather still in its store package, the other some edible fire lotion and a massive vibrating banana.

Amazing what those crystals can do.

MARCIE TOSSED HER BAG on the table, then yawned and stretched. Shawn trotted into the master suite and put Scallywag on his heating pad. The place looked magnificent, one of hundreds of houses Shawn owned, this one down an exclusive drive on the bay side of Galveston Island, south end. A team of servants had been in, every room left immaculate, the kitchen stocked, a small fleet in the garage tuned up, waterlines flushed, attic ventilated, fresh-cut flowers arranged, pillows fluffed.

Plenty of macaroni and cheese.

Shawn went for a soda, wondering what Marcie might want.

"That young couple with the purple hair," she said absently. She'd spent a lot of her time at The Gaseous Giant trip-dancing with those two, Shawn watching from the side with a cadre of hangers-on swapping drinks and stories and knowing glances.

"It's late. I'm beat," he said.

"You could've had several of those ladies tonight, Shawnee. You were quite the item. I don't know if it was just your charm or the power you got from touching that crystal." She accepted the soda, sipped, announced she'd been "holding it" too long, and scampered off to the potty.

"They figured me out," he called after her. "That's all it was. They saw we were VIPeed, whisked right in, allowed to carry a darned lizard, security goons everywhere, Foster's name whispered about. Anybody could see we were important or had money—and most wouldn't know the difference." He took several more sips and wandered over to the glassed-in veranda, watching the lights play across the water.

Flush, splash splash. "It's such a rough life you lead, Mr. Fix-it."

"*Fixer,*" he corrected. He knew the flubbed moniker was a joke, the comment not. She understood why he wanted to be taken at face value, no labels, no ulterior motives, no expectations except that people regard him as an honest man with a good heart.

"Shawn, you need to learn that sometimes pretty chickies'll nibble your ear because they like it, not because they're lookin' for gold coins like some matinée magician."

Shawn didn't say anything. He sat on a divan, still looking across the water, yawning a few times.

Marcie turned down the lights and scooted in beside him, pulling her legs close, resting her head on his shoulder, catching his contagious yawns. "You were already questioning people's motives at barely eighteen, that night I first met you at the quad," she said quietly, referring to her sophomore year at Berkeley as a thirty-something heiress. "It's refusing to trust people to like you for what you *are* and not what you *have*. I know you don't think you're not good enough—"

"Well, what's *your* deal?" he interrupted. He didn't like where she was going. "You were disappointed when *you* first figured out I had money."

"I *know* my baggage. I grew up watching others wield the power of wealth to buy and sell people, their fates, their hearts . . ." She trailed off, then took a sip, adding, "I was attracted to your mystical power, your rainbow aura, what even *you* couldn't see in yourself. I wound up disappointed that you had a gazillion bucks because I was afraid it had corrupted you. Now I know it's made you pure. That's one reason we're friends for life—you understand I care about you despite what you have; you care about me because I'm like the free spirit inside *you* that you won't often let out; and we love each other because we trust— I know *what you are*, Shawn D'Fixx." She smiled, reflections of light through the glass playing across her face. "I'm one of the few you feel safe to let see the real you."

Shawn smiled sheepishly. "And I can't for the *life* of me figure *you* out."

"When you think you've got it, run like hell," she warned, getting up to put the bottle on the counter, "because for *damn* sure it'll mean the end of the world."

Shawn followed, rinsing both bottles before putting them in the recycler. He yawned again. "I need to crash."

They paused and looked at each other for a moment, she smiling just slightly. Suddenly, he felt self-conscious, unable to figure out what seemed so funny. She'd always described him as someone who looked earnest, maybe sensitive and even a bit vulnerable. He never considered himself handsome, but not butt-ugly either. A few inches shy of six feet, somewhat lanky, he could blend into a crowd without trying—sometimes whether he wanted to or not.

She stood tip-toe and kissed him on the cheek. "She's out there, Shawn. But you can't wait for one as wealthy as you—there probably aren't any. Ain't much difference between a woman who wants a guy for what he can buy her, and a guy who wants a rich woman so he doesn't have to worry about what she wants."

He kissed her back. "My flame-headed philo-shrink-sopher . . ." It was a touching moment until he added, "I'm gonna drain the lizard and hit the sheets."

MARCIE STAYED TO SIT ALONE, watching the bay. After a while, she fetched the jawbreaker crystal from her bag and took it back to the couch.

She touched it gingerly, studied it, brushed it against her face, then held it up to watch it refract light. She found it very puzzling.

She walked to Shawn's room and pushed the door open, whispering, "Shawn? Shawnee? You asleep?"

Soft, regular breathing answered the question. She walked quietly to the bed, knelt beside him, and gently stroked his hair. She passed the crystal around over his head several times, then set it on the nightstand and stole quietly out.

SHAWN NEVER STIRRED, too far gone, floating and dreaming, carried back in time, a mere lad—what? Ten—no, eleven years old?

Where was he? Spain? It was Málaga, the village of Torrémoliños on the Mediterranean, straight north from Morocco. Spring break, sixth grade, Kinte taking big-brother Jeremy and little Shawn and Foster B there for a week. There dwelt a lady, an old friend of Kinte's, a fabulous estate on the hill just upriver from the sea. Kinte encouraged them to explore; three rich boys would be safe and very welcome.

Jeremy must have been fourteen, the handsomer D'Fixx lad enamored with Maricíta, a sweet Spanish girl from the village, nearly four years his senior. The older of two sisters and very poor, she thought Jeremy to be a nice boy, taking him off to a small room over the boarding house where they would savor the mysteries of life and love. The grinning sixth-graders stayed behind to explore the market, anxiously awaiting their chance to make him recount everything he'd learned about "doing it" with a woman. Maricíta must have quickly learned that Jeremy could be as generous with money and presents as with his heart.

All three scootered to the village on their last day, but they couldn't find her. Then she emerged from the boarding house with a businessman from the city, embarrassed to see three boys watching gape-mouthed as he kissed her roughly and stepped into his fancy car, driving away in a cloud of dust.

Jeremy went inside with her and spent several hours upstairs, but he wouldn't speak of it afterward, except to admit he was glad to be leaving again for school.

That night, in darkness and quiet, Shawn took his pillow and sheet and crept to Jeremy's room to sleep on the floor beside his brother's bed, something he'd done many times when younger, those nights he maybe felt a little scared. Jeremy always understood, usually saying nothing, reaching down to squeeze Shawnee's shoulder as if to say good night, it'll be all right.

Shawn drowsed for a while, then realized he could hear Jeremy. His big brother was crying.

Shawn felt confused, understanding only that it must hurt very much. He reached up and squeezed Jeremy's shoulder and told him it would be okay.

After all these years, Shawn's dream seemed just like it had really happened, except when he tried to look around, the room appeared different, shifting and refracting, the moonlight through the window changing colors. That night so long ago, Shawn had lain awake for hours, listening while Jeremy cried himself out, his breathing slowing and growing deeper, softly asleep with his hurts and dreams, but this time . . . he could see Jeremy's face, peering over the side of the bed, eyes glistening, watching his little brother.

She was a hooker, Shawnee—a whore, slut, prostitute. It's who she was.

Shawn knew what that meant. It was hard to imagine that sweet young woman as one of *those.*

She had a kid, too. A fatherless little boy.

More than that at eleven years old, Shawn understood what Jeremy was trying to say.

She didn't like me. She wouldn't just give me her most precious gift; she needed to sell it to me. And yet I was willing to give her mine. Tears shined on his cheeks.

"That's not bad, is it, Jeremy? I mean, if that's what she wanted to do."

He shook his head. *It wasn't what she wanted. She was dirt poor, and nobody would love a prostitute or marry one with a "bastard" child. But she had to live, to take care of her little boy, so she did what she thought she had to.*

"Why is that bad?"

'Cause she didn't see in herself what I saw in her. She thought all I saw was her, um—

Shawn nodded. He and Foster had devoted much energy to imagining what Jeremy had seen, had touched.

All she saw in me was a horny boy who could afford to buy her. She thought it was all she had to offer.

Jeremy started sniffling again, embarrassed even in front of Shawn. He pulled his shoulder from his little brother's grip and rolled over, burying his face under the pillow. Shawn climbed up on the side of the bed . . . but Jeremy was gone! Frantically, he started peeling back covers, flinging the pillow aside, searching . . .

Shawn woke with a start, the bed a mess, that crystal on his nightstand scattering reflections from the window.

He studied it for a moment, then picked it up with a pillow case and hurried through the living room, depositing it gingerly on the kitchen counter.

Seeing nothing extraordinary, he shook his head and went back to bed.

MARCIE WATCHED SHAWN get rid of the crystal and hurry back to bed. She sat quietly, folded into a yoga position by the veranda, never noticed by her friend.

Something important had happened . . .

She put her hand to her mouth and nodded.

"I'M SORRY, MISS GEISS, but one of the requirements of the foundation is that we *not* take funding from other sources." Vivian Podrassky never thought she would say something like that. Her advisor in the Master's social-work program had warned she'd chosen a career destined to begging for budgets, competing for paltry grants, scrimping and stretching to perform miracles on a shoestring. Here in Houston she'd found a way to make a real difference with seemingly limitless resources, and now she was telling a very wealthy woman offering a blank check that she couldn't take it. "I can recommend other—"

"Come on, Viv, you know I give my share. Let's cut to what I *want*."

"Your interest in Chaleeshia Poeky must have been more than simple charity."

"I admire the work of the foundation, but too much is wasted because fundamental conditions stay the same. While *you* try to attract people trapped in the cesspool who want a way out, you have competition out there—from the people who have a vested interest in keeping these prostitutes down. I've been helping certain people who want to, um, *diminish* the competition. Chaleeshia's sister was helping *them*. She didn't care so much about herself, but seeing her little sister get pulled in, that her little nephew had so much stacked against him . . ." Carly Geiss trailed off, a faraway look in her eyes. Just as quickly, she resumed a hard, business edge. "I don't know how or why she was killed—it might not have been related—but I owe it to her to do what I can for her sister and that little boy. I want your help."

Vivian studied her for a moment. Yes, this is social work, the kind you don't get a plaque for. "How much are *you* gonna tell *me*?"

Carly shook her head.

"I suppose that's best," Vivian concluded.

"You do your part—very well, in fact. You should be proud. I don't question your methods."

"How can I help?"

"Surely others have been approached, maybe a friend of Chaleeshia's. I need to know who these people are, how to get close, to be offered this phantom opportunity myself."

Vivian Podrassky pondered for a moment. "Yes. Yes, I see. If anybody knows . . . Allow me to bring in Mr. Suggly, our director."

"Thank you. Now, here's the story I'd like to tell him . . ."

BJ AND THE OTHER FOUR seated themselves around the conference table, all dressed in casual business attire, holo-tablets propped in front, curious and eager. All understood that being selected for one of Mr. Garbus's "exploratories" often led to career-making key roles in the management of some new enterprise, an expansion of the vast business empire helmed by their young mentor.

"Crystals and gems," Foster pronounced. He stood at the massive window, watching birds circle over the cliffs, his back to the group. "Don't have any specific plans yet, just want to learn the biz."

Nobody spoke. A million questions hung in the air, but the handsome young tycoon hadn't asked for them yet. They would let him finish.

"Beej, you're heading the team. I want you to coordinate a fact-finding. ID the current status of this industry with a lot of emphasis on *what* they are, where we get 'em, ownerships and politics, markets and applications. You know everybody here; you'll see I pulled in people with good background in each of these areas. Let's pretend I want to get inside in a big way but don't know how. Where's the money being made, who's got control, branding factors, if it's all about jewelry or industrial use or what. I'm real curious about cutting-edge stuff, research going on, anticipated future markets, anything that looks interesting. Just be careful you don't look too acquisitional; I don't want to stir up speculative investment competition."

He left the window and walked to the head of the table. "One other thing. I'm interested in anything—*anything*, no matter how obscure, about crystals channeling psychic energy."

BJ and the biz-wizzes looked surprised, puzzled. But whatever Foster B. Garbus wants . . .

Leave no gemstone unturned.

Foster just smiled. "Any questions?"

"NOPE, IT'S ONE-WAY. Gotta go around." Shawn was trying to navigate, Marcie at the wheel negotiating morning traffic. FuturePlan had to be *somewhere* around here.

"What was her name?"

"Who?"

"The girl in your dream—the one in Spain with the beautiful eyes and long brown hair."

Shawn shrugged, trying to read street signs and watch for traffic at the same time. "Don't remember."

"Is this why you want to see exactly how your foundations are helping people in her kinda situation—young mothers risking their lives to sell their bodies because they don't know any other way to survive?"

Shawn just nodded.

"How we playin' this?"

"Kinte said I've had conferences with this coordinator, Vivian Podrassky, so she thinks I'm his assistant just taking an on-site look-see."

"So maybe an hour? In and out, then off to the airport?"

"Yeah, I'm ready to go home."

"You're *always* ready to get home, anxious to see if the lost episodes of some goofy old TV show are in yet." She sighed. "I'm sure we'll both have some biz to get done, too, before we go on our trip. I wanna talk to Foster about marketing the crystals."

"What trip?"

She shrugged. "I'm guessing Central America because Bulagrét talked about cracks from the meteorite and Pacific ocean rushing in."

Shawn mock grimaced. Marcie was gearing up to drag him off on another futile search for enlightenment.

FuturePlan, right there all along. They parked in a small lot next to the building.

Shawn fussed over Scallywag, wanting to bring him in, Marcie strongly discouraging him.

"Come on, Shawn—soon as we told Kinte hold the jet, he's probably buying downtown Houston and hiring everybody in it just to keep an eye on us."

A HANDFUL OF TEENS watched Shawn and Marcie from across the street.

Check out that van! *¡Nos lo gusta!* A couple of *bomars* getting out, going inside the program place.

The teens waited a minute, then strolled casually toward the lot, a few indifferent pedestrians sauntering by, nobody paying attention. With three hovering close, the other two eased around back, looking in the window, the side, checking out the stereo, any cargo, maybe an alarm. A bum wandered through the lot, no big deal. One of the youths tried the back door.

The bum appeared right beside him—that fast?—something under his coat.

"Stay out of the lot."

"Hey, muh-fu—"

Bum gestured toward the street; a van pulled over, side door open, two armed men.

Shit, there was a woman across the street, her hand in her shoulder bag.

Bum acted casual. "This lot, this building—*sacred* ground. *Never* gonna be worth it."

They agreed, thinking it prudent to move on. They would come back several times over the next few days to look around, but every bum looked suspect, every vehicle a threat. Got the jitters, they did.

Afraid of the unknown.

SHAWN AND MARCIE WERE GREETED by the plump director and led straight to Ms. Podrassky's office upstairs. Everybody gushed, thrilled to have visitors from the foundation, never suspecting for a moment that Shawn was the one who created and financed it, that Kinte merely acted as front-man with the regions as a way to help out and keep busy since Foster had taken over managing their business interests.

Vivian knew her stats, reciting numbers and rates and costs like stilted dialogue in a community-theatre play, proud but concerned. She was worried about losing women to this mysterious new opportunity, but she wanted to be clear the program boasted a phenomenal rate of success. After all, this was the first foundation visit by that D'Fixx guy who seemed to rank way up there just under Mr. Kinte Bilal. Why the surprise inspection?

Shawn kept reassuring her without patronizing. Marcie professed interest in support services—substance-abuse assistance, job training, housing, things that would help participants succeed. Shawn wanted to know about self-esteem, self-concept, self-love. What was being done to help young prostitutes, especially mothers, understand everybody has unrealized potential?

"We try to do much of that in the orientation," Vivian explained. "We're having one in a few minutes. I could move it to the observation room if you'd like to watch through one-way glass and listen over the speaker."

They liked the idea, encouraging Vivian to leave them alone.

They watched as the director interviewed two very nervous young prostitutes, explaining what the program offered. She emphasized taking control, the power within, fulfilling one's potential, blah blah. It seemed to work, instilling confidence, motivating, convincing them FuturePlan must be the best thing ever, the unparalleled opportunity.

Marcie was impressed, Shawn distracted, fidgety, unsettled. The orientation over, he made no move to exit, just sitting there, lost in thought.

Marcie studied him. Finally, she reached into her fanny-pack, producing the jawbreaker crystal.

Shawn started to shrink away, almost scared of it, but then held firm, looked at it, at her, back at it. "It's just a *crystal*, you know," he pointed out. "No big deal."

"Convince me," she said evenly, watching him very carefully.

He reached over and took it from her, holding it in his hand.

"Don't you see it?" she whispered.

"No."

She waited a moment, watching him gaze into it like some kind of crystal ball.

"What now, Mr. Fixx?"

"Find her and save her."

"Who?"

He looked sheepish, shrugging and handing the crystal back. He couldn't explain what he'd felt, so he didn't want to try.

"C'mon, Shawnee. Let's go stroke Podrassky and get to the airport. I wanna hit the jet and stretch out on a waterbed, relax a little."

"Yeah, relax," he agreed.

"Get on home, maybe try to figure this out," she added.

"Yep," he said absently.

"*Okay*, then." She opened the door and waited.

He looked around, shook his head, then got up and followed her dutifully out. "Don't know who she is," he said quietly.

Shawn didn't like Marcie studying him so intently. He realized he was acting strange, not like his normally alert and *intense* self, so he tried too hard to act casual about what had happened. What *had* happened?

He could hear the director's voice in one of the activity rooms, Vivian Podrassky wishing somebody luck.

Two women were leaving, obviously sex workers, too much make-up, provocative clothes, tight leather skirt on one, skimpy shorts on the other, halter tops, heels . . . They moved toward the end of the hallway, opened the door, stepped outside, unaware Shawn had stopped to gape.

One turned and looked right at him.

The one with beautiful eyes and long chestnut hair!

Damn! She was a *prostitute*.

She looked at Shawn, seemed to recognize him, looked embarrassed, then turned and hurried away, disappearing into the harsh glare of day.

Shawn started to follow, but Marcie's hand on his arm held him back.

"That's *her*—"

"From the club?"

"Yeah, but . . . I mean, *she's the one*."

CHAPTER 3

GULF OF MEXICO, Yucatan Peninsula, long stretch of water, jungles of Honduras then Nicaragua, spectacular coastline of sand beaches and mosaic sea in patchwork blues, banking west of volcanic mountains—they finally landing at San José, Costa Rica. Chaleeshia Poeky sat glued to the DC-9's window, stealing occasional peeks at the napping toddler strapped beside her. The plane carried a full complement of tourists winging in for surf and sand, snorkeling and trekking, food and drink—the excitement infectious, the tiny liquor bottles potent, the deliberate flight-plan down virgin coast tantalizing. Chaleeshia had been to Galveston Island, but this was a whole 'nother world.

"Hope you had a good flight, Ms. Bulagrét," the attendant whispered.

The beautiful businesswoman, resort owner, and charter-service operator had sat in *front* of the partition, the big seats of first-class. She traveled with a beefy Hispanic man, his skin dark and oily, his bushy black hair and mustache cropped short. He followed her dutifully down the portable stairwell, then waited beside her while she greeted the new recruit and little boy.

They took a golf cart to the ramshackle terminal, then a back door past customs and immigration. Nodding to the man loading tourists and baggage into the resort's van, Big Man led them instead to a newish Caddy parked off to the side, and away they went.

Her boy awake and cranky, Chaleeshia remained quiet and curious, all eyes everywhere. She had never seen mountains or dense tropical jungles, had never been far from Houston. They drove a zig-zag route, laboring over steep ridges, dipping under dark canopies, their ears popping as they worked their way down into a lush valley. Eventually, the road opened into a flat gravel stretch curving east to the coast and north along the shoreline, passing several resorts walled or fenced off from the jungle.

They turned into Tsala-Pu, a compound of time-share condos and two-story balconied el-buildings, gift shop, pool and spa, tennis courts, water-sports marina, restaurant and bar, spectacular beach and gentle waves. Ms. Bulagrét had been right . . . nothing short of paradise!

Lyla DeCivvio was introduced. The pretty young blonde would be Chaleeshia's housemate and show her the ropes. Leading the tour, Bulagrét suggested the little boy be left for a while in the children's area under the watchful eye of round-the-clock caregivers, normally $32 an hour for parents who drag their little ones to paradise then don't spend time with them.

They took a four-seater golf cart, the silent Big Man silent at the wheel, and headed out of the resort, down a rutted road into the jungle until they came to a cluster of buildings, public-style housing. Miss Poeky would share Lyla's two-bedroom, third unit from the end. Big Man helped carry the suitcases Ms. Bulagrét had provided, clothing and most-valued possessions packed inside. The apartment wasn't bad, certainly nicer than she'd had in the barrio, surely safer.

"Can we get my son now?"

Lyla gestured her toward the couch, sitting in a chair opposite. Bulagrét and Big Man remained standing.

"The deal we made," the older woman explained, "I will honor. One year service, all expenses paid, and you return to States, any city you choose, with a bank account of one-hundred-thousand dollars in your name. But it is risky work we do, so I cannot afford betrayal. For me to be sure of loyalty, we must keep your son apart—"

Chaleeshia jumped up. Big Man stepped forward. She stopped, eyes wide.

Bulagrét continued, "Lyla will explain how things work. You are starting in a few days. If you are performing well and giving us no reason to worry of betrayal, you will be allowed to spend time with your son. The more you are pleasing us, the more you will see your boy. He is to be well cared for and returned to you after the end of the year. If you cause problems, visits are to be stopped. If you try to leave or to seek help or to tell our secrets to anyone, you will never see him again. And then *you* will not be allowed to go home."

She left the threat hanging, Chaleeshia to her own speculation.

"He's okay," Lyla soothed. "I promise. My little girl is there, too. I see her all the time. It's a very nice place."

"Sit down," Bulagrét suggested.

Chaleeshia looked pleadingly, tears welling in her eyes. She started to speak, but thought better of it. She did as she was told.

Bulagrét nodded. "Very good. Once you learn how things work, you will find it to be a very fun year, one well worth the sacrifice. I will leave you two to get acquainted. Start learning how to do your job."

She turned and left, Big Man behind her.

LYLA WHISPERED, "WAIT HERE—DON'T MOVE," and followed the boss-lady out. She stopped her at the foot of the stairs. Desperation in her eyes, she began, "My little girl—"

"I told you," Bulagrét whispered. "You get Señorita Poeky broke in with no problems and you can see your girl again. Long as you are keeping her on track, regular visits."

"What if she don't work out?"

"Then it's not just *her* child at risk."

LIZARD-SHOULDERED, SHAWN ENTERED his private quarters just south of Monterey, a custom-comfort suite as big as the entire mansion at Galveston. He lived in the penthouse level of the sprawling complex, a section along the upper cliff where underfloors dropped more than a dozen stories, terraced outward and built back into the rock. Directly under his sprawled Marcie's level, then Foster's, Kinte's four floors below.

Eschewing the voice-command modules that controlled functions in the other suites, he touched panels to adjust temperature, illuminate foyer mini-office, activate comp-message center, and dis-opaque the glass wall. It revealed his balcony veranda overlooking spectacular coastline and a gray-sand beach secluded by towering cliffs at each end of a private cove. He held his finger there a few seconds, watching the windows change from tinted to clear, bright yellow sunlight washing over the room. He darkened it slightly, then activated the media system—one of many throughout the premises. An early episode of the sitcom Taxi started playing. Another touch, and one of the huge glass panels slid open, a rush of salty breeze filling the room. He walked out and put Scallywag in a six-meter low-sided oval terrarium boasting sand and rocks and shrubs, a small waterfall with stream and pond, beetles and other lizard treats scurrying here and there. The iguana snatched a cricket, then climbed up on a branch in the warm sunlight, winked at his master, and closed his eyes to relax. He never passed up a chance to grab some rays.

A lizard who knows what he likes.

Shawn sighed, then walked back to the foyer to check deliveries. Yes! More *WKRP in Cincinnati* episodes, plus Canadian Broadcasting's *Dead Like Me*, a good sixty hours' worth between 'em. The remainder of his mail had already been opened, perused, discarded or catalogued or filed, listed with summaries and recommended actions. He usually appreciated assistance with his personal affairs, but sometimes he felt smothered. It reminded him of that miserable fancy-restaurant dinner when he was six years old. He had to "hold it" all evening because he'd seen an attendant in the restroom and was afraid the man would follow him into the stall and— and—

Sometimes you just don't want any help.

Lunch would be served down on the beach patio in ten minutes, so he changed clothes, combed his hair, used a fully automated toilet, washed up, combed his hair again, and took one of his private elevators directly to beach level. Foster and Marcie sat casually, already sipping drinks, nibbling herbed and spiced cheese strings, dipped in various sauces, and giggling.

A server hurried over to hold Shawn's chair for him—good thing, it beat puzzling over how to operate it . . . or maybe having it scamper away and hide. Shawn quickly switched to the other chair before the man could react.

Just messing with his head.

Kinte joined them and nodded permission for the courses to begin.

"So what'd you get?" Marcie asked Shawn. "More episodes?"

Shawn excitedly recounted his new acquisitions, confident that if anybody were truly interested, it would be these three.

"Your boxes of crystals came in," Foster confirmed. "I played with a few—can't say I detected anything particularly powerful about 'em."

Before Shawn could agree, Marcie explained, "They're not." Eyebrows shot up around the table. "Their power comes from the person. Everybody has different levels of psi, and of how much they understand it. Shawn just happens to have more than anybody I know, but he can't control it. All the *crystals* do is channel."

"Hmmm," Foster concluded in his non-committal way. "Well, either way, the team's report didn't interest me enough to recommend we wade into the precious-jewels market unless it's retail. Production is concentrated in several regions of the world, especially in southern parts of Africa. The bigger industry is precious metals, but the companies in control have been around a half-century or more and have deep ties to government or military. It's a very political business, one potentially dangerous to naïve interlopers who move too fast. Not that we couldn't pull it off, but with such a volatile market, fluctuating prices, and the upsurge of very convincing imitations—why bother?"

Delicate strips of sautéed barracuda filet—no spices on Shawn's, thank you—slowed the conversation some. Then Kinte asked, "Is there any value to the gems Ms. McNaught purchased other than as baubles for embracers of paranormal superstition?"

"Not as gemstones," Foster responded. "Their composition is so unique they're rare, but fast-cooled geode crystals are badly flawed, subject to cracking, not good for cutting into jewelry or using for industrial applications."

Marcie looked disappointed, so Shawn did, too. He'd hoped for something exciting about the acquisition to shift her interest away from channeling *his* alleged powers.

"There's one thing, though," Foster added. "Your lab tech seemed fascinated by what happened when spectral energy—light—was shined into them. His tests showed that output might have somehow *exceeded* the beams. He also measured electromagnetism and radiation, but couldn't explain some of the readings." Foster wagged his eyebrows and grinned. Intriguing, if not impressive, news. "So I sent him one of the cases of crystals, promoted your tech to project director, and put the resources of all the other labs at his disposal. It fits right into the spectral-energy program."

"So what about promoting them for psi-power channeling?" Marcie asked.

"Got a woman compiling data on the competition, though there's not much, none claiming to sell authentic *meteorite* crystals, mostly cut glass and crystal balls and prisms mounted in wizard or castle statues. We could package and merchandise 'em for your stores within a few weeks, plus we already have excess mail-order and internet-operations capacity if you wanna advertise in specialty publications or buy air-time on paranormal-style shows. I recommend you put 'em in the Herbs & Oils outlets first, then expand and promote the stores as the easiest, maybe even cheapest, place to get 'em. Then you build foot traffic who'll see what *else* you offer."

"Will that woman be handling it?"

"No, she'll study demographics, chart the competition, recommend media skews and so forth, but I assigned a merchandiser—somebody who'll capture *your* style and flare, put the kind of spin on that *you* like. I'll have him come see you this afternoon, if you want."

"Did you get anywhere on the source?" Shawn wondered. He rooted through his vegetable medley to make sure there were no carrots. The others had some, making him suspicious they'd been cooked together, then sorted, maybe one or two slipping past. Gotta be on the lookout.

Kinte answered, "Though Ms. Bulagrét may have tried to mislead you with her meteorite theory, she did inadvertently mention living with an abundance of iguanas. That eliminates the United States except for South Florida—not a source for gemstones—and suggests several regions. Mr. D'Fixx's lizard, that unusual streak of colors on its neck notwithstanding, is Central American. Because the Asian variety looks different, I would expect her to comment if hers were. You believe her appearance and accent are Hispanic, so I agree Central America is where she must live, possibly near the source of those crystals."

"Well, that certainly narrows it down," Marcie kidded.

"Actually, it does. We are checking all common modes of transportation between Texas and those regions, particularly air traffic. Because she plans to call you weekly for possible delivery the following week, her schedule should be easy to flag. I would start by checking the weekly charters."

"What are those?" Shawn wondered.

"A travel service leases an aircraft one day per week for transporting tourists to a cluster of destinations, then cuts deals with proximal resorts to offer all-inclusive air and room packages at discount prices. They fly each group there, then return with the group from the week before. It is efficient and cost-effective."

Foster grinned. "Enough to give me goosebumps."

"Think you'll ferret her out?" Marcie asked.

Kinte just gave her a look, sipping his wine. Of course he would. Ask a silly question . . .

Next came shoestring shrimpmeat, jumbos sliced over avocado, and capers swimming in taramosalata caviar with olive oil and garlic. Even Shawn liked it.

"So, *Kinte!*" Shawn started. Many an ambitious undertaking had started with those words. "I wanna roll out programs in all the bigger cities with prostitution problems, especially targeting sex workers with children. We didn't get to see much at FuturePlan, but Podrassky seems to be on the right track."

"She is very good at producing results and keeping costs under control," Kinte allowed.

"Rather than just dumping money and letting them sink or swim, maybe we should designate a national director, somebody who can look at successes, then work with each coordinator to tailor something to the needs of those regions."

"Maybe Podrassky," Marcie suggested.

Kinte looked pensive. "She could contribute, but I would be reluctant to lose her as coordinator. There are no strong candidates there, like most regions have, ready to take over the job."

"That director, the plump guy—" Shawn couldn't remember his name. He looked to Marcie, but she couldn't either. "He's not next in line?"

"She considers Mr. Suggly able in his function working with clients, but not as an administrator. From what I have seen, I would agree."

"Don't you guys use region floaters?"

Kinte nodded. "I will identify one with relevant background and begin planning your project, Mr. D'Fixx. I assume you are willing to allocate substantial—?"

"Let's start with eight or ten million, see if it pays off."

Foster smiled. "Mr. Fixx sure is good at spending whenever he sniffs a good cause."

"Something bothers me about that so-called opportunity," Shawn continued, "the one where they're losing people in Houston."

"Ms. Podrassky has mentioned it," Kinte confirmed.

"It can't be good," he said, lost in thought. "I mean, the more I think about it—what else could compete with what *we* provide? It would have to be something with a *big* payoff for very little effort. That usually means illegal, immoral, dangerous, or all three."

It was Kinte's turn to be lost in thought for a moment. Shawn knew he must be right, and that the old man was annoyed at himself for not having been more concerned about it.

Shawn suggested, "Let's do a major fact-finding. Announce through the regions that big grant bucks are coming down for sex-worker mother programs, hint jobs for social workers will be opening, put out RFPs to see what kind of proposals float, identify contacts within and outside the regions, then talk turkey, see if this is happening in other cities—losing clients to mysterious opportunities, I mean. It might be any prostitutes, or just the mothers, or even that might be a coincidence."

"I will begin today, but I think I should exercise considerable discretion asking about this mysterious opportunity. If something nefarious is afoot, I prefer not to reveal my interest."

"If something *nefarious is afoot?*" Marcie chuckled. "Sounds like The Arranger is in his secret-agent mode!"

Kinte looked like the jab got by him, but Shawn had learned over the years that nothing escaped the man.

Crème brulée, fresh raspberries, whipped cream with cinnamon, shaved peppermint leaves . . .

"So, Marcie," Foster started. "What makes you think these crystals have some kind of effect on Shawn? Do they make him irresistible?"

"It's his aura, mostly—it makes the rainbow swirl and dance. Plus, when we went back to The Gaseous Giant, I convinced him to touch it again—and babes were all *over* him." She produced the crystal from her fanny-pack, urging Shawn to take it until he finally, reluctantly, relented.

"Don't you see it?" she breathed.

Kinte looked indifferent, disinterested, even uninterested.

Foster studied him, obviously not able to see any aura. Then he batted his eyes and sing-songed, "Golly, now he *is* the sexiest man I done ever saw!" With that, he reached over and grabbed Shawn around the neck, catching him totally off-guard, and planted a big wet one on his cheek.

Beet-red, wiping his face furiously, he flung a raspberry at his lifelong friend, Marcie and Foster highly amused.

Even Kinte smiled.

The crystal sat beside Shawn's plate.

"There was a woman at the club I want to find," Shawn said softly. That quieted them down.

"The *sex worker*?" Marcie gasped. "The one we saw at FuturePlan?"

He nodded. He picked up the crystal and started massaging it in his palm. "She's *not* a sex worker," he pronounced.

"Ol' Shawnee wantin' to get some lizard tail?" Foster teased good-naturedly.

Shawn seemed distracted, serious, earnest.

"If she was at FuturePlan," Kinte offered, "Ms. Podrassky or the director may know—"

"No," Shawn said. Then he looked at Kinte, asserting louder, "No."

Kinte looked puzzled, waiting to see what his friend, his adoptive son would say.

"You can't let on we're looking for her."

"Why not, Shawn?" Marcie whispered.

"We could put her in danger."

"OH GOD, IF WE MAKE this work, it could be my chance." Riding in the dark-windowed limousine, Swallow Gagnon could barely contain her excitement about Carly's offer.

"Driver, take us around so we can talk," Carly Geiss instructed, her barrio accent near-perfect.

"Yes, Miss Morey," he answered stiffly. Carly had become Judy Morey, one of her preferred aliases, one for which she could provide documentation out the wazoo.

"There is no time limit on your man's limo?" Swallow asked.

"No, he always goes to sleep after doin' me. I usually take a ride for a while before I get dropped off somewhere."

"I'm thinking it would work, Judy. We look so much the same that one of *my* babies could be *yours* easy."

They were both young white women, mid-twenties, with long straight chestnut hair. Swallow Gagnon's father had come from Salvador, her mother California. She'd Americanized the name Gañon and changed

Solíta to Swallow when she ran away at fifteen—only to wind up "kept" by a cruel older man who took her in and eventually sold her to a now-dead *palo rota*—"rotten stick," meaning *cafiche*, or barrio pimp. Though careful about birth control while working, she'd been raped a number of times over the years by her "boyfriend," a man who liked her working *púta* on the streets for the drinking money it brought in. The result: two adorable little girls, the youngest a year old, the other not quite three.

"I don't want to be putting them babies in *no* kinda risk," Carly worried. "You sure this woman don't know you got *two niñas?*"

"I heard we's allowed only one baby because it costs a lot of money to pay for the child-care while we's working, so I didn't say nothing about having no two babies. *Hay Díos*, I'm needing to get away from Houston and have me some good money saved up, but you's got *the* high-class, rich-rich men you's working for and no *palo rota* beating you and takin' no cut—how come *you* want to leave?"

Carly shook her head, gazing out the window. "I got me so much put away, I coulda quit a long time ago, except some of these guys I work for is *real* possessive-like. I want to stop working in a year just like you, too, but if I stay here, one of them is sure to find me and then he won't leave me alone."

Swallow appeared to be buying it. "It's a *good* plan."

"Why gotta have a kid to be in the program?" Carly wondered.

"They say it's keeping the rich mans from taking girls away when falling in love with us. When they find out we gots a baby, they don't want us no more. If one *still* wants us and we decide to leave, we lose the money we had in the bank."

"Swallow, since you's helping me out, I will put fifty-thousands in the bank for you and leave you a plane ticket at the airport. If you don't like it there, you get your babies and go wherever you want. If you stay the year and get their money, you can still keep my fifty-thousands, too."

They entered the south barrio again, driving toward Swallow's flat. It looked squalid, but it offered an old woman upstairs who looked after the babies so Mama could turn tricks.

"I need to be living with you," Carly reminded. "The younger baby gots to be used to me, not acting like she don't know her mama, and peoples need to be seeing me around in case they's suspicious I'm not from here. No *púta*, though, just saying I's kept by a rich man."

"We can go *mañana* and say we's both ready to leave end of this week."

"You can let us out this time," Carly instructed the driver. She'd carefully copied Swallow's name and address on a slip of paper for him, to be passed along to Becky, documentation of where she could be found.

"*Sí*," Swallow said. "It's gonna work *good*."

Carly grew pensive for a moment, finally revealing the distraction most on her mind, disappointed to learn nothing from the answer. "Do you know about that guy that done a walk-in at FuturePlan? That skinny man with the *rosa*-haired woman who called him Mr. D'Fixx?"

EIGHT OR TEN GATHERED AROUND, gushing, tearful, congratulations and good wishes for Maria. Lyla DeCivvio attended, along with Chaleeshia Poeky, other newcomers, and several nearing the end of their indentured year. The Caddy pulled up outside, Big Man at the wheel, Joelle Bulagrét in back. Another quick round of tearful hugs.

"You memorized my mom's address, right?" Lyla prompted.

Maria had, promising to pass along where she settled, to get together someday when Lyla got to go home, too. The young Mexican-American mommy had finished her year, earned her hundred-thou, and was ready to start a new life.

One last round of hugs and out she went, to get her little girl, to go home.

Bulagrét beamed—"call me Joelle"—never friendlier.

"Please consider one last time my offer to stay six months more for sixty thousands added in your account."

She felt tempted, but no. Time to go home, to start that new life and be a full-time mom for a while.

To look for the right man she could love.

Joelle seemed disappointed, but happy for her, grateful for what she'd done. "Please remember not to be telling about what we do so not to cause problems for other girls who want the opportunity you had."

She understood. She would never jeopardize her friends like Lyla.

"Your airplane is to leave from San José Airport," Bulagrét explained, producing a ticket. "It is bad roads, so after we get *su niña*, we will take my helio-copter to the jungle for to pick up many magic crystals and then fly you to San José! It is a *fun* ride and you will get to see *más bonita* cave *en el mundo!*"

Mommy was excited, too. Take her through the sewers, for all she cared; just pick up her little girl on the way.

They drove many kilometers down a rutted dirt road before pulling into a turnabout, then down a side trail through a security gate into the barbed-wire compound. Parking next to one of the corrugated residence buildings, the car was mobbed by urchins, none older than seven or eight, all begging for treats. Big Man produced a sack of goodies and started handing them out.

Reunion!

Her little girl had just turned four. Yes, she would get to stay with Mommy from now on. This wouldn't be a short visit like all those other times.

They boarded the beat-up Jet Ranger. Everybody strapped in, Big Man on the stick, up and over the trees. Bulagrét had grown used to it, and the little girl did fine, but Mommy grabbed a sack and tossed her cookies until she felt better.

They flew over dense jungle streaked with high rocky ridges in shades of charcoal and gray, flying northwest toward Nicaragua. After thirty minutes or so, they picked up a river and followed close to a series of cliffs. They ascended over another ridge and continued to climb, a series of broken hills taking them higher. At a spectacular ribbon waterfall plunging some two-hundred feet into a ravine, Big Man circled so everybody could admire.

Finally, they set down on a long, rocky stretch with no signs of civilization any direction. Big Man powered down the craft, then grabbed a large backpack and stepped down, strapping it on. He helped Mommy and the little girl out, then Bulagrét and a large water *botá* for the hike.

They hadn't traveled far before Mommy had to pick up her daughter, the path rough and uneven, the stifling humidity and intense jungle heat enveloping them.

"Just a few minutes more," Bulagrét assured.

The path sloped down, zagging back and forth into a densely treed ravine.

And there he waited, lounging in a low-slung vine-woven hammock-chair in the cool shade beside a well-ventilated log-and-thatch cabin.

"¡*Hola, Litál!*" Bulagrét greeted. Then to Mommy, "This is Takú Litál, Tsala shaman, the last pure descendant of my peoples. He is more than one-thousand years old."

Yeah, sure, whatever. Time to get the crystals and run. *Way* too hot to play fairy tale.

The old man had dressed in a colorful frock, adding a choker necklace of carved and dyed animal bones, polished beads, and tiny colorful feathers. He wore modern, though worn, rubber-soled leather sandals.

"Pretty child," he said, peering at the little girl. "Young."

A gesture from Bulagrét hurried him. He stood, a gaunt man not quite six feet, wrinkled and mottled, surprisingly nimble for a junglemeister supposedly past the millennium mark. He led them down another path, descending to a series of deep cracks in the rock, hundred-foot drops, occasional ribbons of gurgling water below.

Narrow footbridges of rope and planks spanned the crevices. Bulagrét crossed first, leading the little girl. Then Mommy, then Takú Litál, Big Man bringing up the rear.

At the second of three bridges, Bulagrét crossed with the girl; then Big Man said something. Mommy turned and saw it in his hand.

He held a gun, pointed right at her.

Where was her little girl?

And then she realized how this could happen.

Betrayal.

Afraid, she began to panic.

Her little girl . . .

Boom!

She fell, blood spreading across her chest. Right at the edge, holding the bridge for support.

Unbearably hot, salty taste, coughing.

Dizzy.

Another shot would finish her, but . . .

Bulagrét held the little girl, keeping her turned so she couldn't see. Crying—the loud boom had scared her.

Everything spinning, can't hold on, trying to crawl away from the edge.

Tired, just rest. Lay head down.

Cough. Blood.

Slipping over, raining loose pebbles.

Couldn't hold on . . .

"WHEN DID YOU HAVE *that* made?"

"About an hour ago," Marcie answered Shawn. She held out a pendant, the crystal suspended in a platinum spider grip on white-gold chain. "Had a woman come down from Sausalito to make it—for you."

Shawn paused his stroll down the gray-sand beach and turned to face her, eyeing the gift suspiciously. Then he smirked. "A *gift*? For *moi*? Outta the goodness of your heart?"

"Hell, no! Devoted friendship, deep and personal love, loyalty and commitment, tolerance for your quirks—those are just sweetness and spice. I want you to wear this so I can figure out your power over it—or its power over *you*."

He chuckled, turning to continue his walk. He'd already gone a quarter-mile to the north end of the crescent beach and was heading back toward the compound. "You're nothing if not straightforward."

Without breaking stride, she started to put it around his neck. He shrunk away like it might burn. "Shawn D'Fixx! If you really don't believe, then what are you afraid of?"

She had him. After all, it was just a shiny rock. Nothing special. Try this: "Because *you* act all weird when I have it." So there.

She snorted. "It takes a *rock* for me to act weird?" She had a point. "Shawn, at least admit you have visions—there's been too many times, and they've always been right. Just like your brother used to."

"Intuition, predictions, fantasies, dreams; everybody has 'em. When you try *that* hard to interpret 'em, you'll find *something* you think makes sense. Then you ignore all other explanations. The only difference between me and anybody else is I had a brother who believed that stuff, and now I've got a friend who lives and breathes it." Touché.

They'd had similar arguments many times, but she wasn't about to let him off the hook. "Shawn D'Fixx, I'm telling you I see your aura change when you hold this crystal. You don't believe me? Am I lying?"

He shook his head. The last thing he wanted to do was insult or hurt Marcie. He loved her, and often enjoyed her metaphysical view of the world—he just couldn't embrace it. All he could do was leave her to her beliefs. "I *do* think you see something," he offered quietly. "But that doesn't mean it's real—" That didn't come out right, and certainly wasn't helping.

"You're humoring me," she said quietly, quickening her pace to walk ahead.

Stupid stupid *stupid!* He wasn't very good at getting out of social gaffes. Neither spoke until they approached the compound. Finally, not able to think of anything else, he quietly offered, "Marcie, I'm sorry."

She stopped and turned, her face flush, eyes moist. He'd not seen Marcie McNaught get this upset more than a few times, and always for good reason. "You don't owe me an apology, Shawn. It's not your fault. We've been bantering about this since the day we met—and we've always tried to respect each other's way of looking at things. It's just, well, I think we're close to figuring it out." She held the necklace out. "You can tell me

I believe silly things—sometimes I think you're right—but now we have a chance to learn more, to finally have proof, so you should help me pursue that. What's wrong, Shawn, you afraid it's true? You afraid to find out Jeremy was right?"

That was a poke in the eye. Could it be? "Okay, I can't explain what Jeremy could do, but he never had a crystal."

She surprised him with a quick hug, probably for treating her assertions seriously. "Maybe his powers were more developed. Or maybe the crystal just makes it easier—like binoculars stretch the natural ability of your eyes. Or maybe it focuses, like a magnifying glass can turn sunlight into a beam that sets fire to paper."

"Or crinkles up ants." Shawn chuckled. He and Foster were very young when they learned that, his friend feeling bad, Shawn practically in tears over what they'd done.

"Use your powers for *good*, Mr. Fixx," she clucked, her hand holding his arm.

The water sloshed close to their feet, the tide coming in.

"Maybe that thing can help me fulfill my destiny—" He wasn't being serious. "Of holding back this water."

"You may joke about that now, but we still don't know why your brother believed someday you'd *need* to hold back the waters *and* harness the power of your rainbow. Look, Shawn, I don't know if this thing will do it, or if we'll ever find the answers, but you take what you can get. It's like being Rich Mr. Fixx—" She said it right, must be very serious. "You can't fix everything, but *you* try to fix everything you see. And for what you *can't* see, which is why your foundations reach all over the world, helping you do more than any one man can alone."

Shawn looked at his feet, the gentle laps almost reaching his sandals. He didn't know what to say.

"Jeremy knew you'd be Mr. Fixx. Since then, you've done more than you ever thought possible." She studied him carefully, he still looking down; then she held the pendant out for him to take. "Maybe this can help you do more."

He put it around his neck, the jewel hanging like a medallion against his chest. He looked to her for approval.

Her eyes grew wide, her expression rapt.

She whispered, "Oh, Shawnee, I wish you could see this."

"YOU ARE SURE NOBODY will come to look for this baby?" Takú Litál asked, his voice powerful and deep.

"I *know* the rule," Joelle Bulagrét snapped. She glanced at the sun overhead. "We should hurry, or we will miss it."

The old shaman shrugged and crossed the bridge. Bulagrét and Big Man eased up to the edge of the crevice and peered down. No sign of the little girl's mother. Predators and scavengers and eternal jungle would swallow her up.

"Hush!" Bulagrét snapped to the whimpering child, pulling her by the hand as they worked their way down the path.

"Did you sell that American woman the crystals?" Litál asked.

"Yes. She would not yet agree to buy more, but she is a very strong believer. They affected her friend, and she knew this right away. She will want more when she sees how people will buy them."

"If these crystals are worth so much to her," Litál scoffed, "should we not be worried she would come here and take them herself?"

"My lawyer now has documents proving this land was set aside by the government for indigenous peoples. Americans cannot legally take from here, and they could not come steal without you knowing. This is why you must stay here to protect the cave from *touristas*, and so if thieves ever come you may kill them. I will bring that woman here only if it is needed to convince her the crystals are genuine so she will buy more. I will handle the business, Takú Litál, and you will be very rich someday."

They crossed the third ravine, then threaded down more zags, sometimes descending rough-hewn wooden steps, no consequence to iguanas sunning themselves here and there. Finally, they passed into the shade of trees again, Bulagrét worrying about snakes.

And there it waited, the faint odor of sulphur, cool breeze blowing from a narrow crack in the rocks, the opening ringed by shiny six-sided crystals ranging from clear to deep purple, glistening even in the shade.

They found a lantern just inside the entrance. Takú Litál ignited it with an expensive jeweled lighter from under his robe. It made the crystals sparkle and glow, filling the passageway with shifting hues ranging the full spectrum. The little girl stared in awe, finally calming some, used to seeing her mother for brief periods and having her suddenly gone.

The passageway sometimes required them to stoop single file, occasionally opening into crystal caverns punctuated with shiny smooth stalactites and stalagmites. The walkway had been created by breaking or grinding shards until relatively smooth, sometimes with planks crossing deep crevices, once with a stair-like descent that required holding a rope. Big Man had to carry the youngster several times. The farther into the side of the cliff, the deeper underground they went, that sole lantern still seemed inexplicably to illuminate as far as they could see, to give iridescent life to every crystalline formation.

The roar of rushing water could be heard echoing through the chamber ahead. Climbing down a steep grade, handing the child down, they found themselves in a great room hundreds of meters across, crisscrossed by several deep cracks lined with crystal structures, many several meters long. In the middle stood an odd formation, a raised area with hollow depression directly below a pointed shard about a meter long, needle-sharp, crystal clear, and refracting every color. The shard jutted up from the base of an enormous six-sided crystal, several meters thick, four or five meters high, pointing straight up.

The far end of the cavern broke into several more cracks, then seemed to drop away into void. A waterfall gushed from thirty or so meters above, ribboning down and disappearing into the depths of that biggest crevice. The mist it churned kept the crystals in that end wet and even shinier. The lantern light penetrated the vapor to create wondrous rainbows shifting and flickering.

The most interesting feature, not evident unless one looked straight up, was the opening. Several hundred meters above them loomed a crystal-lined crack similar to the one they'd entered, a glimpse of blue sky beyond, sunlight filtering down through the rainbow-mist waterfall.

The rushing water had one predictable effect: the little girl started to squirm, whispering, "Potty."

Bulagrét sighed, looking up at the crack high above. "How much longer?"

"Hour," the shaman guessed.

Bulagrét grabbed the tot's hand roughly and pulled her back the way they'd come until she found an easy place to sit her on a pair of planks over a deep crevice. By the time they returned, the men were bare-chested, pendants of jawbreaker crystal around their necks. Each had found a smooth spot to sit and wait.

Bulagrét removed the little girl's pullover, leaving her in shorts and sandals. Then she removed her own blouse and bra, laid them aside, and accepted one of the crystal pendants from the shaman. It found its niche nestled between two voluptuous breasts, tan-lines nowhere in sight. She and the girl sat in another smooth spot to wait.

Litál asked, "You will stay two days for Tsala-Pu?"

"Maybe. You still think seven, eight more days until it is time?"

"The sun is *very* high. I am always right. One time each year, Tsala-Pu; soon it will come. Seven, eight days."

Takú Litál had been accurately predicting Pu for many years—claims of a thousand or more notwithstanding. Like a solstice, only on one or two days per year would the angle of the sun be perfect for shining straight down through the crack, striking the big crystal in its center and refracting 360 degrees with a burst of light that filled the cave and set every crystal glowing. For most of the year, the sun would hit at least one side, creating a similar but incomplete effect. Litál, like his ancestors, believed this to be when the crystals would come alive—and could transfer life—but that Pu was the apex, when all power of the universe would channel through Tsala, the shaman and his people, giving immortality to the worthy.

For the right price.

For it to work required regular payments—and a larger payment on the big day. They were here to make a deposit, and the moment was drawing near.

"You are not doing the ceremonies anymore?" Bulagrét asked.

"The peoples, they wanted those. Is not needed. You may do them if you want." He waved her off, apparently not interested in participating.

Suited Bulagrét. Just make the offering, watch the light show, and head back.

"Do I get a necklace?" the little girl asked.

Bulagrét looked to the shaman. He just shrugged, produced another from under his robe. The little girl liked wearing it, thinking it looked pretty—that the whole cave looked pretty.

As they waited, the angle of sunlight sharpened, the beam firing bursts of colored light from the crystals down one wall and across the floor. As it neared the big crystal in the center, Takú Litál announced, "Soon it will be time."

Big Man and the shaman took positions on each side of the depression, the latter producing a long, crystal dagger from under his robe and laying it before him.

Bulagrét led the little girl, lifting her to stand over it, the protruding shard pointing straight at her back. She unstrapped the girl's sandals, had her step out of them, tossing them off to the side. She removed the necklace, leaving the little girl disappointed and confused.

Big Man and the shaman gazed upward, watching the sunlight.

The little girl started to ask Bulagrét something.

"Hush, it's almost time."

A CHIRPING SOUND SIGNALED a call. Marcie looked at Shawn, lost in his thoughts on the beach at water's edge.

"I'll see what it is," she said quietly. He nodded.

She walked to an outcropping of rocks, then touched a spot that opened a panel to reveal telephone, vid-screen, mini-printer/fax. Kinte's face appeared.

"Mr. D'Fixx is with you?"

"Over by the water." Yeah, like the big Jamaican couldn't activate a monitoring system that would show him Shawn's exact location on the estate.

"We have identified your crystal vendor. Her name *is* Joelle Bulagrét, if she is the same woman. Her passport shows her as a resident of Costa Rica. Is this her?"

Kinte's image changed to a photo of a woman.

"That's her. *All right, Kinte!*"

"Mr. Garbus has already discovered she owns a resort on the Caribbean coast called Tsala-Pu and a charter travel company that makes weekly flights. What else she might have will require more time to uncover."

"Good work. We're gonna take the jet down there and sniff around."

"As I feared."

"Where's the airport?"

"At the capital, San José, in the Central Valley region. People of means tend to live in the surrounding hills because the climate is very comfortable year-round. I have a friend who lives there at Escazú, though she is in Europe this time of year."

"You've got women all over the world, old man. It's a wonder your jet doesn't get lagged."

"I would dissuade you—"

"Not likely, Jamaican dude. Shawn'll want a day or two to get ready, knowing him; then we're off. We should find a resort other than Bulagrét's so we can check things out without tipping her off—at first, anyway."

"I will make preliminary arrangements."

"Thanks, Kinte."

She closed the panel and turned to walk toward Shawn.

At least she started to. Then she stopped dead, amazed at what she saw.

AS THE CAVERN FILLED with light, the waterfall roared louder, the ribbon gushing furiously, misty spray billowing like fog. Rainbows beamed from every side of the enormous center crystal, brightest on the water side, striking a million smaller formations and splintering so many directions that no eyes could focus on the shifting, swirling colors. The little girl stood rapt, the adults entranced.

"Close your eyes, child," the shaman whispered.

The colors exploded brighter, an electromagnetic buzz rising louder than the water, everybody's hair standing on end, skin rippling with static energy.

The shaman took the little girl's hands, whispering, "Keep your eyes closed." He squeezed for a second, then gently gripped her shoulders.

Suddenly, he thrust her body backward.

She squirmed for a second or two and tried to cry out but couldn't, the narrow shard impaling her torso, protruding from her chest, stained with blood instantly oil-slick iridescent.

He used the dagger to slice deep just above her ankles, blood gushing down over her feet, a crimson pool slowly forming in the basin.

Bulagrét could feel intense heat from the biggest crystal, the chantry growing unbearably hot, steam rising from blood starting to boil.

"Now!" the shaman pronounced.

They dipped their pendant crystals in the broth, then lifted them dripping high in the light. They dipped again several times, each crystal caked with a thick, brown coating, then replaced them around their necks.

They were seized by the power, electric sparks dancing around and through them, bathed in sweat and panting from the heat, the crescendo deafening.

The waterfall burst like a water main, spraying every direction, boiling and steaming at the chantry; a thunderstorm underground, washing and cleansing; the water now ankle deep, rising, rising, to the knees, deeper and deeper . . . Hold on, don't be afraid.

Difficult to breathe, standing in a carwash, trapped in a steamy dishwasher, frozen in headlights.

As the sun eased across the sky, the light in the crack slowly faded, the waterfall slowing to a ribbon, electric buzz grounding to naught.

Within minutes, the water drained away, only wet crystals belying its torrent, the chantry washed clean, three soaked people standing with sparkling jewels around their necks, rejuvenated again in their obsessive quest for immortality.

A cavern of crystals with very special powers.

A small lifeless child impaled on this beautiful, natural wonder.

THE PACIFIC TIDE HAD COME way up, waves crashing against rocks, mist rising to the sky. The sunlight created shifting rainbow colors in the air around and above Shawn.

Marcie stood by the rock-panel in awe. Shawn faced the sea, a dozen meters out, a horseshoe of sand around him, the water parted to leave him dry.

Her eyes couldn't focus, tricked into seeing electric sparkles dancing around his body. His rainbow aura came alive, expanding every direction, furious in its frenzy of swirls. Yet a black streak permeated it, also growing, fighting the colors and swallowing them whole.

Marcie felt scared. But she was drawn closer, walking in a daze until she stood several meters behind him, mesmerized by the rainbow beauty, yet sickened at the black streak threatening to engulf even her.

"Shawn! Shawn!"

It sounded like he said, "Costa Rica!" without turning. "The crystals! We have to go—*now!*"

Marcie: "Why do—?!"

"No!" he wailed. "It's too late!"

She saw him snatch the pendant from his neck and fling it out to sea, the blackness rippling every direction.

Then she felt it, a sense of pervading evil like nothing she had ever experienced. Suddenly cold and afraid, she could only stand there transfixed, watching as the blackness spread and blotted out the sky and the sea, stalking toward her, closer, closer, threatening to envelop and carry her away.

Shawn's aura flickered and faded, consumed by everything wrong in the world, the blackness surrounding and trapping him, overwhelming the last vestiges of resolve her friend could muster.

Then the blackness became everything everywhere, leaving Shawn as the only image she could see.

Mr. Fixx fell to his knees in the water, his face buried in his hands, waves of black rushing and washing over him . . .

And his rainbow colors flickered and disappeared.

CHAPTER 4

MUSTA BEEN ONE *HELLUVA* WILD and raucous party, that's all Marcie could figure. She studied the scene: both of 'em passed out on a chaise-longue, Shawn still wearing sunglasses against the harsh afternoon glare, Scallywag nestled against his arm and soaking up rays, debris scattered on the table and balcony deck. Half-eaten mac and cheese, open jars of macadamia nuts and sweet cashews, trail mix, several cans of fruit nectar, ice cream puddled under the carton, saucer of water, shipper box of Peruvian grubs, episode of *Time Tunnel* playing on a recessed monitor ... It sure didn't seem like Shawn to doze off before cleaning up after himself.

Careful to be quiet, she pulled a chair over for herself, setting a small package on the deck. She fished sunglasses and a small tube of face cream from her satchel, Scallywag watching while she put lotion on her face and arms. They winked at each other before the lizard went back to sleep.

"Marcie," Shawn said quietly. She smiled, Scallywag winked, and Shawn asked, "What's in the box?" By his tone of voice, he'd already guessed.

"Had 'em made." She opened the package to lay pieces on the table, jewelry with shards of cut crystal sparkling in the sunshine. "Kinte accepted one but won't wear it. Foster went for a collar tack. I like the ankle bracelet." She rolled down her footie to show him. "What about you?"

He sighed, not quite rolling his eyes, but the effect was the same. "Is that a money clip?"

She grinned, having guessed right: solid white gold, plain the way Shawn would prefer, a simple border of shaved shards laid end to end. He seemed reluctant to pick it up.

"Afraid touching it'll make you wanna go to Costa Rica?"

"I said I'd go—soon as Kinte's got it arranged," he defended. Picking it up and looking closer, he seemed relieved that nothing unusual happened.

"He would've hustled if you'd not turned wishy-washy. He's waiting for you to back out."

"Give him time. You can't buy the whole country overnight." A running joke.

"*Kinte* could. Anyway, we're goin' tomorrow." She checked her watch. "In fact, we're supposed to be down below, meeting about it right now."

"Can't talk you out of it?"

"*You're* the one who declared that we needed to go there—right away, you said." She added quieter, "You were having a vision or something?" She'd tried unsuccessfully to get him to talk about it several times.

"I just meant let's hurry up and get it over with."

Not buying that. "Why'd you throw the crystal in the water?"

"Sun was making it hot, starting to burn my chest. Shoulda hit the beach. Sorry."

"Why'd you say *Costa Rica?*"

"That's where you wanna go—where the crystals are from."

"But *you* didn't know that."

"Yes I did; you told me."

"I never said that. You said it first."

"No, *you* said it first."

They looked at each other, Scallywag watching, experience telling them both to drop it and go below.

KINTE AND FOSTER B WERE BUSY in the control center, pausing when the well-sunned pair walked in, plus the shouldered lizard.

"I have shipped the helicopter to Panamá City," Kinte explained, getting to the point. "Mr. Brinkley will fly it up to San José before you arrive tomorrow. Mr. Moolhuizen will accompany you—" Sam was an operative The Arranger liked to send for bodyguard and related duties. "As well as an anthro-archaeologist from Purdue."

"Why him and not a *geologist?*" Shawn wondered.

"If there are indigenous crystals believed to exhibit extraordinary properties somewhere in the countryside, you will find local people who know about them. Unless you want to devote years to an exhaustive geologic survey of the entire country—possibly with unsuccessful results—it seems prudent to work with someone who understands the culture." He *would* have sent a geologic team, too, but he knew Shawn would balk at any more than one "nuisance," so he'd selected carefully. Seeing that Mr. Fixx looked satisfied, he added, "Mr. Garbus would like to send somebody as well."

"Oh?" Marcie prodded. "Got a deal brewing?"

"I've arranged accommodations for your stay," Foster explained. "Found a resort for sale—cheap. It was owned by a drug dealer who built it to launder cash before he got popped and signed it over to his lawyer, somebody in my network. He doesn't want it, prefers fast cash, and knows taking his time selling could let the business devalue. I'm making it part of Shawn's chain of high-end resorts, hotels, and convention centers, changing the name to D'Shawn Costa Rica."

Marcie smiled at Shawn. "You do know that D'Shawn Worldwide and D'Shawn Resorts International are *yours*, don't you, Shawn?"

He gave her his patented don't-patronize-me look.

"I want to send a lady down to take over management, adapt it to our system, determine what kind of team we need to send in to clean house, retrain, whatever." Then to Marcie, "I'm setting it up to look like you, as Melinda McNair, are the muckety-muck from corporate—in case you attract Bulagrét's attention. She already sees you as a tycoon, thinks Shawn's a nobody."

"A nobody with a lizard," Shawn corrected. "So where is this place?"

"Caribbean coast, north of Limón."

Marcie smiled. "Close to Tsala-Pu, Bulagrét's place?"

"Right up the beach."

"YOU BEEN DIPPIN' YOUR WICK more this week than the whole rest of your pathetic life," accused Wally. He pulled a wad from his Bermuda shorts, peeled off a thousand-colón bill—about $8.00 U.S.—and slapped it on the waitress's tray. "Try to get some ice in 'em this time, sweet-lips." He grinned leeringly. She had the hots for him. Hell, they *all* had the hots for him. Ever since those crystals.

Chuck nodded for another of the same and returned her smile. She seemed to have the hots for *him*, too. They *all* did, ever since the crystals.

Of course Fraidy Chuck and Wally Flaunt-yer-wad had been there several times before, now known as flamboyant mega-tippers, show-off *presumidos*.

"And that ain't *shit* for how it *can* be."

Chuck sighed and gazed across open veranda toward the sea. Wally noted a mean-looking storm brewing on the horizon. Probably blow through in less than an hour, dump a lakeful of rain, been doing that most afternoons.

"I agreed to four-hundred K for a couple crystals," Chuck argued, "because you said we could write 'em off—microchip conductor research or whatever. But I *know* we can't call some trip to a cave a *biz* expense."

She returned with the drinks, flirty, grateful for several more thousand-colónes.

Wally acted polite, waiting for her to leave before he farted. "Hell, you can afford it. Whatta you gonna *do* with it if not have fun? Give it to some church? It's only another two-fifty apiece. I wipe my *ass* with that much."

"Oh, that's a nice image," Chuck snorted. "Look, I would if we could write the cave trip off, too."

"Come on, Fraidy. Bean counters'll find a way. If not, so what? I ain't been laid so many times so many ways since college—" Wally hesitated, realizing Chuck knew him quite well back then and probably couldn't recall him *ever* having a woman. Still, it had been one momentous week for Chuck, too. Skeptical at first, he'd have to agree the crystals were doing *something* right.

"But we already got matched with the ones to take home—" Chuck started.

"She ain't steered us wrong yet. Those is like putting on a toupée—why settle for a wig when a half-hour at peak time in that cave'll make you grow *real* hair? Turns these crystals into jump-starters instead of just batteries."

Chuck sighed again. Wally knew he was winning. They'd been a team since way back, Chuck doing the detail, Wally making things happen. Wally *always* got what he wanted—and then some.

"Well . . ." Chuck had given in. "If tomorrow's the cave trip and then our last night, let's take tonight off. I'm *spent.*"

Wally sat back and grinned. He was, too, but wasn't about to admit it. Good, tomorrow the cave, then sexual power to rival the gods.

Wally held up the dregs of his drink in toast. "Here's to crystals and sweet booty!"

The waitress appeared with two more. She had the hots for him.

Hell, they *all* had the hots for him.

WITH FABULOUS WEALTH comes inevitable ostentation, but Shawn always tried to avoid being flamboyant about it. Around people he liked, too often he felt embarrassed by his riches. Around those he didn't, sometimes he felt embarrassed *for* them.

When people care how *much* they have, and dollars and baubles are short, they usually compensate by inflating their own self-worth. It might be that obsessive quest for a buff body or enhanced beauty. Others find pride in erudition and experience, travel and exposure, esoterica and obfuscation. *So what—you got all the beans, but I got a secret even you don't know.*

So it was with this insufferable twit. Shawn didn't like him, but he knew Kinte would only send the best anthro-archaeologist available—spare no expense—an expert fully versed in Costa Rican culture.

There aboard Shawn's private jet winging toward the Caribbean, it became obvious the twit hadn't parlayed his knowledge into any sort of income-generating business consultancy, thus had been relegated to teaching, writing boring journal articles, and sniffing for paltry grants to pursue the dream of becoming head of his department back at Purdue. Much as he *tried* not to show it, he was nevertheless impressed by Shawn's custom-built Boeing 757, privacy lounge, conference room and several offices in front, then luxurious living quarters with sunken conversation pit and dining area, four private bedrooms behind, modest kitchen facilities at the rear. Bathrooms boasted enough space to dance in, with showers and mirrored vanities. None of that gold-fixture hooey could be found—Shawn wouldn't have that—but with appointments of elegant simplicity, it was furnished so you could find just about anything at the touch of a button, or voice command, or just ask.

Or we can land this puppy at the next airport and have whatever you want waiting on the tarmac, his Gulfstream ready to jump puddles.

All but the flight staff gathered in the pit for a briefing. Operative Sam Moolhuizen sat close to Shawn and Marcie, the silver-haired Afghanistan-era CID veteran more dangerous than he appeared, keeper of the gadgets Kinte's unlimited budgets let him stock or develop. The D'Shawn Resorts International manager sat next to the twit, a laid-back woman in her fifties with mousy business 'do and very alert eyes. Shawn had seen her work before, so he knew she could charm an irate customer, threaten or dismiss thieving staff, soothe the union steward, and convince the wine vendor never to try peddling his substandard shipments their way again—all in the space of a minute. She remained quiet, taking it all in.

The twit looked like a real frump, baggy clothes, a tall and lanky fellow with severe waves of hair across his head and hanging too long over the sides. He had nicotine-stained fingers and teeth, but hadn't been seen smoking yet, probably his private vice, one of those cultural things. Anthro-twit was supposed to be orienting everybody about the land of the "rich coast," but he persisted in bragging about his vast knowledge of cultures, his trips around the world, famous people he'd met, his where-withal among the highest or lowest in any caste system.

Shawn wanted to drop him unprepared into some jungle for a few weeks, then pick him up and ask for his scholarly analysis of the relative role of toilet paper in civilized societies.

It was the little speech about sultans and shahs and princes and pooh-bahs with their luxury yachts using their wealth to become tyrants over their people that most rankled Shawn. He interrupted with, "Ah, but did they have trap doors?" He waved his hand in the air; a panel appeared at his side. He touched a button; Anthro-twit's seat started to vibrate and move, causing the good professor to leap to his feet in fear, spilling his drink.

The ground-rules about twiticism established, the time had come for useful information about Costa Rica. Anthro-twit proved a bit long-winded, and Shawn had to vibrate his chair once or twice, but he managed to cover the historical highlights.

"—Smaller than West Virginia—early peoples were Indians—Nicoya pottery dated earlier than Christ, Mesoamerican in style—imported jade from Guatemala—gold from South America—worshipped the Mexican god Tlaloc in Guanacaste—"

He went on too long about the various pottery and housing styles over the millennia, Shawn slipping away to the microwave, returning with a tub of mac and cheese to share with Scallywag. "Dinner will be ready in twenty minutes," he explained by way of acting the host. The luxury crew had been left behind, so everybody drifted toward the bar for their own drinks.

"—Was Christopher Columbus who discovered Costa Rica in 1502 during his fourth voyage, chased by a storm to Uvita Island just off the coast from Limón—not much settlement for another half-century—Juan de Cavallón came in search of gold but eventually gave up—Juan Vásquez de Coronado brought Spanish settlers who cultivated crops and lived in harmony with the natives—no prosperity, but grew coffee and banana—"

Scallywag was enjoying his mac and cheese, Marcie her wine, the resort manager a spritzer. Shawn had made a tiny TV screen appear in his armrest, silently watching an episode of *The Monkees*, only Marcie the wiser.

"—Turning point in the 1940s, bitter civil war, big social changes, the democracy they enjoy today—constitution—electoral tribunal—women's right to vote—outlawed discrimination against the minority population of black immigrants—outlawed capital punishment—made primary education both compulsory and free, *not* run by the churches—"

"How's business, the economy?" Shawn wondered.

Anthro-twit hemmed and hawed about agriculture, coffee and mangoes and such. Shawn touched his panel several times. A large viewscreen floated along one wall where all could see. Within seconds, Foster B. Garbus's handsome face smiled at the group.

"Playin' with your lizard in mixed company, I see," Foster greeted.

"Sorry to bother you, Mr. Garbus," Shawn apologized, putting on a show for manager and twit. Moolhuizen knew the charade like he seemed to know *everything*. Shawn wondered if the operative was briefed first whenever Mr. Fixx needed to pee.

"That's all right; I was hoping you'd check in." Foster greeted the others, then to Shawn's next question explained, "Costa Rica went fully democratic in the forties, then immediately started asking a dozen other countries to lick its nuts. U.S. went at it hard and heavy, floating billions in economic-development loans which have been refinanced for two generations now. U.S. influence hasn't paid off much; there's nothing economically or militarily strategic about Costa Rica that Panama just to the south can't do better. Some good development around San José and the west coast, Nicoya Peninsula. *Very* agricultural, probably never get out from under that foreign debt, good for eco-tourism. Lots of U. S. retirees are starting to cluster up and down the Pacific Coast. Sniff around if you like, but focus on the resort we just bought. Next one'll probably go up on the Gulf of Nicoya, possibly some development outside the capital at Alajuéla or Cartágo."

"Thanks, Mr. Garbus."

"Enjoy your trip!" He seemed to wink to Marcie, though it was hard to tell with a flat-screen.

Anthro-twit quickly grabbed the stage, pointing out, "One under-exploited economic opportunity is horticulture—flower and plant export. There are more than a *thousand* varieties of orchid down there alone—and I mean just growing wild, everywhere you go."

"We *must* do an orchid trek," Marcie announced for Shawn's benefit. She reached over and caressed his shoulder, she and Scallywag winking at each other. Shawn would have made a smart remark about the psychic power of orchids except for the others present.

The pilot, John Guyton, wandered back to join them. A good-sized feller with a friendly face and slight southern drawl, he'd come as a package with Moolhuizen and Chopper-Pilot Brinkley way back when, ostensibly working for Foster B's corporate empire. "Thought you might want to know it's a good time to peek out and see the Mayan ruins at Yucatan."

"John!" Marcie called. "Who's *flyin'* this thing?"

Surprise! Recognition! Guyton grinned and hurried back to the cock-pit. He really did have a co-pilot up there, but Marcie always liked to play that on guests—when Shawn didn't beat her to it.

The views offered a nice respite, but before long, they found them-selves listening to that self-important drone again. "Lots of birds like tou-cans and macaws, monkeys like white-faced and howler and spider and marmosets, big cats like jaguars, ocelots, pumas—"

"A threat to the resorts?" worried the manager.

"Any built *that* close to the jungles are usually walled off to discourage—"

"What about the people?" Marcie interrupted.

"Most are of mixed heritage, Indian and Spanish. It's not derogatory to call them *ticos* because of their unique variation on the Spanish language. The diminutive in most of Latin America is *tito*. Like *segment* translates to *segmento* and short segment is *segmentito*, in Costa Rica they would say *segmentico*. They even call *themselves ticos*."

"If you have a son someday," Marcie whispered in Shawn's ear, "they'll call him *Señior Fixxtico*."

Without missing a beat, he returned, "You lean over any farther with that loose halter top and I'm gonna get an eyeful of *your* little ticos! *Ouch.*" Nobody could see what she did, but it sure got his attention.

"Okay," Marcie interrupted Anthro-twit, "so we're not worrying about lack of due process or being swept up in a revolt or civil war or becoming political hostages; we're pretty safe overall—"

"Well, they have a deadly snake, but they also have some of the finest medical facilities in the world. In fact, many from the U.S. seek treatment there—especially for procedures like plastic surgery—because of the high quality and low costs—"

"So we're free to travel and all we have to worry about are snakes and big cats?"

"And crime and maybe a little police corruption. It's not uncommon for the authorities to stop tourists over the smallest inexplicable infractions, problems solved by a modest donation to the local youth league or whatever. But crime, especially against naïve tourists, can be *very* high. You leave valuables in a rental car on the street *anywhere* and they *will* be gone when you return."

Moolhuizen snorted. Shawn knew he begged to differ. Not with the contingent Kinte probably had waiting for them.

"Prostitution?" Shawn asked, a peculiar, intense expression on his face. Scallywag regarded him curiously, then climbed up on his shoulders.

"Oh yes, especially in the capital and surrounding villages. Some *very* young girls for sale—at least from what I *observed* on previous trips," he hastily added, actually blushing some.

"That's *your* job, then," Shawn said quietly.

"Excuse me?"

"During this trip, with Mr. Garbus covering your expenses to further your studies, what he wants in return is a thorough report on the prostitution problem and your recommendations for solving it."

"But that is just a characteristic of culture worldwide—"

"And I have no moral problem with consenting adults, um, you know—*consenting*, but if children are being used, or people are doing it against their will, or poor families are turning to that because they don't know or have anything else—that's what, um, *Mr. Garbus* wants you to help solve."

"But as an academician, my job is to remain impartial, to study—"

"What good is *knowing* if you can't *help*?"

"But history has shown that some of our best-intentioned efforts at *help* wreaked colonialistic havoc on—"

"I'm not talking about wholesale cultural transformation, just helping people who *want* it."

Anthro-twit looked befuddled. "I'm not sure how—"

"Look at it from every perspective—cultural, religious, educational, health, economic . . ."

"But isn't economics the ultimate driving force—?"

"Sure, that's why I want you to consider *any* option. Screen out no ideas, whatever the cost. If these young sex workers—especially those trying to support children—if they have better ways to earn *more* money, then the pool of labor for illicit services will shrink, prices will go up, demand will drop due to exorbitant cost. It's a business." He hesitated, then sat back and relaxed. "I don't know," he admitted. "Just work on it."

"Could lead to a Nobel," Marcie jested, but the twit was taking that thought seriously.

"Who we gonna meet when we foray into the jungles?" Shawn wondered, changing the subject. He knew Marcie wouldn't be satisfied until he was up to his butt in *something* outrageous.

"There are still concentrations of Indians, the Chorotegas at Nicoya, the Borucas on the west coast down near Panama, a few Guatusos scattered about in the northeast. The Talamanca group, including the Cabécar and Bribri, are pre-Conquest tribes north of the mountains." He grew pensive for a moment. "There *was* some talk years back about descendants of Tsala still living in the volcanic highlands of the Tilarán Mountains, the middle of the Sierra Madre-Andes chain. It was never verified, though. Seems I read something once where an anthropologist lived with them near a sulphuric lake at the bottom of which could be found their ancient city, buried Atlantis-style after a massive eruption and earthquake. Strictly legend, though, supposedly peoples who had emigrated all the way around the world."

Scallywag winked at Marcie.

"Religion?" she asked.

"Who? The *Tsala*? Um, something about the power of light I think, light shining through crystals in magic caves."

Shawn and Marcie looked at each other, Scallywag waiting patiently. Moolhuizen scowled like he'd already mentally packed for a jungle trek. Kinte wouldn't like this.

"What else do you know about that?"

Anthro-twit just shrugged. "I'd have to look up the article he wrote, the man who claimed to find these peoples."

Shawn sat forward, hand poised on his console. "Can we talk to this man?"

"Oh me, no. He's been dead ten, fifteen years."

Shawn and Marcie both exhaled. Shawn suggested, "Let's get that paper he wrote."

Almost at once, Kinte Bilal appeared on the flat-screen. The Arranger was on the job.

"Hey, old man," Shawn greeted.

"Greetings, Mr. D'Fixx. I trust you are well?"

"Just playing with my lizard. Hey, we need a journal paper written by some professor—"

"An *associate* professor," Anthro-twit corrected.

"About the Tsala people of Costa Rica." To the twit, "What was his name?"

Twit had to think. "Um, oh yeah! Frenchman. Milo something."

Scallywag was watching him.

"That's it: Associate Professor Milo Bulagrét."

BY THE TIME SHAWN'S nondescript jet skimmed the mountains and rolled to a stop on the tarmac at Aeropuerto San José, it had been settled.

Anthro-twit would investigate and try to locate the legendary Tsala people, or refute their existence. Then he would concentrate on humoring Shawn's desire to rescue sex workers from their circumstances.

The entourage was met by a customs/immigration official and Les Brinkley, the wiry black man with graying beard. Their documentation was handled quickly and efficiently, admittance for Scallywag having been pre-arranged by Kinte. Brinkley offered a satchel of colónes to be used for pocket money.

Then the visitors golf-carted over to inspect Shawn's classic Bell Jet Ranger, 900hp Alliss turbo, a luxuriously appointed six-seater chopper decked out with state-of-the-art electronics, the least of which were satellite communications (relay transponders on French-launched FosCom, Shawn's private "bird") and military surveillance starting with the basics: thermal imaging, infrared, sonar-tracking. Boasting the best emergency-medical technology, it could also be a life-saving air-ambulance if the need arose. Soundproofed and set up for entertainment, it offered discs of *Parker Lewis Can't Lose* episodes ready for viewing.

Reminded how to contact Brinkley, Anthro-twit selected one of the waiting private cars and headed off to the college to look up old contacts.

Rather than head straight to the resort, Shawn wanted to look around San José a bit first, get the lay, feel the pulse. Les Brinkley lifted off in the helicopter with the manager so she could get to work. Sam Moolhuizen pulled away in another private car with Marcie and Shawn. Marcie made noises like she might want to drive, but decided not. Moolhuizen breathed a sigh of relief. So did Shawn.

They were followed, two men in a van, but Moolhuizen seemed unconcerned—must work for Kinte. They parked downtown, a covered garage not far from the main square, and set out on foot. They discovered a bustling market area, very Central American in character, vendors and hawkers, tinkerers and soothsayers, craftsmen and artisans, wholesalers and food servers. Many worked from trucks and vans, or stalls and shops from semi-permanent to ramshackle; others roamed, carrying their goods, thieves and cons, musicians and tour guides, prostitutes.

Scallywag a-shoulder, Shawn wandered around aimlessly, stopping to admire, Marcie selecting while he dutifully paid for baubles to load her tote. Moolhuizen strolled not far behind, casual and relaxed, mirrored shades to hide his eyes, more alert than he appeared. Marcie wanted to sample a few of the foods, but Shawn worried about Montezuma's revenge—or worse. Spicy garlic bread, rolled chocolate treats, and bottled sodas served as a sanitary compromise.

At the far west end, on the outskirts of the crowd, they found a lone lad in a rickety wooden wheelchair. He stammered that he was nineteen, but he looked younger and, when he spoke with that deep silky voice, sounded a good bit older. He appeared very thin, dark-skinned like the native Indians, with big brown eyes and a well-practiced earnest expression. Shawn was drawn to his infirmary, wondering why such a young man couldn't walk, if maybe something could be done about it. Marcie was drawn to his wares, a piece of cardboard held in his lap, adorned with pendants hanging from thin strips of rawhide, small six-sided pieces of wood onto which he'd painted rainbows, then glued bits of broken glass.

"I will allow each of you to buy only one for to bring good luck," he said very seriously. "One-thousand colónes for each of you, and also your friend." He gestured casually toward where the operative leaned against a wall.

Moolhuizen's cover blown, he wandered close, staying behind the young Indian.

"Buying these will help a handicapped—a physically *challenged* person—care for himself?" Shawn asked, trying to keep the words simple.

The Indian looked hurt, not insulted, but maybe embarrassed. "You must want to have these not for helping *me*, but for *you* to have good luck. My legs do not matter."

Surprised by the approach, Shawn had expected the sympathy pitch. *Sure, I'm selling junk, but it's for a good cause.*

Marcie knelt and looked closer, intrigued by the rainbows. "How will these bring us good luck?"

"Rainbow light," he answered firmly, drawing his shoulders up as if proud of the answer. "It can be for the badness or it can be for the goodness, but *you* are the goodness so you may buy one each."

Shawn smiled. He liked the attitude. "What is your name?"

"*Me llamo*— I am called Tsoo-Ki."

"Tsoo-Ki, I'm Shawn; this is Marcie, and that's Sam. Why are you in a wheelchair?"

Tsoo-Ki's shoulders and face dropped. He stared at his lap, taking a deep breath. "What I am *no está importante*. Please, you must have a rainbow." He seemed frustrated, not impatient, just that somehow this had become very important to him.

Moolhuizen dropped something behind the wheelchair, stooped to pick it up and surreptitiously poked the young man's leg with a needle. Getting no reaction, he stood, appearing mildly surprised.

Still kneeling in front of him, Marcie looked into Tsoo-Ki's eyes, at the intensity of his feelings. Smiling reassuringly, "I believe you," she offered quietly. "But the luck these will bring is worth *far* more than you ask. We want to pay one-hundred thousand colónes each—but that's a limit of *one* per customer," she teased, allowing a wide grin.

Tsoo-Ki grinned, too, his face lighting up. Shawn wondered whether to attribute the financial windfall or Marcie taking him so seriously. While Marcie selected three pendants, Shawn produced his money clip and started to peel off bills. Instantly, Tsoo-Ki's eyes went wide, but rather than looking excited about such a wad of cash, he seemed to shrink away, afraid, confused. He breathed hard, his eyes darting furiously between his three customers and possible routes of escape.

Marcie stood with the pendants, then saw what was happening and paused. All three visitors stared at Tsoo-Ki, the young Indian gazing toward the wad of bills.

Or was it the money clip?

Marcie realized it first, whispering, "Shawn, take off the clip and put the cash back in your pocket."

He did, but Tsoo-Ki's reverie persisted unbroken, the lad staring fixedly at the clip.

"Touch it, Shawn," she insisted.

He didn't want to. Nope, didn't want to at all.

She gave him that look, the one that said he was going to wind up doing what she wanted eventually, so why not get it over with?

He shifted the clip so the crystal inlay touched his hand.

Tsoo-Ki gasped, almost panting, then started to . . . *cry?*

Tears brimmed in his eyes as he breathed, "Tsawa-Ki! Man of the rainbow, I am to be your prince!" Then he lowered his head again as if unworthy.

Marcie gazed at Shawn like so many times before, rapt, mesmerized. She looked to Moolhuizen, gestured toward Shawn as if asking did he see it, too? The operative seemed befuddled, hands open and apart to indicate that whatever she meant had gotten by him.

Shawn wanted to ask the obvious questions, but then again, he didn't want to see Marcie getting caught up in more superstitious hokum.

She beat him to it. "*His* prince? And what is a Tsawa-Ki?"

"Tsawa-Ki is the man who makes the rainbow, the man who will come for my Tsala peoples. As was my father and his fathers, I am the Tsala prince, waiting to serve Tsawa-Ki."

Okay, too far gone, Marcie wouldn't let this get by. Might as well focus on something practical. "Tsoo-Ki, what happened to your legs?" Shawn asked.

"I have fallen from the rocks, from searching for my cousin with *las cristales.*"

"Did that happen a long time ago?"

He shook his head. "Not long. I left my family because I am no longer able to work, to grow the food and do my part." He looked sad, wistful, almost ashamed.

"Have you seen a doctor?"

He shook his head no. "I wait for Tsawa-Ki and hope someday to swim under the rainbow."

Numerous urchins and several street people gathered, trying to get their attention, pitching their wares, offering favors. Shawn wouldn't be comfortable staying there much longer. "Where do you live?"

"I sleep in back of the snake museum. I am helping the man clean at night."

Snake museum? Cool. Shawn offered reassuringly, "I want to have you examined by a doctor to see if your legs can be healed. We have a nice place you can stay for a while. Would you like to come with us?"

A broad, sparkling smile answered for him. He had remarkably straight white teeth for somebody who'd obviously never seen a dentist. "Is it okay if I take my things?"

"Is it okay if I see the snakes when we stop to get your stuff?"

Glancing at Scallywag still on Shawn's shoulders, Tsoo-Ki offered, "*Su amiga iguana* will see his cousins there, too." Everybody smiled.

They stopped at the car; Shawn made a phone call; then they walked toward España Park, pushing Tsoo-Ki in his rickety wheelchair. The Serpentario turned out to be fairly nondescript, second floor up a flight of stairs. Tsoo-Ki explained how he normally arrives at dark, waiting for the caretaker to come take his chair up then return to carry the crippled young Indian. Moolhuizen eased him, chair and all, backwards up the steps until they entered a large room full of snakes and lizards and frog-and-toad displays.

A python more than five meters long the highlight, Tsoo-Ki led his benefactors around for the full tour. At the iguanas, he explained that some Indians still believed them to be magical beings, very intelligent and able to understand what certain people are thinking. Scallywag poked his head out the front of Shawn's shirt as if listening patiently. Tsoo-Ki rolled himself to a back room and returned with fresh beetle grubs for Shawn's pet, the lizard winking his gratitude.

The sat-phone in Shawn's pocket chirped. "Day after tomorrow?" Shawn spoke into the handset. "Hmmm . . . Okay, we'll be leaving here in another fifteen. Is Les back already? Will it be there by the time—? Yes. Sure, old man. Uh huh. Oh? Um, you're gonna laugh— We lost him. Yes,

I mean Moolhuizen. We sent him on a wild-goose chase and gave him the slip— Oh. Um, okay. Thanks, Kinte."

Marcie was smiling. "Did you have him going?"

Shawn looked sheepish, turning to Moolhuizen. "You've got a blipper in your pocket, don't you?"

The operative put on his innocent look, gazing around the room. He'd been signaling The Arranger that all was clear even as Shawn tried to fool him.

Tsoo-Ki's possessions fit in a small satchel, toothbrush and comb, spare rags of clothes, a tiny hand-carved flute, more of the hand-made pendants, plus tools and paints for making them.

The caretaker wished Tsoo-Ki luck, the young Indian promising he would come back one day soon. By the time they reached the street, their car was inexplicably parked right by the entrance. Moolhuizen helped Tsoo-Ki into the back seat with Marcie, Shawn climbing in the front, the wheelchair left next to the door. Off to the airport, they found Les Brinkley waiting with the chopper and a shiny new *electric* wheelchair.

"It's going to be two days before the specialists will arrive down here to examine you," Shawn apologized. "We have a nice resort on the coast where you can stay until then."

It took the lad a few minutes to get used to the feeling of riding in a chopper, finally settling down and relaxing, gazing in awe at his countryside below.

"We have much to talk about, you know," Marcie said.

Tsoo-Ki smiled. "Much to do," he agreed.

"Shawn's Rich Mr. Fixx. He helps people."

"This is why he is helping me."

She nodded. "He's also got the power of the rainbow."

"I know."

"We came here to understand it."

"We have been waiting a long time for him."

THE TEMPORARY SIGN READ, *Coming Soon! D'Shawn Resorts International*. It looked like a nice place, though it could use a bit of work and would require certain additions to meet corporate standards. Occupied only to one-third capacity, as soon as it went on-line with the D'Shawn International reservations system, it would be full in no time.

The entourage followed as an earnest manager led Marcie on a complete tour, bowing and scraping and reporting more than anybody wanted to hear. Afterward, Tsoo-Ki chattered his gratitude for the new chair and everything else, but he wouldn't talk about the Tsala or rainbows or why he called Shawn "Tsawa-Ki." Moolhuizen disappeared, but Shawn knew he'd only have to whisper, "Sam, *help*," and the silver-haired operative would be all over him.

Two things did come out as they finally relaxed on the veranda watching moonlight reflect in the gentle waves. One, Tsoo-Ki had been ashamed his injury prevented him from contributing to his family and the remaining few dozen of his people who still farmed in the valley, a tiny community that avoided using the Tsala name around outsiders. Shawn made several calls, then hired Tsoo-Ki as a temporary tour guide in exchange for a tractor, plow and several years' worth of diesel fuel delivered at regular intervals. Tsoo-Ki could go home and bring his people something to benefit all, something he'd earned honestly.

The other thing was about those crude rainbow pendants the young Indian had made. Marcie was wearing her own and had Shawn's in her pocket no doubt awaiting a chink in his reluctance to encourage her fantasies. With permission, she went to Tsoo-Ki's barrier-free suite and got another one from his cardboard display.

Then, glowing with a lunar corona, Tsoo-Ki admitted they were nothing more than trinkets, just bits of glass and wood and paint.

No powers, nothing mystical.

She convinced Shawn to try his on, obviously disappointed when nothing happened. Tsoo-Ki didn't want to wear the one she'd retrieved for him, either. Much like Shawn, he seemed almost afraid of it.

"This only be glass," he argued again.

"Then it can't hurt," she offered gently. "And what do we lose if we try, *maybe* something *can* happen. Right, Shawn? Isn't *anything* a *maybe*?"

He shrugged, trying not to disturb his lizard curled up in the warmth of his lap. "Open-minded people believe in *maybes*."

"Believe in *maybes* with us Tsoo-Ki."

The young Tsala prince draped the proffered pendant around his neck.

No rainbows or explosions, no epiphany—just a gentle salt breeze blowing across the water, reflections shimmering in the surf.

Tsoo-Ki whispered, "*Maybe*."

DESPITE THEIR PLATINUM cards boasting no limit, the manager had to make a phone call to clear such a large amount. After all, Wally and Chuck had been spending quite a bit this past week, sometimes in suspiciously huge lump sums.

Approved and recorded. Between them, they had dropped more than a million dollars.

On crystals.

She started gluing their super-duper custom-psi, perfectly matched and harmonized shards to the backs of their watches. "*Está importante* that you understand you will not feel this power as much—now it is becoming part of you. When you are in the light of *la caverna*, it will fill your psi for always, even without these shards, no matter where you go."

Sprawled in one chair, Wally scratched his belly while Chuck sat stiffly in another. They'd spent a lot of money, but they were having one phenomenal week.

"Different bitch every night for the rest of my life," Wally pronounced, grinning.

"I wouldn't mind, you know," Chuck explained apologetically, "getting married."

"This man has the wisdom to use this power for good," she said, shooting a look toward Wally. "To use the crystal for fun—" She shrugged. "That is okay. To use for being happy, that is the wisdom."

"Different bitch every night," Wally agreed.

She sighed. "You should be here in *dos horas*—two hours. The van will take you to helio-copter, and you will fly *a las montañas* where you will be hiking to *la caverna*. You should wear sturdy shoes for the jungle."

"We'll be here," Wally announced, getting up and gesturing to Chuck that it was time to leave.

She watched them go, shaking her head. Butt-ugly fools with too much money.

She'd forgotten this time to act like they made her hot.

LOCAL CABLE WAS SHOWING some good stuff, an early episode of *That Girl!* at the moment. Shawn hadn't bothered to arrange for sat-streaming his collection, but this would work. He had couch cushions and extra pillows piled against the headboard, a makeshift back-rest for himself and Marcie, tray of munchies between them on the king-size bed, lizard lounging at the foot. Their first night in Costa Rica.

Commercials. "You sure do humor me, Shawn."

"Who's humoring whom?"

"But *your* foibles are usually fun. Mine rush us off in every direction, trying to find answers to questions *you* don't even wanna ask, with you trying not to encourage me, but goin' along anyway."

"You keep it interesting," he said, smearing a dab of guacamole on his toe and sticking it out for the lizard to snarf.

Scallywag accepted graciously, Marcie chortling mid-gulp on her soft drink, burning her nose but not quite spraying the bed. "You and your iguana."

"If'n a feller cain't enjoy his lizard ever' now an' then—" he drawled. Then he couldn't think of an ending.

Final jokes, closing credits, remote control; he shut off the TV. Marcie extinguished the lamp, a slash of moonlight cutting through the screened balcony doorwall. Warm breeze enveloped them, salty air, the rustle of swaying palms just outside, gentle lapping of waves washing over yellow-white sand.

She sighed. "It's the cosmic tease," she said softly.

"Huh?"

"You're the one's got the power; I'm the believer. I get *this close* to proving something, and it just slips away." She shook her head. "But still, you humor me."

"Who's humoring whom?"

They took turns yawning, both shifting lower in the bed.

"Suppose I oughta wander over to my suite and crash," she mumbled.

"Um."

After a few minutes, "Did I leave?"

"Not unless it's your aura speaking," he mumbled.

"Silly Mr. Fixx, aura's don't talk."

"Marcie, if *you've* got an aura, it'll find a way to run its mouth—Ouch!"

"Auras can't pinch, either."

"Then you're still here." Silence. "You asleep?"

"I don't know."

"So stay here. I'll make my lizard behave."

She kissed him on the cheek and settled in. "G'night, Fixx-dude."

"Night, space-chickie."

"You're quite the smoothie."

They faded within minutes, the sound of their gentle breathing keeping rhythm with the lapping waves.

Scallywag eased over to the side of the bed and up onto the nightstand. From there, he climbed to the dresser where Shawn had tossed his pocket change.

And the money clip.

The iguana made a full circle, not unlike a cat settling in, then lay flat on his belly, directly in the slash of moonlight, his head resting on the crystal-laden clip.

It was probably the moonlight reflecting in his eyes, but they glowed, almost sparkled.

The colors of a rainbow.

CHAPTER 5

"NOTHIN'S GONNA HAPPEN TO HER, is it?" Lyla DeCivvio was obviously worried about the new girl, Chaleeshia Poeky.

"No, but she will just lose the money," Joelle Bulagrét assured her.

Big Man stood off to the side, eyes shaded, unmoved.

"She and her *niño* are to go back on the flight today," Bulagrét added.

They paused to listen, voices on the tape again. It sounded like Chaleeshia had come out of the bathroom.

Lyla's voice was trying to convince her to stay. "But you *can't* run. You got no money, no way back to the U.S."

"Yes I do. I got somebody I can call. I just gots to get my little boy and ride on outta here. I don't be wantin' no problems. If I can get to a phone, all I gots to do is axe and I be gettin' all the help I need."

"Well, when you gonna do this?"

"Supposed to get my first visit with my boy in the next day or two. Soon as I can get him." There was a pause on the tape. "You won't tell nobody, will ya?"

"You can trust me," Lyla said.

The recording fell quiet for a moment; then came the voice of Chaleeshia thanking Lyla again before heading off to bed.

Bulagrét stopped the tape, removed it from the micro-recorder and pocketed it. "Do not tell her I know, or that I will be sending her home. I do not want the other girls to know of this. We will take her to see her *niño*, and *then* she will find out we are going to the airport. She must leave her clothing and things."

Lyla had been wringing her hands, worry in her face. That seemed to satisfy her, though. "Um, you said if I could prove any, you know, um, that I would get a month off, be able to go home sooner and still get the money?"

"You are doing good. You will go home one month sooner."

Lyla was pleased, very pleased. She opted to stay at the resort while they went to the apartments to pick up the unsuspecting mother.

Chaleeshia looked surprised when she opened the door. "Oh! Hello. Come in."

Bulagrét smiled. "Good news, Señorita Poeky! We are going to visit *su niño!* Let us go right now."

Obviously thrilled, she locked up and followed, Big Man bringing up the rear. They drove toward the children's compound, but pulled into a turn-off before reaching the gate. Big Man shut off the engine and walked around. He opened the door for Bulagrét, who stepped out and gestured for Chaleeshia to follow.

The young prostitute hesitated, looked puzzled, then stepped out. Standing with her back to the car, she noticed Big Man had a gun pointed toward her.

Smack! Bulagrét hit her! *Smack!*

Chaleeshia glared, coiled to fight back, but her eyes drifted back to the .357, her face awash with dejection and fear.

Smack! Bulagrét figured she had her attention.

"What?!" Her lip oozed blood.

Bulagrét showed her the tape. "If you are wanting to leave, you should be asking, not be running away. I cannot let you take your child with you."

Chaleeshia began to cry. "No! You can't—"

Smack!

"If you want your child, you must tell me who you called to come get you."

"No one. Ain't *nobody!* Just talk, is all."

Bulagrét looked to Big Man. He handed her the pistol and stepped forward, the young sex worker cringing.

Crack! Open-handed, aside her head, the blow spun and dropped her. She cried out, then struggled to her hands and knees. He grabbed her hair and lifted her bodily into a standing position. One hand on her throat, he pulled back with a massive fist aimed at her face.

"You better tell me," Bulagrét said calmly.

Chaleeshia sobbed, trying to get her breath, hands pulling fruitlessly on Big Man's arm. "She—ain't—nobody," she choked out.

Big Man released her throat.

"Who is she?"

"Just someone my sister knowed, said I could call if I ever needed help."

"You will give me her name and telephone. Then you will call her while I am listening, and tell her you are okay. So do not lie to me. *Who is she?*"

Chaleeshia was panting, wiping her face, still cringing from Big Man. "You'll—you'll let me and my little boy go home?"

"Not with this woman, but to go with *me* on the plane, yes. You will not call anybody else or tell where we are."

"Oh! Oh, I won't tell no one. Promise! You can trust me. Won't tell *no*body."

"Who is this woman?"

"Um, Carly. Carly Geiss. The number she gimme—" She had to think to get it right, an 800 number in the U.S.

Bulagrét smiled. "See? That was not so difficult. Now we will get *su niño.*" She gestured toward the car.

Chaleeshia turned and opened the door, then started to climb in. Big Man stepped behind her.

All at once, his arms surrounded her neck and torso.

Pull and twist.

Snap.

Her head lolled, a quick gasp, her breath slipping away. She shuddered once and went limp.

He pulled her lifeless body around the back. Bulagrét reached in and pressed the trunk release. Loaded and locked, they drove toward the compound.

"We will drop her in the jungle now and come back to take those fat gringos to *la caverna.*"

As the old Caddy pulled in, kids scurried from every direction, gathering around and looking for treats. The car drove on through, pausing so Big Man could open the gate that admitted them to the helicopter pad. Positioning the vehicle so nobody could see, he loaded the body aboard.

Bulagrét reached in and pulled Chaleeshia's hair to twist her head around and look at her swollen, lifeless face.

"It is good this happened now. Her *niño* will be another child to give life for Tsala-Pu."

"USUALLY EIGHT ROOMS, sometimes nine or ten," the manager explained.

Shawn picked at his breakfast fruit plate, wondering how this woman with her severe features and hair pulled back so tight it stretched her face could wear a wool business suit in such humid, stifling heat—and still come off laid-back and relaxed. Marcie tried to look interested, the big-shot from corporate who cared to pick nits.

"Changing to different rooms every week," she continued, "always for young, single women, a block of advance reservations and paid for by—get this—the competition next door."

"That place called Tsala-Pu?" Marcie got interested, Shawn watching quietly.

"What's more, I asked around a little and have come to the conclusion this is for illicit purposes, the vile debasement of women." Not so laid-back now; other women trading her body for cashola apparently offended her brand of feminist sensibilities.

"Vile debasement?" Shawn asked matter-of-factly.

"*Prostitution!*" There, she'd said it. Laid out for scorn and derision.

Marcie looked puzzled, glancing over to Shawn. "Prostitution doesn't have to be a *vile debasement.*"

The manager looked stricken, glancing toward Shawn for support.

Sensing both waiting for his reaction, he shrugged. "Honest and fair exchange of services for goods or money has been the basis of economies throughout recorded history."

"But I thought—"

"Hey, *I* don't like it, certainly wouldn't be a customer, but it's not my place to decide for everyone else—"

"But you wanted to—"

Marcie cut her off. "I think my friend here is against people being *forced* into prostitution, or feeling trapped so they have no other choice, or putting their children at risk because they need to support them and have no other way."

The manager obviously didn't agree. Prostitution and pornography, in her mind, degraded *all* women—like some successful supermodel being paid handsomely to pose *au naturel* for a photo spread somehow could diminish a fat frump in Toledo with a trailerful of squalling brats, swilling beer and chain-smoking generic cigarettes while she feverishly scratched a pile of welfare-check instant lottery tickets.

"We had a friend who hookered her way through college," Marcie explained. "She enjoyed it. She had other ways to make money, too— probably didn't even need the cash, but she liked excitement, took pride in being very good at it. Made oodles of money from some very grateful customers who went on to become captains of industry."

"And made some friends in the process," Shawn added. He sort of blushed.

The manager might have wondered if they were talking about Ms. McNair—the role Marcie played as D'Shawn Resorts VP—but she didn't ask.

"I'm more curious *why* the resort is booking them," Shawn pointed out. He'd been trying to toothpick-stab a grape, accidentally sending it flying into the manager's lap.

"Probably making a cut, swinger's kinda place, send their tourists home happy," Marcie conjectured.

"But why at the competition?" Shawn puzzled. He still had several more grapes. Oh, what the hell, it wasn't like they could put somebody's eye out. Lost two more, only one left.

"They could be doing the same at other resorts around this cove, too," Marcie pointed out.

Flip. Shawn slipped over and grabbed a fruit platter from an empty table. Fifteen or twenty more grapes. He spotted Tsoo-Ki on the veranda, Scallywag on the rail sunning himself, the young Indian watching the white-caps rolling in. Shawn calculated the distance and flipped a grape. Damn, missed by a meter or more. "What're you thinking, Melinda?"

"Well, I don't know. I guess people travelling all the way down here must have *some* money, a bit classier than the Motel 12 in Kalamazoo." Marcie had grown up in the western Michigan city, sometimes referring fondly to that motel, but had never offered to explain why. "Can't be sending 'em to seedy brothels; may not wanna be known as using their own rooms for sex workers—families and all, you know—so could be they just keep rooms in several of the locals, but not too many in any single one."

"Regardless," the manager sniffed, "I was planning to cancel—"

"No," Marcie instructed. "We have no reason to cancel honest, paying bookings."

"But we oughta learn more," Shawn added. "Hey, Sam?" Moolhuizen had been discreetly lounging at a nearby table. He appeared at Shawn's side in an instant. "You got some guys can check out some of the women staying here?" The operative nodded. "We think they might be sex workers. See if you can find out their game—get the lay of the situation—" He grinned, but only Marcie seemed to appreciate his pun. "Um, anyway, don't get in too deep—" At least Marcie stayed with him. "Just find out how things work. She can give you their room numbers," he said, referring to the manager, "and help you ID the women we're after."

Moolhuizen nodded and went back to his table.

"Another thing," Marcie added for the manager's sake. "Contact the right person at Tsala-Pu, intro yourself, get friendly, look for mutual respect, a reliable place to send our best overflow customers where we know they'll be treated right. When you're in, broach the subject of these, ah-hum, *bookings*—but don't explain what you think they're for—and make a pitch for getting a bigger piece of that action away from some of the other resorts they use."

"Assume this is happening around the cove?"

"Sure. *So what* if you're wrong. I'm betting you'll be right, though. Then play it out and learn as much as you can."

The manager with severe features and too-tight hair and too-hot suit obviously didn't like it, not one bit, but she had a *really* good job with one helluva corporation, and whatever the skinny lady with the red hair and her goofy friend flinging grapes off the balcony wanted . . .

Shawn let fly, right off the top of Tsoo-Ki's head, the young Indian turning to grin. What a shot!

Even the lizard looked impressed.

ANTHRO-TWIT RETURNED SHAWN'S CALL just as they readied to leave. He didn't have any new information; his colleagues and contacts in San José said there had been rumors of a Tsala people some years back, but that's been debunked. He wondered whether or not Shawn had come up with Milo Bulagrét's paper yet. Of course, the good professor had been too busy to give much thought to sex workers or various social ills in Costa Rica.

Shawn found Marcie and Tsoo-Ki waiting in the lobby, Scallywag on the young Indian's lap, Moolhuizen hovering nearby. Les Brinkley powered up the chopper across the road.

"Can I call Kinte from that thing—from Costa Rica, I mean?" Shawn had held many multi-continent videoconferences from the chopper over U.S. airspace, but he didn't know if his satellite's "footprint" covered this far south or not. "I wanna check in."

Moolhuizen used a hand communicator to ask Brinkley, confirming that yes, despite being at the periphery, he could because microwave relays had been set up to make the signal redundant.

They climbed aboard and lifted off.

"You are sure it is okay to see *mis tías*—my aunts—and then leave right away?" Tsoo-Ki had been very nervous about going home for the first time since his accident, since convincing a neighboring farmer to leave him at the capital so he wouldn't be a burden on his family. He wanted to zip in while the men worked the fields around Lago Amarillo— the Yellow Lake. This initial contact would give the women a chance to prepare the elder shaman, Tsala-Tsoo, for Tsoo-Ki to return the following day with the gift of tractor, plow, and fuel. Marcie reassured him he could call the shots, that they were simply his guests and grateful to be a part.

It took nearly a minute for the connections to be made, Kinte's face appearing on a small screen in the soundproofed chopper.

"Hey!"

"Hey!"

"Hey!"

"Hey!"

Shawn and Marcie alternated the word every second or so, a tiny camera in the console swiveling back and forth to follow their voices. It focused on whoever was speaking, so the rapid-fire tomfoolery had the effect of giving Kinte a gyrating shot of the group. He always found it exasperating so, therefore, they considered it fun.

"Hey!"

"Hey!"

"Hey!"

"Greetings, Mr. D'Fixx, Ms. McNaught; I trust you are well." He never waited for them to quit goofing off—or gave them the satisfaction of showing his annoyance.

"Hey, ol' man," Marcie returned, Shawn busy making faces, the lizard atop his head.

"Having grown tired of your adventure, you wish me to arrange your flight home."

"Yeah, *right*," Shawn interjected. He knew damn well Moolhuizen and Brinkley and even Guyton back at the jet had been checking in with the old man constantly, that his plans and intentions were quite known, thank you very much.

Kinte sighed for their benefit. "And this native fellow between you must be Señor Tsoo-Ki."

The young Indian was too busy freaking out about the satellite communications. "He is *hearing* me?" he breathed.

"And I am able to see you, as well."

That made him self-conscious. He straightened his new fluorescent-orange *I been to Costa Rica and I'm goin' back to stay* shirt.

"Yeah, he's the dude you're setting up the doctoring for," Shawn confirmed.

"Please be sure his expectations are realistic, that these specialists will assess his condition but cannot yet promise relief."

Shawn wanted to word his response so Tsoo-Ki wouldn't understand. "Already anticipating futility, the patient's expectations are on par with an atheist's at a revival."

"It is best," Kinte allowed.

"Anthro-twit wants to know about that Tsala paper by Milo Bulagrét."

"It was transmitted to him just moments ago, copies for you to the D'Shawn resort." He looked distracted for about two seconds, doing something at the console below-screen; then pages started appearing in a slot near the chopper's floor.

Shawn pulled them out—a dozen sheets of journal text in fine print. "What's the short version?"

"The associate professor was attempting to trace the migration of various Indian peoples, looking for a connection between what we call the Native Americans who traveled across the Bering Straits and those found in South-Central and South America. He claims to have found several of the Tsala in Costa Rica, worshipers of *las almas joyas*, the jewel spirits."

"¡Si! ¡Las almas joyas!" Tsoo-Ki confirmed, fingering the crude pendant around his neck.

"Obviously, that is the Spanish moniker, these people having lost most of their earlier language through assimilation. He describes six-sided

Jewels of the Earth through which they claimed the power of the spirits would visit for purposes good or evil, depending on the intentions of the people touching them. It was during his next exploration through Costa Rica that Bulagrét and his daughter were killed in a boating accident, his research left unfinished."

"So have your snoops found a connection with my crystal vendor?" Marcie wondered.

"She is his widow. The daughter was his from a previous marriage, the mother having died in childbirth."

"Was Joelle down here with him when the accident happened?" Shawn asked, typically suspicious.

"In the boat, the only one who managed to swim to safety. It happened on an inland volcanic lake, during an expedition in search of a lost city."

"Wow. What else do you have on her?"

"Most is from a man who worked with her husband, and Mr. Garbus has a team running down her business history. After Bulagrét's wife died, he used to leave his young daughter in the care of his own mother during research trips. He apparently met your crystal vendor during one to Costa Rica, married her, and brought her back to the U.S. Shortly after, his mother died of a stroke, and her cousin—my source can't remember the man's name—came to live with them near Houston. I did find they had registered their marriage with the state of Texas. The Bulagréts took his daughter and the cousin with them on the ill-fated trip. After the deaths, she and the cousin returned here long enough to cash in his inheritance and sell off his estate before moving back to Costa Rica."

"How old was the little girl?" Marcie wondered.

"He thinks she was three or four."

Foster's face peeked around Kinte's on the little screen. "Her business dealings look clean," he cut in. The camera swung up to capture him fully.

"She owns the resort outright?" Shawn asked.

Foster nodded. "Used the cash-out, got several small investors in San José—nothing dirty about *that* part—and built that plus some apartments on an adjacent parcel. It wasn't very successful—it rains and storms too much along the Caribbean coast compared to the resort trade on the Pacific side, Nicoya especially. Her occupancy ran low on both developments, struggling to cover costs. Her investors—I talked to one of them just a few minutes ago—he got to checking things out and found both places more full than the books showed. He confronted her, so she made a low cash offer and bought him out, then the other two investors right after. Can't figure where she got the money, but the transfers came from off-shore. After that, she bought a chopper for tourist excursions down there, then set up the travel-charter service to feed her resort, and has done fairly well. Can't see where she has anything else except a modest condo at Splendora, Texas, not far from Houston's Intercontinental Airport."

Tsoo-Ki was trying to give directions to Brinkley, but he was limited to following rivers and mountain landmarks he knew, a circuitous route at best. They were getting into high altitudes, crossing between ridges and irregular peaks, heading toward the massive mountain spine that ran the length of Costa Rica. Shawn knew GPS and satellite-grid tracking kept *somebody*—several somebodies probably—constantly updated with their precise location.

"Anything else of interest, Jamaica-dude?"

"Yes, one. I scanned the marriage registration in Texas and found out her maiden name. She had also Americanized her first name, had changed it from Joléa to Joelle."

"So?"

"Her birth name was Joléa de Tsala."

WALLY WAS SWEATING PROFUSELY, Chuck nearly as much. Neither were up for this hiking-through-the-jungle crap. No sir, Wally didn't like it at all. Damn rocks. Hot, too.

Takú Litál led the way, a dart-paralyzed spider monkey slung over his shoulder, its hands and feet tied. Something bigger would have looked more impressive, but this one would do.

Wally and Chuck followed next, Bulagrét bringing up the rear. Crossing that first ravine had slowed them down some, Wally being too afraid. He said he didn't trust the boards, but then had finally clomped across fast and heavy, obviously distrusting his own ability to keep balance. Fifteen minutes they'd lost on that one, ten on the second. Now he was holding them up at the third.

Litál watched the sky, getting angry, threatening to go on without them.

"If we leave you here, we will return for you after having the ceremony, but there will be no refunds," Bulagrét warned.

Clomp clomp clomp. Chuck did it a bit more gracefully.

Continuing on, Wally kept slowing down, especially during the climbs. Several times, she had to push his fat carcass from behind and remind him of her threat.

"I don't understand what the damn hurry is!"

"There is only one time each day when the sun will shine directly on the crystals—and you are making us miss it!" she snapped.

Exhausted by the time they entered the crystal-lined crack, he finally stopped bitching. It looked awesome, like nothing he'd ever seen. He'd started to suspect a scam, maybe to get them out in the jungle and murder them, then keep the money, but this was obviously the real deal.

Wally believed, and Chuck did too, so this became their temple of the gods.

In awe, Wally whispered, "All that pussy . . ."

Litál used his crystal-encrusted lighter on the lantern, then kept a brisk pace leading the group to the great room crisscrossed by deep cracks. Wally and Chuck first noticed how the far end broke away into void, the ribbon waterfall disappearing deep into the earth; then they saw the chantry, its giant six-sided crystal towering over the meter-long shard jutting across the hollow depression. All eyes gazed up toward the crack, sunlight streaming almost straight down. Where it struck crystals along one side, tiny rainbow beams of light filtered through waterfall mist to create a shimmering, mosaic image.

"There is no time!" Bulagrét hissed, pulling Wally by the arm toward the chantry, gesturing Chuck to the other side. Litál already had the pendants out.

"Fast, remove your shirts!" She had hers off, her natural bounty spilling forth and distracting Wally for a moment. She boasted beautiful breasts, Wally thinking maybe he'd use his power to have her right there in the steamy jungle. "Now!" she ordered. The leering hunk o' love complied.

Litál impaled the tiny monkey backward onto the shard, then rushed off to scoop handsful of water from a low spot near the fall, pouring them into the depression.

It grew very warm, the light striking the edge of the giant crystal. The pendants were passed around and hastily donned.

Takú Litál produced a dagger of hewn crystal from under his robe, Wally and Chuck flinching as if ready to bolt.

Litál gazed up, then grinned. "It is time."

TSOO-KI LOOKED CONFUSED. They passed close enough to San José that Brinkley decided to stop and refuel, letting everybody have a bathroom break.

The route took them over Irazú and its volcano. Brinkley identified it, Tsoo-Ki realizing he'd confused it with Poás. Never in his life had he been so far south. They flew over ruins from the 1910 earthquake, then passed close to the actual volcano, the highest in the country. It was steaming, boiling and fuming, a time bomb waiting for the day it might destroy the city of Cartágo yet again. Several yellow-green lakes had formed in large cracks, water colored by high levels of sulphur seeping from deep inside the earth, making the area look similar to where Tsoo-Ki was trying to take them.

They made their stop, grabbed some quick sandwiches from an airport vendor, Shawn not so worried about food poisoning for a change, and headed north. They found the craters of Poás, an impressive display. Trails and a roadway wound through the jungle to a visitor's center, open slopes covered with *sombrilla del pobre* with its giant two-meter leaves, a series of cracks and fissures, then the slope. Extinct crater Laguna Botos had filled with bright green water, also churning, steam rising from one end.

Marcie studied a guidebook Brinkley had brought, announcing that it was named after an extinct Indian tribe thought to have been wiped out by eruptions some three-hundred years before. The main crater was fuming despite a thin layer of yellow water in the bottom. His bearings finally straight, Tsoo-Ki directed Brinkley along a set of ridges heading northeast. They could see it in his face . . .

He was going home.

Marcie, still thumbing through the guide, announced, "Cool! Says here that Lake Arenal at Tilarán, not far from someplace called Cañas, has at least a dozen pre-Columbian settlements underwater, wiped out a thousand years ago when Arenal erupted, recently mapped by satellite photo-radar tracking."

"That one is much farther that way," Tsoo-Ki explained, pointing westward. "*My* fathers' homes are under Lago Amarillo, near where we farm even today. It is water you cannot drink, and it smells *muy mál.*"

"Sulphur," Shawn conjectured. Scallywag gave him a look. Another brilliant deduction.

"It is said," Tsoo-Ki explained, "that the volcano took most of the Tsala peoples into the earth, that it was also swallowed into the earth and is waiting for the day when it will come again. Some believe it will take the *last* Tsala peoples; some believe it will *bring back* our fathers' homes. It is to be decided by Tsawa-Ki when the rainbow brings him to us."

"What do *you* believe?" Marcie asked quietly.

Tsoo-Ki shrugged. "I believe to work hard and feed my family, but then I am hurt—" He looked painfully at his limp legs, again somewhat embarrassed. "I cannot let myself become a burden. It was not easy for me to believe more, but now I have found Tsawa-Ki. Now I am bringing him to my people." He gestured toward Shawn, who was busy watching the fuming volcano receding in the distance.

Rich Mr. Fixx wondered how far they would need to flee to escape the concussion of a full-scale eruption—and if they would have time. Kinte sure wouldn't like them flying so close to something so potentially deadly, yet tourists stood right up on the rim looking in, several tour-copters hovering in the air, several more flying in from San José. Playing extremely long odds, he figured. Sure, they'd risk the lives of their families to gawk at a real volcano, even with chances for harm much greater than the odds of winning a lottery. He was trying to ignore the discussion about his supposed destiny, not that Marcie would let him.

"What is the Tsawa-Ki supposed to do?" she asked, pressing the young Indian on a subject he seemed to consider personal or private or even embarrassing.

He shrugged again. "He is to make it right."

"To fix things?"

"He is to fix."

"Yow!" Marcie had poked Shawn in the ribs. "Watch it, McNaughty. I give good wedgie."

"There!" Tsoo-Ki announced. "It is that way, past the big rocks and deep cracks. There is my home."

"And they're waiting for Mr. Fixx," Marcie emphasized, poking Shawn in the ribs again.

She became the reluctant recipient of one *atomic* wedgie.

CHUCK LOOKED AMAZED at what he was seeing, admitting he could feel it all over, pulsating right through his body.

Wally tugged at his clothes to make room for a throbbing stiffness pressing against his pants. He leered at Bulagrét's bosom, rainbows glowing from the crystal pendant nestled between those round, quivering—

The waterfall started to roar, a crashing torrent cascading into the cavern, distracting Wally enough that he finally noticed prismed beams shining from the huge six-sided crystal behind the spiked monkey, the lights breaking into a zillion refractions all about the cave, swirls of color through waterfall mist. The water in the depression began to steam and boil.

Takú Litál picked up the shard dagger, holding it ominously in the air, then slashed hard! The monkey's genitals dropped into the boiling cauldron, a trickle of blood discoloring the evil broth.

Ripples swept over their bodies. Chuck instantly got an obvious erection, Wally's pressing even harder. All four started panting, riding waves of sexual energy, higher and higher, reaching toward the pinnacle of orgasmic climax.

The water rising around them, not even the dweebs cared anymore. Still rising higher, to their knees, climbing their legs, wanting a piece of this action.

Wally could feel his crotch getting soaked, cooling his throbbing love lizard but not slowing it down, the water to his waist now, tickling his chest, kissing Bulagrét's hard nipples, the colors blindingly bright, the roar deafening.

Wally screamed out, Fraidy Chuck whimpering scared, Bulagrét droning a low moan, Litál smiling knowingly.

The water began to recede, the roar fading, their eyes adjusting to the dimming light, the colors shimmering and merging into white before dying away.

Wally and Chuck swayed on their feet, spent.

Bulagrét was looking at the crack high above, the sunlight streaming in. She whispered to Litál, "*¿Cuatro más días?*—four more days?"

He nodded. "*¡Tsala-Pu!*"

THE CHOPPER APPROACHED Tsala Valley, Lago Amarillo appearing below the fissured volcanic peaks and vertical canyons beyond. It looked hot down there, with steam rising from patches of jungle, the sun high in the sky.

Then Shawn saw it: from cliffs on the horizon, through billowing mist, a giant rainbow reached into the sky, arcing straight toward the chopper. "Wow!"

"What? What is it, Shawn?" Confused, Marcie searched the direction of his gaze. "What do you see?"

"*You* can't see it?"

The rainbow glowed brighter, vivid colors filling the sky.

Brinkley looked confused, too, craning his neck every which way, trying to figure what Shawn could see.

Tsoo-Ki seemed to be in a trance, his mouth open, watching the same mysterious vision as Shawn.

The colors washed over them, filled the chopper with light, danced across Shawn's skin and through him . . . difficult to see, so bright, Marcie's voice fading but still asking, "What? What is it?"

Shawn could feel himself being swept away, a million tingles, all emotions and feelings, the past and future and—he was, what? Oh, geez! *Aroused?*

A low moan escaped Tsoo-Ki's lips. Shawn could see only colors, but from where the young Indian sat, eyes looked at him, looking through him, telling him something. They were the eyes of a very old and wise man.

And they knew. Dammit, the eyes knew what Shawn couldn't figure out.

Then they blinked, and the rainbow faded away, the world returning to that reality to which Shawn clung so desperately, four people in a chopper hovering over a steamy jungle in Costa Rica.

"What the hell happened?" Marcie demanded. "*I* didn't see anything."

Brinkley shook his head and studied his instruments.

Shawn looked at Tsoo-Ki. The young Indian's eyes brimmed with tears as he fought to maintain his composure.

With the backs of his fingers, Shawn reached out and wiped the tears from his cheeks, whispering, "Tsoo-Ki?"

The Tsala prince smiled. "*¡Tsawa-Ki!*"

CHAPTER 6

TSOO-KI SUFFERED LAST-MINUTE jitters. The chopper had come in over Lago Amarillo from the west to avoid the Tsala villagers—all of the men and most of the women—toiling in fields over the next ridge. They could see a cluster of rectangular buildings on a flat area just up a gentle slope from the colored lake. A small stream meandered close, passing through rocky crevices and stairstepping down a series of small falls, obviously the village's source for fresh water. Several older women worked in the shade between houses, a half-dozen youngsters helping or playing, all looking up at the approach of this whirly-monster in the sky.

Tsoo-Ki, increasingly apprehensive, warned them that outsiders are generally unwelcome in his village.

¡Maldito helicóptero! ¡Malditos turísticos! Damned tourists!

The Tsala didn't like their privacy breached, their world invaded, and they didn't want to be on display for rich gringos, people who come to see a different culture but alter it merely by their own presence.

"Go that way, *por favor!*" Tsoo-Ki suddenly begged, urging Brinkley to head up toward the cliffs. He was breathing hard, worried or even scared about going home.

"Take your time," Marcie whispered.

"*Está bien.*"

Brinkley followed a small box canyon between two cliffs, ascending to see a series of deep cracks in the rock, drop-offs of fifty meters or more, streams running through these narrow confines.

"I want for you to see where I fell and hurt my legs," Tsoo-Ki explained.

"Why were you climbing around up here?" Shawn wondered. "It looks dangerous."

"I was seeking *las almas joyas*—the spirit jewels. There!"

Brinkley circled around an area of jagged, low ridges with three nearly parallel crevices only a few meters wide at their narrow points and at least a hundred meters deep, water flowing through them far below. The area abutted dense jungle, a faint trail leading to a series of three narrow, wooden footbridges. The path didn't appear to lead anywhere, though, except to a series of crumbling rises with hundreds of splinter cracks, stairstepping another hundred meters before leveling out briefly and breaking into jagged ridges that sloped off to the east.

"I was climbing from there," the young Indian explained, pointing toward a treacherous route up from the direction of his village, the only way over toward the footbridges.

"Can you set her down?" Shawn asked Brinkley.

The pilot studied the area and chose the only safe place, a brief flat spot between numerous cracks at nearly the highest point. He brought the chopper in deftly, then powered down.

"This whole area could crumble," he warned, "and those cracks could be near bottomless."

Nobody offered to get out, just scanning the scene.

"This is about where I saw that big rainbow," Shawn said, not catching himself in time.

"And where Tsoo-Ki went in search of the crystals," Marcie pointed out.

"And where I fell and hurt myself," the young Tsala reminded.

"Where?" she asked. "Where did you fall?"

He pointed over the precipice. "There is only one way to go down from here. I was coming here many times before I learned that way. I was as far as that *grande* crack—" He pointed off to a lower level, one of the widest though not very deep fissures without a footbridge to cross. Granted, it probably dropped only a dozen or so meters to the bottom, but it was a sheer descent, no way to negotiate without the kind of equipment and training a young Tsala obviously would not have.

Bringing their attention back to the slope before them, Tsoo-Ki explained, "It was here that I fell, on the day I reached that crack and asked the rainbow to carry me over to find what I seek."

"Then you fell on your way back?"

He nodded, his head down. "The rainbow knew it was not for good that I wanted *las almas joyas*." He didn't seem to want to look that direction, suddenly asking, "Is it okay if we go now?"

Brinkley powered up and they lifted off, Tsoo-Ki directing to where they could land near the village, not too close so they wouldn't rotor-wash the cornmeal several women were grinding for bread.

Brinkley powered down again, everybody waiting for a cue. Tsoo-Ki shouted his name several times. Finally, one of the oldest women slowly made her way close to where the chopper rested, the children following.

She stood a good ten meters away, her dark and deeply lined visage impassive, considering what she saw. The children weren't shy, coming right up and greeting, dark-skinned barefoot urchins in ragged shorts. Several called out "Tsoo-Ki" while a very young little girl stood in the open door, calling him "Whale-tico."

The old lady spoke something ominous in an unusual dialect of Spanish, Tsoo-Ki responding in same. Neither Shawn nor Marcie, with their customary four semesters each, could follow what anybody said.

"She say I should not come here if I am bringing the bad on them all."

She said something else, harsh at first, then softening toward the end.

He responded again, adding, "I know he is mad at me. But I am learning from *las joyas* for the good. I will return with a tractor and the plow and the fuel. *Mañana.*"

She nodded, trying to look stern, the façade melting to reveal deep love in her eyes. She asked something else, this time tenderly, gesturing to the other faces watching from the chopper.

"*Están mis amigos.*"

She nodded recognition.

He gestured toward Shawn, pausing dramatically. "*¡Está Tsawa-Ki!*"

She looked disappointed, shaking her head piteously.

"Please touch your colónes hold-thing," he whispered to Shawn.

"Hurry," Marcie urged.

Shawn didn't want to, but, well, whatever. He reached into his pocket and caressed the money clip with his hand.

The old lady's face lit up; the children stopped chattering, all gazing at the funny white man with the rainbow aura.

The old lady wagged her finger, then intoned, "*Mañana,*" and turned to walk back, summoning the children to follow.

Watching his villagers—his family—head back for the shade, Tsoo-Ki beamed. Apparently this was a good beginning.

The young Indian sat quietly during the flight back to San José for refueling and out toward the coast. He didn't speak until they neared the resort north of Limón. Finally, he said, "It is good I am hurt."

"Why?"

"I am bringing Tsawa-Ki."

There was no arguing with that. He'd never have found Shawn—or attracted his attention—except for being in that wheelchair in the marketplace.

Except that Shawn was just some rich dude and not a spiritual crystal channeler. Don't try to convince Marcie of that, though—or the young Tsala.

Marcie had to ask. "Why was looking for the crystals bad?"

"For why I would be using them."

"Why?"

"To be alive forever. To be young forever."

"Youth and immortality," Shawn breathed. "Ponce de Leon and so many others before and since. An impossible dream." He looked off into the distance, an image of bed-ridden Jeremy in his mind.

"Why did you think you'd find them there?—where you were looking, I mean," Marcie prodded.

"Because my cousin looked there for *las cristales*. He has used them already, but for the badness."

"You have a cousin who *found* the crystals?"

He nodded. "My youngest cousin—Takú Litál."

"SO WHERE'D YOU TELL HER?" Chuck was ready, Wally still in the bathroom tweezing hairs from his ears and trimming more from that mole on his neck.

"The Pink Parrot."

"And she offered to set up a tab to run on her account. A classy last-night thank-you."

Wally snorted, pulling on his shirt and checking his teeth. He could see Chuck through the open door. "Yeah, *right*. For the bucks we dropped on her, she oughta *buy* us The Pink Parrot." He dug around in his nose, trying to retrieve a glob that made him whistle when he breathed.

"Were you serious? What you told her, I mean."

"What? That I wanted to taste some black cherry and taco salad with my whitebread tonight?"

"Yeah. You *did* mean a white woman, a black one, and a Mexican babe, right?"

"Hell, throw in a slanty-eyes, too—except I ain't seen none down here yet." He sniffed his armpits, decided to roll on a thicker layer of goo, and took his shirt back off to apply another coat. "What was all that horseshit you was talkin' about?"

"*What?*" Chuck sounded defensive. "*So what* if I wanna meet some-body nice, maybe fall in love or something."

"Screw that!" Wally stopped and grinned at his partner/friend, amused by his inadvertent pun. "Look for that back home. Here you oughta be sampling some exotic babes—ones who don't know your address and won't be comin' round whinin' some shit later."

Chuck shook his head like his friend just didn't get it.

Wally put his shirt back on, saw the underarms were stained, then pulled it off and went to rummage through the dresser for another. He came up with one covered with tropical flowers—bougainvillea, it looked like—not that he cared. "When we get there, let's split up, each get our own table. You look all pathetic and lonesome and see if Cinderella comes along. Me?—I'm gonna round *me* up a *pussy* posse!"

Chuck shrugged, dutifully following Wally Flaunt-yer-wad out to the waiting courtesy shuttle.

They walked into The Pink Parrot, instantly thrilled. Even Chuck had to grin. The place was *crawling* with babes, big tits and tight asses, skilled lips and pouty nipples, a whiff in the air.

There she sat, all by herself, a petite blonde with a hint of *something* in her face, maybe South Pacific, Hawaiian? Her beautiful brown eyes made her look lonely, almost sad. She seemed surprised at herself, making eye contact with Chuck, too mesmerized to look away, drawn in. Finally, she gazed down at her snack plate, then glanced up again shyly. Yes, he was still there, their eyes locked.

"Go get her," Wally whispered. "She's a *little* thang—be gentle and don't break her."

Chuck wandered over, wondering if it would be okay for him to sit down. She seemed a bit embarrassed, but decided she'd like that.

Seemed like all the other babes had stopped to watch Wally. He was checking out the action, liking what he saw. Sweet black cherry, taco salad just *waiting* to be slipped the ol' Wally burrito, coupla white girls, some licking their lips, one fingering her nipples . . .

This was gonna be their lucky night.

He grinned, spread his arms wide, and waddled into the thick of things. They surrounded him in no time, the power of the crystal drawing 'em in like moths to a light.

"Which one of you babes got a room here? Let's stock up the bar on *my* account and take us all in for a party!"

A key landed on the table. Black Cherry's. Yow!

Wally stood motioning for them to gather round, an open invitation to get hot and sweaty.

He held one on each side, caressing and kissing, nipples pressed into his back. They couldn't wait.

Lucky bitches.

He grinned again and let out a whoop.

"Well, let's *go!* It's *Wally time!*"

MOOLHUIZEN WATCHED THREE TARGETS from his seat on the veranda, his carafe and a glass of papaya juice sitting on the rail before him. He'd had two "misses" so far, leaving only three chances to catch one of the women leaving a room on his list, usually about ten minutes—clean-up time, presumably—after her customer left.

One of the doors opened, a touristy-looking fellow stepping into the bright glare clad in garish golf pants and crew shirt. He looked around nervously, adjusted his collar, then hurried off the other direction.

Moolhuizen checked his watch and waited. Five minutes.

Six.

Seven.

He picked up the carafe and glass, then sauntered casually down the walkway past the room.

Nothing.

He wandered back toward his seat and repeated the process.

Nothing—

The door opened just as he started that direction again. He looked back toward his seat, like maybe checking to be sure he'd not dropped his keys or something, and bumped into the young woman as she stepped into the bright glare . . .

And spilled papaya juice all down the front of her clothes!

Ooops!

The light chiffon summer dress proved no match for the sticky ade, soaking right through and making it cling to her contours in a rather sexy way, even plastering some of her long brunette tresses to her shoulders.

A wet t-shirt effect, the alluring expectedness of her now-glistening nipples contrasted with the frown gracing her delicate features.

Moolhuizen had a job to do, one already offering a nice little respite from following Shawn and Marcie.

"OH! I AM *SO* SORRY, MA'AM! Oh me!"

Annoyed for a moment, she relaxed and sighed after the initial shock.

The man who had spilled juice on her *did* have a rather disarming smile. "I'm sorry, but you look beautiful—even wearing papaya," he charmed. "Please, let me pay for a new set of clothes, or to have those cleaned— Look, let me pay the tab for your room. I want to make this up to you."

She stood there dripping, not sure what to do. No spare clothes in her bag, she couldn't duck back inside for a shower and change. Finally, she smiled, too. "It's okay. It was an accident."

"I got a really nice, brand-new robe in my room there." He gestured toward another door. "I'd like you to have it, something to change into. Use my shower if you like. I can have your clothes cleaned in an hour or two, and maybe see about getting you a whole new wardrobe just to make up for any damage."

Hmmm . . . She wasn't sure. She didn't want to let on that she used her suite for business purposes, no place a typical vacationer's luggage could be found. He appeared to be rich and classy, hitting on her in a polite, gentlemanly way. She *did* need to clean up. What's the worst that could happen? She'd profit? He'd wanna get laid? She might have some fun? She didn't have to be anywhere until that night.

She smiled. "That's very generous."

He did have a luxurious suite, and he looked quite handsome with his silver hair and rippling muscles, a quietly elegant-yet-relaxed style about him.

He gave her the robe, offered use of any shampoos and what-nots in the bathroom, then handed her a plastic bag for her soiled clothes so he could have them picked up and cleaned right away.

He didn't try to shower with her, didn't even touch the bathroom door, not even a peek. He *was* a gentleman.

By the time she came out wearing his robe, still pulling a brush through her long damp tresses, he had a clerk from the gift shop there with a huge selection of clothing—women's undergarments, casual skirts and tops, all manner of sandals and vacation footwear.

"Gimme everything you got in her size. She can keep what she wants and toss the rest. Put it on my account."

"Yes, señor. As you wish."

She wound up with several stacks of goodies. She changed in the bathroom, emerging in a very nice skirt and blouse, low-heeled open-toes, nude pantyhose, and a pretty necklace/ear-pin ensemble of carved abalone. She'd fixed her make-up and worked a bit more on her hair.

She decided she would be Marla, a cosmetic rep, down with her friend from Madison, Wisconsin. Her friend had hooked up with a local man and largely ignored her all week.

"Don't I know *that* feeling. My buddy talked me down here with him for a week. I'm retired, you know—hung it up when I hit thirty. I'm *real* comfortable, but my buddy's wealthy like you can't imagine. Now that we're here, he keeps running off to San José to do business, leaving me to putter around with nothing to do."

It sounded like blah blah blah blah *wealthy* blah blah.

Before she could respond, Moolhuizen introduced himself as Car-lysle Hizen. "I got a car here; we can be in San José shopping for your new wardrobe inside of ninety minutes." She hesitated, so without missing too long a beat, he added, "Or I can arrange to have some of the more exclusive shops send selections *here*." Yes, he had money—and it was no object.

He kept at her until she decided; she really didn't need a new wardrobe, but breakfast and maybe a walk on the beach before it got too hot would be nice, thank you very much.

They got to know each other fairly well. Turns out his rich friend was a young guy, a bit of a dweeb who didn't have much of a way with women. No, Carlysle hadn't heard what everybody was talking about, this thing with crystals where they help channel power and make you attractive, people having a good time and swearing by them.

"I've heard it's expensive, though," she said.

"Hey, if something like that works on my friend, I'm sure it would be worth the money. I might even pay for it myself, make it a gift, get him to relax and quit thinking about biz long enough to have a good time. Maybe loosen him up for some future trips, too."

They walked the beach for a while; then she begged off and said she needed to meet somebody, then to return some important calls. "Hey, while I'm at it, I can ask around and, like, maybe find out where to get in on those crystals."

"Would you? I mean, I'd really appreciate that," he agreed as they headed back toward the rooms.

"Sure, no problem," she said, smiling demurely. "It's the least I can do for a gentleman who bought me some wonderful new clothes. Hey, I could find out if there's a deal on two people, in case you wanna try 'em out, too."

"Oh no, not for me. Thanks anyway. But definitely for my friend."

Back at her room now, she suggested, "How about if we meet here at three?" That should be long enough to make sure he'd gone, then to move some things into her room so she'd look more like a vacationer, and to alert the manager to prepare for a possible customer.

"I can't say enough how grateful I am, you helping me like this," he said, bidding her good-bye, "—when I'm the one owes you for my clumsy mistake."

3:00 came quickly enough, and her new friend knocked precisely on time.

"It turns out," she explained, inviting him in for a drink, "that it's a big secret. But I got you an invite by vouching for you. I promised you'd be discreet. They don't want people who can't afford to play coming down here trying to get in on it."

She led him to the manager's office, making sure to look wide-eyed and excited at this new concept in sexual attraction. The guy turned out to be an easy mark, barely batting an eye at the price, a cool quarter-mill.

"What the hell," he said. "I've come this far. I can't wait to see the grin on my friend's face—that's if they work."

"Your friend," the manager said with a wry smile, "he will find this very much the fun time, these crystals and how he will attract many women."

She cleared the transaction on his platinum card. "You will bring your friend here at seven o'clock for the big surprise."

Back out on the veranda, Carlysle asked his new friend, "Afterwards, you think maybe you and I could get together?"

"I'm sorry," she said, obviously disappointing him, "but I have plans. How about tomorrow afternoon?" That would give him time to be impressed by his friend's crystal experience, another chance for her to pitch him. Carlysle Hizen was just sexy enough that she might actually enjoy climbing all over him—as long as he wore his crystal.

"I can't be sure, but I'll check in with you, if that's okay."

"I'll be around," she agreed. She'd wait for weeks to realize an opportunity like this. Delivering Carlysle's rich dweeb friend would earn her a month deducted from her go-home date. Snaring Carlysle would earn her another. One more sucker after that, and she'd be on the next plane, train, boat, whatever. She'd walk through the jungle if that's what it took to get her son back, to start a new life with a pile of cash.

She'd have to find out who the dweeb's seeing on business, maybe get number three signed up by the end of the week.

What a stroke of luck.

Papaya juice!

TSOO-KI TRIED NOT to look scared, putting on a brave face, coaxing everybody to smile, optimistic and hopeful. Shawn didn't buy it, though. Exchanging glances with Marcie and Les Brinkley, he could see they weren't either.

Shawn understood how scary a bustling hospital could be, the noises and odors and bright lights and strange machinery and threatening instruments—and that would be for people who understood. But what about a young man who'd lived his life in a patch of deforested jungle? One who'd never seen more of the world than the streets of San José? Who'd never experienced Western medical care at its harshest?

Blind trust in his new friends had brought him here, confidence in the people who cared, belief deep in his heart, in the Tsawa-Ki . . . Rich Mr. Fixx.

And it was driving Shawn to distraction. He wanted there to be a solution, a way for the young man to walk again. It had been just an accident, not a punishment, yet he knew Tsoo-Ki would never believe that. Why did he deserve paraplegia—for going off on a quest in the dangerous rainforest to find magic crystals? Was that so bad?

Wasn't that why Shawn and Marcie had come here?

And this young Tsala had put all his faith in what Shawn could do for him. Forget the silly myths and superstitions; it all depended on what the best doctors and the best diagnostic equipment and the best research could accomplish. Okay, maybe that's grounded a bit more in reality, in the scientific approach, in tried and proven methodologies, but it still depended on faith—faith and hope and counting on others to do their best to help.

All the help Shawn could buy.

That's what it always seemed to come down to, being able to afford to do as much as he possibly could, his true worth in this world reduced to buying faith and hope for somebody else. That's why he could never be content just to write checks, why he had to get out and see the work his foundations did, to wade in and use his hands wherever he may. That's what helped make it so worthwhile.

And made it hard.

Because then there's a face. And another face, and another. And sometimes it seemed almost more than he could take, because he couldn't always help, or as much as he wanted, or even at all.

And sometimes he tried too late.

But the faces could make it seem right—not the gratitude, not acknowledging his role, but seeing them look ahead to a different future than they'd ever imagined.

Seeing hope in their eyes.

But that also meant seeing something different those times when he failed to help them. And when he got to know those people, the stakes rose that much higher; then when he cared about them personally, everything Shawn was or would ever be seemed to hang on the outcome.

You can't be Rich Mr. Fixx if someone stays broken.

So Tsoo-Ki endured being poked and prodded and mag-resonated and CAT-scanned and electro-something and neuro-stuff and osteo-this and ambulo-that and fluids-in and specimens-out and radio-isotopic intra-spinal mumbledy-gookery, but the best doctors kept looking grim and shaking their heads and acting puzzled and consulting each other and speaking in low voices and ordering more tests and bringing in more equipment and scaring a young Indian who couldn't understand but who believed and trusted because Mr. Fixx had done all this for him.

And it wasn't working.

5:30 a.m. they'd started. Nearly seven hours so far. Marcie stayed close to Tsoo-Ki, encouraging, comforting during the painful parts, entertaining when it grew boring, explaining as much as she could, keeping his spirits up.

Shawn admired this in her. Marcie would've been a great mother, just as she knew how to be a good friend. This was way too hard on him. Several times he had to slip out, just put on that hopeful face and ease on out for a trip to the bathroom, only to wind up standing by some candy machine or staring at a closet, trying to figure out what else he could do.

Les Brinkley followed him on these sojourns. Hell, it was his job, safety for the rich guy, purchased by Kinte, the old man spending the bucks to do what he could.

Les had become a good friend, though, just like Sam Moolhuizen and the pilot, John Guyton. They'd become a team, more than employees, people who had been through some serious times together, a helluva lot more loyalty than a paycheck could buy.

And Foster, too. The man was a biz-wiz who could squeeze every penny out of every possibility, who would put everything he had into saving a few bucks and making that pile a bit bigger. You couldn't torture him into buying a bad investment—yet if Mr. Fixx thought it would help just one needy person, Foster would buy the Brooklyn Bridge from the sleeziest con, no questions asked. *Don't worry, Shawn, we'll make it back on the resell.* And for his part, Foster got to play the rich celebrity playboy, young most-eligible tycoon, all the women and good-times any man could ever want, sometimes enjoying it, sometimes wearing it like a yoke, finding his greatest pleasures in just spending time with his friends, hearing how they'd all played some small part in doing right for someone, knowing the money he generated could make it possible, putting his acumen on the line as one more tool in Mr. Fixx's arsenal.

Shawn found himself sitting in a waiting room, scared people around him all expecting news about a loved one. He wanted to run through the hospital shouting, "Spare no expense, do everything you can, send the bill to me, whatever it takes. *I'm Rich Mr. Fixx!*"

But here he sat, Tsoo-Ki down the hall strapped to some machine, and all he could do was write a check and hope. What if nothing could be done?

Then he'd build ramps in the jungle and get the best motorized chairs and donate to the village and . . . and what? Apologize he couldn't do more? Throw money at the situation, try to make up for his failure? Run off and help somebody else?

What did Kinte do?

The big Jamaican had spent tens of millions of dollars, had single-handedly funded spinal leukemia research worldwide—and still did to this day—but had been forced to watch young Jeremy D'Fixx go from hopeful to scared to resigned, deteriorating to frail and helpless, sickly and in pain, and then through the final stages of acceptance while he died in agony, his last thoughts worrying more about his little brother Shawn than himself.

And Kinte and Jeremy had both left Shawn a burden to bear.

Jeremy had called his little brother *Rich Mr. Fixx*, urging him to carry on, never to walk away when something could be done.

And from Kinte, the responsibility never to hurt the old man the way Jeremy had, never to leave him behind, a failure as guardian, always to wonder if there was something more he could have tried.

No wonder Shawn had grown up such a worrisome mess.

No wonder he cared so much.

Maybe *too* much.

He felt like he just couldn't be Rich Mr. Fixx anymore. Too much, too many were broken. Doing a little would never be enough, and trying to do so much would consume him.

He knew he'd have to back off someday, had seen it coming, would have to settle for what good he'd done and enjoy life a little, maybe get married and have some kids of his own to worry about.

Yeah, right.

Shawn stared at the glass front of the candy machine, a reflection of Marcie standing behind him, and he could see it in her face. No, they couldn't effect a cure for Tsoo-Ki because they couldn't find a cause. Doesn't matter how much money you have; there's nothing can be done.

And that's when he did it, like something he'd never done before.

Crash! Tinkle tinkle.

Put his foot right through the front of the machine.

Brinkley appeared instantly, gingerly pulling Shawn free.

Marcie just stood there, like she understood.

He wasn't hurt, but he'd wasted the candy machine.

So what? He could afford to replace it. He could replace 'em all, every damn candy machine in the world.

He couldn't stop the pain and suffering, people from falling sick or dying young, but he could buy 'em all a candy bar.

So he'll pay for the machine. Just bill him; send it to Kinte or Foster, and somebody'll write a check.

One candy machine, destroyed during childish tantrum. Payment due on receipt.

Just mark it *Mr. Fixx.*

CHAPTER 7

THE CHARTER FLIGHT LANDED, happy travelers heading home, sunburns and snapshots, souvenirs and stories. Bulagrét and Big Man started their three-hour lay-over with a cheap cab ride to the storage lot where she kept a car, then a short ride to Splendora and her condo.

Noting the time on the dashboard, she shook her head. "I hate to miss *las almas joyas* this close before the Tsala-Pu, but I want Señorita McNair to buy more cases *de las cristales*. If she keeps buying regular, I will leave someone working here to handle that for me, but it is not good to use somebody else this soon."

Big Man's silence agreed. It had been his idea to start a legitimate export biz with the crystals, something more stable that would better weather official scrutiny than the rich-geek sex-bait scam.

Not that it wasn't a *good* scam. So far, it had paid off nicely. Wally and Chuck had been the biggest fleece yet, encouragement to up the price and be even more selective in their clientele.

Bulagrét's condo looked nice, sparsely furnished, neat as a pin. Big Man made himself at home, a cold beer from the fridge, iced tea for her. She pulled her business log from a small satchel and headed straight for the phone.

"Ms. McNair's office," answered a young-sounding man.

Bulagrét introduced herself and said Ms. McNair expected her call, then got transferred to an assistant, a deeper voice redolent with sophistication and power.

"Ms. McNair is traveling outside the U.S. at the moment, but I was awaiting your call. I understand you are inquiring about a possible crystal-shard order?"

"We agreed I would check each week to see if she wants to order more cases."

"To be clear, her obligation to maintain exclusivity is four cases every two months; is this correct?" The guy sounded so charismatic, he could pass for Foster B. Garbus himself—a silly notion, that such a celebrated tycoon would deign to answer McNair's calls.

"*Sí*. Yes, every two months."

"Then I would like to postpone making a decision for now. Ms. McNair has been rather busy, but we *have* done some testing and found reluctance from customers to buy such small shards. We suspect their marketability might increase if we have bigger stones to offer, and some even larger ones to put on display."

"I am afraid that would not be easy," Bulagrét hedged.

Before she could finish, he interrupted, "I thought that might not be possible. I'm sorry to hear that; I really was hoping to spark Ms. McNair's interest more. She likes to believe in what she sells, so I thought a large specimen would give her a plaything, something to hold her attention, to put on the dresser, so to speak. If I don't get more commitment for quantities from her, I don't see much benefit in trying to launch any kind of national marketing push."

Bulagrét hesitated. She'd worked too long at getting this set up to watch it slip away. Sure, she could pursue other potential outlets, but none as good as what McNair had to offer. "I am not sure if I can. I will have to check . . ." She considered a moment, then realized she'd been tricked into admitting she didn't have complete control over the source. "If you order four cases now for next week, I will get a big crystal for Ms. McNair."

"Hmmm . . . Well—hmmm . . ." He was thinking it over. That meant he had decision-making authority. "Well . . . I don't know. I still have that problem with the size of the stones. Sure, there *might* be a market for the cheap version, young people and lower income, but these are like any other gem; more interest is generated by having big expensive ones for those who can afford them; then lower-end clients will buy just to have a *piece* of that status."

This assistant obviously understood his marketing and had put some thought into this. He was teaching her something important, that maybe she needed to reconsider her product. She'd been maximizing her quantities by breaking the crystals into as many shards as possible, the smaller the better. Still, she had a problem with Takú Litál's protective attitude over the fact that bigger crystals really *could* channel power in significant ways. Sure, the little ones were good for a zip, but dare they risk putting dynamite on the table at a firecracker party? And could she convince Litál to let her? After all, she'd paid him very little so far, and his reluctance to let her remove crystals from the cave hadn't waned. She couldn't admit any of this now, though. She needed to reassert the image of being in total control, hoping McNair's assistant hadn't already seen through her façade.

"As with diamonds and other jewels," she said, "the bigger ones cost more. I am not able to offer cases of larger crystals for the same price."

"But if you get too expensive, you might kill your market. Maybe I *can't* get more for bigger ones, but those might be all I can sell. I suggest you offer four cases of considerably bigger stones next week for the same price and throw in a free big one—I mean *huge*—for Ms. McNair, then let me test the market. You'll be able to see how customers react and glean more data on how to price. Right now I can't say they're worth even what you're asking, let alone more. If I find out big goes high, you'll be in a position to ask for more, and I'll at least know if it's worth it for us to invest."

¡Maldíto! She couldn't agree without consulting Litál. She hadn't anticipated this. "I already have the next four cases here, and you are exclusive. If you will agree to purchase those next week—"

"Can't do that," he interrupted, getting a bit pushier, making her squirm. "You check in with me next week at this time—ask for, um, Garvey Finster; I'll be your liaison—and let me know what you decided about bigger stones. I strongly suggest you bring a huge one for Ms. McNair, though, so I have a way to get her interested again."

She couldn't counter that. "Thank you, Mr. Finster. I will call you in one week."

She slammed down the phone, a stream of guttural obscenities filling the air. Big Man opened a second beer to her disapproving glare.

"I will try to find out about Carly Geiss," she told him. "You should pick up the two women and their *niñas*. I will take a taxi to *aeropuerto* when it is time."

She gave him the paper with their names, needlessly reminding him to be sure they had their birth certificates—kids, too—and photo IDs and such. After he left, she made another call, the 800-number taken from Chaleeshia Poeky's suitcase.

"Hello? Becky here!"

She hesitated. "Hello? Who is this?" she asked tentatively.

"Private line. Where did you get this number?" The cheerful young woman sounded relaxed, nothing suspicious.

"From my friend." Trying to get info without giving any, she didn't want to use the Carly Geiss name yet, not until she learned more about her.

"What's your friend's name?"

Damn. Might not be smart to use Poeky's. She was dead. But then again, the young prostitute hadn't been able to call before her untimely demise. "She said not to use her name."

"Why ya callin' then?" So upbeat.

"She said to call if I need help."

"What kinda help ya need?"

"What is this place?"

"Private phone, like I said. What's *your* name?"

"I do not want to say."

"Hard to help ya then."

"What is it you are able to do?"

"What do you need?"

Shit, back in Bulagrét's lap. "Are you helping many people?"

"We're talking about *you*. What kinda help you need?"

She hesitated. "I am not sure."

"Need some time to think it over?"

Yes, yes she did. This wasn't getting her anywhere. Suddenly, she remembered technology for tracking phone contacts. She got nervous. "Thank you." *Click.*

She stood there staring at the phone for a full two minutes, waiting for it to ring, for that interminably cheerful voice to mock her, a "Hi again! We know who you are now! Ha ha ha!"

It didn't ring, though.

Googling for custom background-check services, she marked three likely prospects.

"Roux Tumowt Investigations," a woman answered.

"Yes, I have a woman's name and her 800-number, and I want to learn more about her."

She got the same story from all three: day rate, minimum increments, various expenses, need retainer up front, gotta come in and sign—or wire a wad and we'll come to you. Tumowt was the most expensive, so he must be the best. Plus, he was near the airport. She said she'd be there in an hour.

It didn't look very impressive, two small offices and a reception area shared by several other renters. Tumowt seemed pretty sharp, though. Older guy, bit of a cowboy.

"These is usually some kinda scam goin' on, ma'am. You want I should dig deep enough to see how she rides?"

"*Anything* you can find out."

"Now, since you'll be needin' some pictures, I'll see what I can find. May need to travel wherever she is and take some shots."

"Try to find at least one photo of her first, and then I may want to pay for more photos only then."

He grinned and said he had some other stuff that needed wrapping up, but he'd make her a high priority. He seemed to like that she'd cover the expense of him communicating regularly with her in Costa Rica, but she declined his offer to fly down and deliver his report in person—also at her expense, of course. Hell, he thought she meant Puerto Rico. No, Costa Rica is *not* an island.

"Three days," she decided.

"Huh?"

"I will pay only for three days. You will learn what you can for three days, no more."

She knew he would run up some expenses, then try to impress her with how much more info there could be, and get her to extend.

Try to get that trip to the "island" of Costa Rica yet.

The receptionist confirmed Bulagrét's funds on another line, so Mr. Roux Tumowt ended the call a happy man.

Bulagrét arrived at the the airport early and waited for Big Man in the lounge, worried there might have been a snag with the new recruits. She would be furious if she missed *las almas joyas* only to come back without more women.

And more kids.

He arrived at the last minute, leading two Hispanic women and their little girls. She'd met Swallow Gagnon before; Judy Morey was new. The little girls looked cute, brown-eyed moppets with pudgy cheeks, Gagnon's maybe three, Morey's at least a year younger.

Bulagrét prepared to overcome their last-minute concerns, but no problems arose. Both women seemed excited, thrilled for the opportunity, looking forward to paradise. She walked them through processing and let them blend into the group of tourists waiting to board.

Big Man followed his normal routine, going through the back way and pulling the new recruits' luggage, thoroughly searching it. He discreetly reported that everything looked normal, right down to some photos of each woman's family, nothing to indicate any alternate identities, no weapons or communications or tracking devices. Both women had worn tight clothing, and they'd been casual about opening their handbags to produce documentation, so they didn't need to be pulled for a body search—"To be sure you are not bringing drugs or things to get us in trouble at customs" being the usual excuse for a frisk.

At least the trip wasn't a *total* loss.

A ROUTINE LIFT-OFF, it all seemed new and exciting for Swallow because she'd never flown before. To play Judy Morey right, Carly took her cues from Swallow and acted out a similar mix of awe and anxiety. The kids kept them both busy cooing and comforting whenever pressure changes hurt their ears.

Turns out paradise would be Costa Rica, south of Mexico, as Bulagrét described it.

Cool! Neither had ever been there before.

Or even outside Texas for that matter.

Not bad for a couple of hooker-babes.

"GUESS WHERE WE'RE GOIN', Beckster!" Todd grabbed a seat aboard the private Gulfstream jet on the tarmac at Houston Intercontinental, talking on a view-screen. Tall and somewhat goofy looking, a bit shaggy with sparse tufts of facial hair, he could pass for either a street bum or rich techno-genius.

"Don't waste any time, Todd," she admonished. "Get in the air."

"Costa Rica! Ever been there?"

"When are you leaving?"

"Relax, wonder-wench. It'll be another twenty to get our flight plan registered and approved, then we're up and oughta here. We'll beat her down there by at *least* fifteen minutes—or by the time they get a wad of tourists downloaded and processed."

"I don't like this, you know."

"Say it thrice, means no more than twice." He sing-songed it a second time.

"Your widgets better work."

"Don't they always?"

"WHAT'S SO FASCINATING THERE, old man?" Foster was used to seeing Kinte race through piles, dispatching work frenetically. He didn't often pause to stare at his screen for long periods.

"It is not relevant," came the only reply, no "Mr. Garbus," no subtle jab at Marcie's foibles, not even a changed subject.

Foster watched him a moment.

There! He did it. The big Jamaican ran his fingers through his hair. He had to be worried about something.

"What is it?" Foster prodded gently.

Kinte looked up, then touched a panel that cleared his screen, pretending to be interested in some papers in front of himself. Foster wasn't fooled, though.

Kinte absently ran his fingers through his hair again.

Foster B. Garbus didn't like this one bit.

TSOO-KI ACTED NERVOUS as a plucked hen while they circled over the village several times, their chopper spooking all the real hens scurrying below. Brinkley set it down in the same place as before, powering down and waiting. Shawn and Marcie remained quiet as Tsoo-Ki shouted out his name several times.

Expecting him, they'd not gone out to work in the fields, but nobody could be seen outside in the common village area, either. The old woman appeared from one of the modest buildings, staring tentatively for a moment, then advancing slowly. No children, no animals followed. She came alone.

Tsoo-Ki had to translate for his friend. "She is saying the shaman will honor *las almas joyas* today, to be teaching the young Tsala children. I am expected to come and bring you, too, *mis amigos*, because it is a lesson we need to learn. She is saying the shaman does not believe *Señor* D'Fixx *está* Tsawa-Ki, and she is warning me not to say he is."

"Will they accept the gift you bring?" Shawn asked.

Tsoo-Ki spoke to her. She smiled and shrugged, then replied something good-naturedly.

Tsoo-Ki smiled, too, reporting, "She say we may have strong beliefs, but we are not *stupid*."

Shawn had to smile. Time to pay tribute to the gods of gringo technology. He nodded toward Brinkley, who spoke something into his radio, then unfolded and set out Tsoo-Ki's new wheelchair so he and Marcie could help the young Indian into it. The old lady looked impressed. By then, the sound of another chopper could be heard. The children, some of the adults, even the chickens crept out of hiding and strained to see.

It was a *big* bird, with a series of cables dangling a large packing case. Brinkley led the group, Tsoo-Ki motorizing himself along the relatively smooth trail, all heading toward a big flat area on the village side toward the crops, down along the shore of the yellow-green lake. He carried a tool kit slung back-pack style over his shoulder.

He stopped the group, then gestured toward an area where the chopper descended and gently set the box on the ground, the cables hanging loose. Brinkley hurried over and disconnected them, this time gesturing beyond the small ridge toward a corner of the crop field. An okay sign flashed from the open door; then the chopper disappeared into the sky beyond the mountains.

"He's gone to get the fuel tank," Shawn explained. Tsoo-Ki translated for the growing crowd now numbering at least forty while Shawn added *vroom vroom* sound effects, shrugging sheepishly when Marcie patted his hand like a doting mother.

Brinkley used his tools to open the outer layer of the crate, exposing two pre-fabricated concrete horseshoe shapes, each more than a meter across. "Need strong carriers," he explained, Tsoo-Ki translating again. Several strapping young men stepped forward, helping hoist and haul them over the ridge, all but Tsoo-Ki following. Placed U-side up on level stone at the corner of a field, Shawn explained this would hold the fuel tank when the chopper returned in two or three hours. Several younger Indians spoke English well enough to help translate his words, adding a *vroom vroom* and matching Shawn grin for grin.

Everybody back to the crate, it might as well have been a big birthday present wrapped and tied in bows for all the eager faces. The tractor looked quite impressive, with a set of attachable spades and rake plows, plus claws for sifting rocks from the soil. Directed by the old woman, the strapping bucks carried pieces of crate back toward various houses to be pressed into service as table tops or doors. The children climbed all over the tractor like it was some piece of playground equipment. Everybody seemed pleased, the old woman grinning broadly—except for the shaman. He stood solemnly off to the side.

Shawn couldn't help but think the old codger looked to be a thousand years old.

"A gift for my peoples!" Tsoo-Ki proclaimed. "It is to be for the good," he added, watching the old shaman out the corner of his eye.

The old man let everybody admire for a few minutes, then nodded toward the old woman. She clapped her hands and barked out something unintelligible, the children obediently climbing down and waiting expectantly.

"*¡Las almas joyas de Tsala!*" the old man announced.

Everybody headed back toward the houses, Shawn's entourage at the rear. The old coots had managed to throttle the *vroom* out of *this* tractor party.

"If you think there's no danger," Brinkley offered, "I'll start setting it up. I want to fuel and run it before we leave, make sure they know how."

Brinkley set to work while everybody filed into the largest building at the center of the cluster. One of the young bucks climbed up on the roof and slid a platform, not unlike the pieces of crate they'd just salvaged, across the roof to reveal a hole just big enough for a child to fall through. A vivid beam of sunlight streamed down through it, striking some kind of ceremonial centerpiece mid-way across the room.

At Tsoo-Ki's whispered instructions, Shawn and Marcie joined him on the outskirts of the group, back in a corner, sitting on the cool, smooth-stone floor. Everybody found their positions and sat concentrically around the chantry. The old man produced a jawbreaker-sized crystal from under his robe. It appeared almost identical to the one Shawn had flung into the sea.

Shawn rolled his eyes. Hokum time. Everybody get your beads and stoke up the hookahs; let's chant and wax ethereal.

The old man handed the crystal around, each person cradling it a few seconds and passing it along. Nobody offered it to the trio in the corner, not even to Tsoo-Ki, still the village outcast.

Not that the tractor gift wasn't a good first step. *Vroom vroom!*

The shaman placed the crystal on a small pedestal sitting in a bowl of water, perching it just above the surface, a faceted Fabergé egg at the edge of a natural spotlight created by the sunbeam.

The old man spoke sage words.

"He is saying this is for the good," Tsoo-Ki whispered as the shaman glared reprovingly toward him.

The adults all nodded, the children sing-songing his words.

And they waited.

It didn't take long for Shawn to start squirming. It grew quite hot in there, and he had overdressed. The Indians mostly wore gym shorts, t-shirts and tank-tops, some of the women in lightweight saris. Tsoo-Ki boasted his new shorts and sandals, practically glowing in his favorite shirt, the fluorescent-orange Costa Rica tee. Shawn almost envied Marcie's wisp of denim and braless halter. He wore the only long pants and long-sleeve linen shirt.

Sweat City.

The sunlight touched the edge of the crystal, shooting out little beams of rainbow light similar to what they'd seen in the Houston lab. Most in the group touched their hands to the centers of their chests, Marcie playing along in her customary way.

Tsoo-Ki leaned toward Shawn and whispered, "Touching your chest is not necessary."

The water in the bowl began to steam, a slow boil, hot mist rising into the room, shimmering rainbows coming alive as it billowed through refracted beams.

Oh great—*more* humidity. Bathed in sweat, Shawn stripped down to his undershirt.

The sun moved slowly across the crystal, its beams spreading through the room, the rainbows dancing and flickering like flames, reflections in the eyes of serene, glowing faces.

Brighter and brighter, swirling colors, rainbows exploding everywhere, Shawn could see nothing anymore . . . but color.

And a pair of aged eyes, across the room, watching him. The shaman.

He looked down at Tsoo-Ki and saw another pair of old eyes, also watching.

He tried to scoot away, but found himself against the wall, the colors enveloping him.

And still those eyes.

"Cool!" he heard Marcie exclaim, but it sounded from a distance like she no longer sat there beside him.

Or like he no longer existed in this room.

But he must be there. He could see those two sets of eyes, right where they should be, looking at him, at each other, back at him.

Waiting for something.

What could old men's eyes want? They were waiting to see.

But see what?

The colors started to fade, flitting away in every direction, dissolving into the mist.

And the rainbows disappeared.

Shawn felt relieved, but sheepish over the panic risen up inside him, wondering why such bright lights would make him hallucinate, to see visions of old people's eyes.

But the shaman was still watching, and so was Tsoo-Ki.

And so was everybody else.

"What?" he blurted.

Marcie nodded her head.

Tsoo-Ki looked toward the old woman, then the shaman. The old woman shrugged, then nodded to the young Indian and turned again to look toward the shaman.

Oh no, not them, too.

The shaman shrugged, rubbed his chin while deep in thought, then let a wry grin creep across his deeply lined face.

Everybody looked at Shawn again. *Stop looking at me!*

The shaman laughed. So did Tsoo-Ki and the old woman, then the children. Soon, everybody—even Marcie—began laughing.

Shawn didn't get it. What was so funny?

The shaman came toward him, standing in front, reaching out to poke and prod, feeling his arms, looking at his hands, tousling his hair, then turning to grin while the laughter grew.

Finally, the shaman backed away, put his hands on his hips, and gestured toward Shawn while mumbling something to the group. More laughs, Tsoo-Ki having a good time, Marcie playing along, Shawn trying to straighten his hair while everybody watched.

"What?!"

The shaman regarded him top to bottom, then shook his head resignedly. Finally, as if it must be the last thing ever expected, he made the call.

And the crowd cheered.

"¡Tsawa-Ki!"

THE FLIGHT TO COSTA RICA impressed Carly's companion, mountains and jungles and sandy beaches and old-style Spanish towns . . . and volcanoes! Swallow Gagnon hadn't realized volcanoes still existed, or ever had for that matter, the substance of myths.

Carly had already grown weary of playing Judy Morey, of acting awestruck over every little thing. It was time to find Chaleeshia Poeky, make it worth Swallow's while to leave, then get out of there—or find out the opportunity really was legit, a great deal, the chance of a lifetime.

Yeah, right.

Carly Geiss had been around the block too many times to buy *that* one. Still, though, there *were* some good people in the world, people who would do anything for others, no matter the cost, whatever it took . . .

This she knew for a fact.

Though sometimes it seemed hard to believe.

Processing took a while, the tourists loading into busses and courtesy vans. Once Judy Morey, Swallow, and their kids were cleared, Big Man and Bulagrét led them to the waiting Caddy. Good thing Carly had provided complete, though fabricated, documentation on her "daughter." Swallow hadn't thought about getting through immigration on a verbal lie about whose kid belonged to whom. Carly hoped the good-hearted but naïve barrio sex worker could keep it together long enough not to blow their cover.

By the time they wound over and around the mountains to head through jungle toward the Caribbean Coast and Limón, a storm began to stir.

"You cannot have a rainforest without the rain," Bulagrét explained with a smile, excited about the fabulous fun her new friends were going to have.

Carly relaxed, enjoying the views through dense foliage. The route wound circuitously, the driving slow, affording opportunities to observe and study.

Wild orchids! A toucan. Was it?—yes! A sloth! Some kind of wild pigs, a whole bunch of 'em, with weird noses.

The valleys stretched out longer, the rises less daunting, jungle giving way to cultivated fields and orchards. The rain let up, mist rising from the road and fields, the sun chasing clouds toward the mountains, rays of bright sunlight filtering down here and there.

The sky cleared by the time they worked their way north on the narrow road along the coast, a breathtaking trek offering expansive views of deserted beach and crashing waves, a route punctuated by several walled resorts.

They passed one with a new sign: *D'Shawn Resorts International.* Carly's eyes went wide, but she said nothing. They passed another called *Tsala-Pu,* then headed down a side road inland to a small apartment complex with several buildings.

"This is where you will be living, *all* expenses paid, *free!*"

Looked like a dump to Carly, but Swallow stood mesmerized by the exotic countryside. With her flat in Houston as a point of reference, this must look like Shangri-la.

Swallow would be roomies with a woman from Detroit named LaTisha. Judy Morey would be sharing with Lyla DeCivvio. Big Man stayed with their kids at the car while Bulagrét helped them inside with their luggage and made introductions. Leading them back out, she explained that the children would be living someplace else, with liberal visiting privileges, better not cause any problems and all.

Carly waited quietly, taking it all in. Swallow started to freak, demanding her *kids*—like she had more than one—announcing she didn't like this after all and wanted to go home.

Bulagrét listened politely. But . . . no.

Faces at the apartment windows watched, several women standing quietly on balconies. Carly ached with the realization that this must be standard procedure. Once a week new arrivals came. Same show, different actors. Sometimes a drama, maybe some action, always the same ending.

Swallow tried to get past Big Man to the car. Big mistake.

Smack!

Open-handed, the blow spun and dropped her.

"Stupid! Now you will not be able to work with your bruised face for days. It will delay when you may see your child."

Swallow rose to her knees, sobbing.

Bulagrét helped her up, soothing her, assuring all would be okay once she learned how things work.

They stood there watching while Big Man drove off with the children, Swallow distraught, but not daring to resist.

They started toward the apartments, Judy Morey still quiet.

Carly had already figured out how things work . . . and all was *not* okay.

CHAPTER 8

Y UCK. IT REALLY STUNK. But it looked beautiful if you could ignore the odor, like a sheet of yellow-green glass nestled between mountains, reflecting the clouds and bordering ridges.

Lago Amarillo.

Not a big lake, several kilometers long and nearly as wide, it seemed placid and serene, except for that distinctive smell always permeating the air.

Shawn was burning up in the heat, still overdressed, not used to this tropical humidity. He knelt and looked closer at the water, the shaman indicating several spots not more than a dozen meters out. Yes, he could see them, the tiniest bubbles, like soft-drink carbonation, rising to the surface from unseen depths, silently popping, sulphuric gas.

The whole village gathered around, watching this man they called Tsawa-Ki and his red-haired and dark-skinned friends. Tsoo-Ki watched from smoother ground, several of the children doting on him, the littlest girl repeatedly calling him "Whale-tico" and doing her best to climb into his lap.

"How can you stand to live so close to this smell?" Shawn asked not-so-diplomatically.

"They do not notice it because they live here all their lives," Tsoo-Ki answered. "It is strong for me now after I was away in San José."

The old lady said something, stabbing a finger toward the water, looking indignant.

"She say our true home is in the waters—*under* the waters."

The old shaman said something passionately, the woman repeating much of it. They jabbered a moment among themselves and with Tsoo-Ki. Finally the young Indian interrupted them with upraised hand, explaining to Shawn and friends, "They want you to understand the village of *abuelos*—our grandfathers, um, ancestors—" He stammered, trying to find the right words. "At the central of the old village *está la alma*—it is where our ancestors kept the crystal that is for everyone. And then the Spaniards came looking for gold. There is no gold here, but they stayed to help our people with growing foods." He gestured toward the crop fields and orchards.

Marcie added, "Corn already thrived here, but Spanish coffee and bananas became big cash crops, plus lots of the veggies common here now weren't yet known to this part of the world—according to Anthro-twit, anyway."

Tsoo-Ki nodded. "Our neighbors shared all for every person, but then some of our peoples traded with the Spaniards for pretty things just to keep for themselves. Young womens and girls, what they did with the Spaniards—it was—what they—" He blushed, glancing at his lap. "So the volcano," he continued, "it was saying no more, and it was rumbling and making the ash fall on the crops, and on the animals, which ran away until we could not hunt them for food. And then the Spaniards left, except for one who came back for the young Tsala woman he wanted to take with him. That is when he saw how Tsawa-Ki used the crystal to make the rain wash the ash into the earth, and the crops to be alive again, and the animals to come back."

"Tsawa-Ki?" Marcie asked.

"The child from the rainbow. He was the young boy who carried the colors with him. All peoples could use their own power *en la joya*—with the crystal—but Tsawa-Ki used *la alma*, the *spirit* of the crystal."

"What happened with the Spaniard?" Shawn asked. He didn't want to set off another round of speculation over himself. Stick to history.

"The Spaniard went after his other men and brought them back. They demanded that we teach them how to use *la alma joya*, but Tsawa-Ki say we should never tell them because they would use for the bad. My peoples were afraid of the Spaniards and wanted to kill them, but Tsawa-Ki say no, this would also be for the bad, that to kill for the crystal ¡está muy mal! My peoples took la joya from Tsawa-Ki, and they tied him with ropes and carried him over the mountain—" He gestured toward where they'd choppered with Brinkley the day before. "And they left him there so he could not stop them from using la joya to kill the Spaniards."

"*Did* they kill them?" Marcie asked.

"After using the crystal to make the Spaniards very desiring of the pleasures of the body, the Tsala women each took one of them into their homes . . ." The young Indian blushed again, picking at a loose thread on his fluorescent tee. "But it was the pleasures of death these men found," he added quietly.

"They killed them with sex?" Marcie looked incredulous and, Shawn thought, just a bit too intrigued.

Tsoo-Ki shrugged, then jabbered questioningly to the elders. Shaman and the old woman spread their hands in a gesture that could have meant they didn't know, or that the answer was too obvious to dignify.

"Then what happened?" Marcie prodded.

"It was the next day when the sun would be highest in the sky, la Tsala-Pu, and the men went to find Tsawa-Ki, to bring him back for the ceremony, but he was gone. Then all the peoples saw him standing up there." He pointed to the high point where the chopper had landed, the area where Tsoo-Ki had been climbing when he suffered his paralyzing fall. "There was a bright sparkle in each of his hands. He held them up, and they were brighter, and the rainbows came down from the sky and filled everything, all with many colors, and nobody could see anything but these colors . . . and that is when it happened."

"What?! What happened?" Marcie was caught up in the legend.

"The ground started to shake, and the volcano started making grumbles, and the cracks opened everywhere, and water came from the ground and covered everything. My peoples had to run to the hills to stay alive— and many did not make it, but were swallowed in the ground or covered with the waters. When it was over and the colors went back to the sky, there was Lago Amarillo, and the homes were gone, and so was the central of the village with *la alma joya*—all gone under the waters. Tsawa-Ki stood up there, watching and saying nothing."

Marcie let out a long sigh. Shawn thought it was a cute story. Brinkley studied the water, probably wondering just where in the bottom of that stinky lake the big crystal might be and how he could salvage it.

"The peoples," Tsoo-Ki continued, "they sent the shaman to tell Tsawa-Ki to use these powers to bring back the village and *la joya*, but he say no, and that he would leave and not return again until the Tsala prove they will use only for the good. He say he would come again when the Tsala needed for him to help defeat the badness. But the shaman tried to grab Tsawa-Ki; then the rainbow surrounded him, and he could see only the colors, and then Tsawa-Ki was gone, and the shaman fell, and his legs never worked again." His face down, his hands gingerly touched his legs, a catch in his voice.

"You think you've suffered the same fate," Marcie said quietly, "that you're also being punished for wanting to use the crystals for the bad."

Tsoo-Ki only nodded his shame.

"Whatever happened to the kid?" Shawn asked, refusing to use the moniker everybody seemed determined to resurrect.

"He never came back until after all this time," Tsoo-Ki said quietly. He looked up into Shawn's face, his eyes shining with hope. "Until now," he said. "And you are here."

Shawn rolled his eyes, scratched his head, shuffled awkwardly, no doubt inadvertently making his rainbow aura shift and swirl. It seemed he and Brinkley were the only ones who couldn't see it. *You'd think a mythical rainbow dude could at least see his own light show.*

"So what is the badness Shawn is here to defeat?" Marcie asked. She loved this, finally getting answers. She'd long insisted that the rainbow around her friend must be there for a reason.

Just eating this up, Shawn thought.

"There was *una familia*—a family—that left here many years ago," Tsoo-Ki explained, "to live in San José. They had *una niña* who grew up to become a woman. She came back looking for *las cristales*. They talked to my cousin, and he left with them in the helio-copter."

"Your cousin?"

"Takú Litál."

The shaman jabbered something, pointing out into the lake.

"He say it is not always just for the badness to seek *las cristales*, but Litál wanted to use them to be young again, and for the woman to become a person with many riches. The woman had her husband with her, and a big man who spoke only to her, and they had *una niña pequita*—a little girl. They brought a boat with them, too, one that had many machines for seeing under the waters, and they went out on the lake to look for *la joya* and the homes of my peoples. One day they were out there and having loud words and shouting—" He struggled with his vocabulary.

"An argument?" Marcie supplied.

"*Sí*. The big man hit the husband until he was dead, then put him in the water. My people were angry, and they started to swim out, but the boat ran from them, and the woman and the big man and Takú Litál took the little girl in the helio-copter and flew away. The Tsala peoples sunk the boat to the bottom because it was used for the badness. We have never seen these other people again."

"Joelle Bulagrét," Marcie said.

"Joléa de Tsala," Shawn clarified.

The jabbering stopped, all eyes watching Shawn.

"You know of this?" Tsoo-Ki asked quietly.

"It's why we're here," Marcie said sagely. "It is why Tsawa-Ki has come."

Sheesh. Shawn was burning up. Late afternoon, it ought to be cooling down. In fact, they needed to lift off and head back toward the coast soon.

But good ol' Marcie persisted. "You've hurt your legs as punishment for going to look for your cousin and the crystals?"

"I took *la joya de la aldea*—the crystal of the village you saw. I was using it to be young always, and to find *las cristales*. It was for the bad."

"Can't *the crystal* help cure you then?" Marcie asked, ever the positive thinker.

His face down, Tsoo-Ki shook his head. "I was trying."

Don't say it, Marcie. Shawn tried to burn a hole in her with his eyes. *Don't say it.*

She said it. "Maybe *Shawn* could get the crystal to work. His name is D'Fixx, but for many reasons we call him Rich Mr. Fixx."

Shawn had to wonder how well the old shaman really could understand the conversation because, on cue, he produced the jawbreaker crystal from under his robe and offered it to the nouveau Tsawa-Ki. Shawn didn't take it, so the old man walked it over to the young man in the wheelchair and said something quietly.

"He say I will keep it until Tsawa-Ki judges me worthy to help."

Shawn felt queasy. Damn, it was hot! He didn't want to leave these people angry or disappointed. Better to show them it wouldn't work. Play along. "What do I do?"

Kneeling beside the wheelchair, he felt silly, but he had a lump in his throat. He wanted to help this young man, this Tsala who believed his infirmity must be more than an accident, a punishment crippling him for life, no one to blame but himself. But he knew it was no use, that nothing could be done. He'd raised the lad's hopes, but would only leave him sad and disillusioned that Shawn, the man in whom all his trust had been placed, would never be more than just that:

A man.

A pretender who fancied himself *Mr. Fixx*, and did do a bit of good here and there; but when it came down to it, he was just a sham.

Tsoo-Ki had put the crystal in Shawn's hands, now holding them against his own chest. Shawn struggled to keep from passing out in the rising heat, his heart pounding, his face and body bathed in sweat. He looked at the young Indian and saw he was drenched, too.

Everything spinning, so many colors, nothing left but the confident eyes of an old man. They believed.

Shawn tried to look away, to focus, to orient himself. He could see the high ridge toward the volcano, shimmering and wavy in the heat. A boy stood up there, arms held wide, hands sparkling.

Shawn blinked, wanting to wipe the grimy sweat from his face, but Tsoo-Ki held tight. That kid up there didn't look like an Indian. He looked like . . . Jeremy?

No. Like little Shawn D'Fixx.

Hallucinating from this heat. He shook his head and tried to keep from vomiting, from fading . . . the colors . . . so hot . . . colors . . .

Darkness.

He floated out on dark waters, then felt himself lifted by a wave of determination before suddenly being washed back, deposited on the shore, drenched but unafraid.

Somebody was holding him, helping him up.

"Tsawa-Ki," came a whisper, Tsoo-Ki's voice.

Somebody lifted and carried him to the stairstep stream of cool water, laying him gently on the stones and rinsing his face.

"You all right, Shawn?" asked Marcie, Brinkley behind her. Everybody stood back, Tsoo-Ki gesturing to stay clear.

"I'm okay," he said.

Tsoo-Ki helped him to his feet, the two *standing* there looking at each other, the young man's legs—*healed?*

"Tsawa-Ki," the grateful Indian whispered.

Shawn could see past him to the ridge. That child stood there, nodding his head, a swirl of rainbow colors and blinding light, and then he was gone.

JUDY MOREY STARTED UNPACKING her meager possessions to make herself at home. Lyla DeCivvio had left for some kind of meeting, so she finally had the place to herself.

Carly Geiss dutifully continued to play Judy-the-hooker. Nobody more than she liked to relax and cut loose, have a good time, walk on the wild side, then dive off a cliff while over there, but Chaleeshia Poeky's *life* hung in the balance—at least she assumed; she'd not seen the young, black prostitute mother yet. *Hoped* she was okay, anyway. Worse, she'd already seen enough to know this "opportunity of a lifetime" had become downright dangerous, and there were a lot more people at risk than the one she'd come to check on.

Carly removed a small make-up kit, touching the wells in a peculiar combination-sequence. The bottom swung open, revealing a touch panel. She activated something inside, a series of small colored lights glowing on a display. She walked around the apartment, "scanning."

Humph. The device helped her discover a micro-recorder running just outside her bedroom door, concealed in a small pouch on the back of a cabinet, positioned to pick up sound from the living area, or from the new girl's bedroom.

Nobody else had been in the apartment for at least the past hour. Lyla must have planted it. She was in on the scam.

Okay, good to know. Good to know.

No other active electronic devices, no toxic chemicals or substances, no unusual electro-magnetic activity—she learned as much as that device could reveal, but outward indications suggested that was enough.

Turning on the small television in the living room, she tuned it to a Mexican music-video station. Then she disassembled her curling iron, dumping three small disks from its shaft into her hand before putting it back together. She massaged the blower on her hair-dryer for a minute and placed it carefully on the dresser, then changed into some loose-fitting jeans and a tight halter top.

No bra. Hopefully, her "charms" wouldn't come into play on this trip.

She left a note indicating she would be outside walking around, not too far, just shout.

She found some wrapped candies in the kitchen, putting a half-dozen in her pockets, along with the dull-gray disks from her curling iron. She locked up and wandered out, feeling eyes on her, careful to stay within sight of the building.

Over the next fifteen minutes, she managed to circle the complex, stopping to admire wildflowers and sprays of bougainvillea and several orchids at the edge of dense foliage. Steam from the afternoon's rain puddles misted around her, damp and sticky, the day still growing hotter.

Every now and then, she'd eat a candy from her pocket, sometimes kneeling to adjust her sandals or smell a flower. By the time she went back inside, all three disks had been carefully concealed in a triangular configuration around the perimeter in places they would likely never be noticed.

Back inside, she used her make-up compact to check the recorder—still running. She went to the bedroom and massaged the blower on her hair-dryer again.

"GOT HER, BICKERY BECKY!" Todd announced.

"Oh, good," came the relieved voice over a speaker at the surveillance console inside the Gulfstream.

"Guess what? I'm parked next to the Foster B. Garbus jet."

"I wonder if Carly knows it's there. I wonder *who's* there."

"Leave it to me; I'll find out. Just waiting for her report right now, though."

GOOD, THE RECORDER had shut down. Carly stood in front of her dresser mirror, massaged the hair-dryer yet again, then started talking in a low voice.

"Small apartment complex just northwest of a resort called Tsala-Pu, due north from Limón on the Caribbean coast. There is no sign yet of Poeky. The children have been taken hostage . . ."

MOOLHUIZEN WANTED SHAWN to go under one of his alternate names, suggesting "Dillard Shaw."

"No, Bulagrét knows me as Shawn. If she checked me out, she's got *D'Fixx*, too, and figures me for a businessman with money, though not as big as Marcie's *Melinda McNair*. If she sees me and finds out I'm using a false name, she'll get suspicious of both me *and* Marcie, maybe even of you, too."

Shawn knew that what Moolhuizen really wanted was to talk his boss out of going through with this. No such luck. Marcie wanted to figure out what was going on, and rich dweeb men were who these crystal-renters wanted. Dweeb was a role Shawn had been rehearsing all his life.

"Put your shoes on," Moolhuizen instructed. He'd learned long ago not to be deferential. He had a job to do, and his boss respected that.

While Shawn donned his sneakers, Moolhuizen activated his own pocket listener in the next room, adjusting it so the transmitter concealed in his ear canal could pick up the test tone just right. "Go ahead," he called.

"I think it's very generous of my good friend Carlysle to pay for my crystal excursion, to try to get me laid," Shawn said in a normal tone of voice.

Moolhuizen came back satisfied, then slung a travel-bag over his shoulder and waited for Shawn to use the bathroom before they left. He'd forgotten to suggest his boss do that *before* he activated the listener.

"Just hope I don't get distracted and pee on my shoe," Shawn said for his benefit, "—probably electrocute you."

They walked over to Tsala-Pu, first scoping the lobby. Moolhuizen gestured toward the manager's office, then toward the public men's room off the waiting area. He left Shawn standing there while he went to use a toilet, no doubt ensconcing himself in a stall and opening his travel bag of gizmos and goodies.

Shawn talked to a receptionist who led him to an office. The manager seemed thrilled to meet him in a broken-English sort of way. She went through her pitch up to the point of applying paste to his wrist; then he suddenly needed to use the restroom, promising he'd be right back.

Having listened in, Moolhuizen was ready. Shawn wouldn't let substances of unknown content be smeared on himself, so the operative painted some kind of invisible sealant on his boss's skin from the knuckles to not far below his elbow, blowing on it a minute to dry, then sending him on his way.

Back to the office he went. She applied the paste, put his crystal-enhanced watch on his wrist, then proceeded to get all hot and horny over him. She had to beg him to leave before she lost control.

He wasn't impressed.

D'Fixx told the shuttle driver he'd be just a moment, then ducked back into the restroom, just catching a glimpse of Bulagrét as she came through with Big Man and headed toward another office.

Moolhuizen removed most of the paste and sealed it in a specimen jar, then put a small amount in a field-test kit and added some concoction. He peeled away the micro-thin film that had protected his boss's skin, inspected the watch and crystal, and decided it posed no other threat. He checked the field test and smiled knowingly.

"There's at least a 'caine, probably coca, and some kind of methamphetamine. Absorbed through the skin, you'd feel it tingling, then get a mind-rush that would last probably an hour or more," he explained. "Watch out, they probably have a way to dose you even more when this wears off. Don't eat or drink or handle things you suspect. Remember to act a bit wired up."

Shawn chose The Pink Parrot and shuttled over. He turned out to be *very* popular. That was *some crystal* his buddy Hizen had provided for a five-thousand-dollar one-night sample fee. He ordered a bottled beer, watching carefully as the waitress opened it and brought it to the table. Several nearby babes openly flirted with him, but he found himself most interested in one at the bar.

He had several more drinks, then noticed her studying him, showing her interest, too. Finally, he got up the nerve and moved over next to her, introducing himself. They had a nice chat, all eyes for each other, obviously smitten.

Turns out she had a place next door to The Pink Parrot, right on the beach.

WATCHING FROM ANOTHER TABLE, Lyla DeCivvio was disappointed; she'd wanted the score. She'd been racking up a lot of points with Bulagrét lately; this would have been another nice feather. Oh well.

When it became clear the mark wouldn't come back, she and the others shuttled back to the apartments. Shortly after, Bulagrét stopped by to check progress. DeCivvio reported that the crystal-geek at The Parrot had successfully picked up a real tourist, not one of the plants.

Bulagrét carped about not having control, wanting to assure he would have the ultimate sexual adventure, to get progress reports on his tastes and style so she could arrange for each successive night to get better. But that happens. Sometimes they really score.

At least there would be authenticity in the lady's story.

SHAWN WAITED AWHILE, enjoying a room-service dinner with his date while they played a game of Scrabble. Later, when nobody would likely see, a car pulled up to take him and his date away, back to D'Shawn Resort, to settle in for the night.

They went to her suite where she removed her blond wig and sunglasses; then she started wiping off the outrageous make-up that matched her sassy clothes.

"Next time you play dress-up, Marcie, come by *my* room and I might *really* jump your bones."

That made it *his* turn to get the atomic wedgie.

"STUPID BITCH," CARLY PRONOUNCED. Her Judy Morey hooker character acted like she just couldn't understand Swallow's behavior.

"I mean, yeah! What's she think?" Lyla DeCivvio agreed.

"You gotta *know* this is some kinda scam goin' down here. I got no problem with that, as long as it's workin' for *me*, too."

"*There* ya go. That's how I look at it. Even if you don't expect it, what are you gonna do when you get here?"

"You're gonna play, and play it straight. Make it work."

"Right. That's why she had to be slapped down, to show her this is serious."

"I think we got her in line now."

"It's good *you* got her calmed down," Lyla praised. "She sure wasn't listening to *me*."

"We come down together, both from the barrio. She figured I was closest thing she got to a sister, I guess," Carly explained. It'd been all she could do to telegraph to Swallow Gagnon to play along for now and not worry, that somehow it would all work out okay. She couldn't afford her freaking and getting somebody hurt, or letting on that both kids were hers, blowing Carly's cover.

"Joelle's real impressed with you already. That's good for both of us. She said get you trained, and you can start tonight. She don't usually trust 'em that fast. That's *real* good."

"Well, let's get to it then. I need to know how everything works so I can start makin' my hundred-grand—"

"And get to see your kid tomorrow."

"And look forward to getting back home someday."

CHAPTER 9

THE HOSPITAL CANDY MACHINES survived unmolested throughout the next day—not that Shawn D'Fixx wasn't cast a wary eye by staff, a few raised eyebrows, several whispers.

Marcie stayed with Tsoo-Ki while the bigshots and kahunas poked and prodded and tested and sampled and scanned him. Sounds like "Hmmm . . ." could be heard occasionally, lots of shaking heads, rubbed chins, surprised expressions.

They pronounced a full recovery with no detectable atrophy. The doctors couldn't have been fooled the day before. No, their tests were infallible. Tsoo-Ki had clearly been paralyzed. Sure, a man could train himself not to react when needles are jabbed surreptitiously into fleshy appendages, but the instruments had thoroughly documented lack of electrical and bio-chemical activity down to the neuro-transmitter level.

And now he appeared healthy, for no logical reason, no explanations.

Must've been psychological. Yeah, that's it. Psych.

Shawn spent that time Fixxing his way around the hospital. He'd had Kinte hire several department heads for private consultation, plus a brassy nurse whose attitude he thoroughly enjoyed. The heads had been assembling and reviewing patient records, financial statuses, sorting by need and making recommendations, all while Brassy Nurse took Shawn on a full tour, visiting patients, giving toys to children and practical gifts to adults. Moolhuizen and Brinkley brought in crateloads of goodies as fast as Rich Mr. Fixx could hand them out.

Brassy kept a list, too, soon to be forwarded to Kinte. This child would need surgery for cleft palate after his legs healed; that woman would need the kind of rehabilitation not offered here; a second dialysis machine would lessen Guillermo's daily ordeal by eliminating these long waits.

Shawn was in his element. See it, find out what it needs, do it. Or bring in whatever it takes. This was Fixxing.

But those doctors kept interrupting him. No, he didn't want any more tests on himself, Marcie's and Tsoo-Ki's assertions notwithstanding. If those two wanted to keep wearing hand-crafted rainbow pendants with bits of broken glass, fine, but that didn't mean any special powers could be ascribed to Shawn. Just flesh and blood and bone. Nothing to see here; move along, move along, go on back to your business. Ouch! That's enough!

They had to admit he was right. Must have been Tsoo-Ki's strong beliefs. Psychological power of healing. Seen it before, always impressive. Hard to itemize on a bill.

Finally it came time to meet with Anthro-twit. Shawn had him summoned to the hospital for a private luncheon in one of the administrators' offices. The expert had nothing on the Tsala people. They didn't exist. 'Nuff said.

He did have two things to report about prostitution in Costa Rica. First, he'd located a man who could arrange to sell him some girls. He thought Shawn might want to buy in, then release them or move them out of the area for a better life.

Shawn found it tempting, but he thought about a time when he and Foster were fifteen: a friend of theirs was stealing rare and expensive wines from his parents' cellar and selling them to his buddies. Shawn and Foster had bought-in several times, giddy and drunk on thousand-dollar vino teenagers had no other way to acquire.

Until Kinte caught them.

The old man seemed upset, *very* upset—but not because they'd been drinking. In fact, some years later he'd actually smiled when recalling the incident, allowing as how they at least had displayed discerning taste in their selection. No, what outraged him was the buying-stolen-goods part. Foster had argued that the kid was doing it anyway. Kinte wondered how long that would go on if none of the friends would buy.

"When you encourage it, finance it, give reason for it to happen, especially to one with no other means or cloudy morals, then you are even more guilty than the thief," he'd intoned.

Man, Kinte looked big, towering menacingly over them, rubbing his hands through his hair, even slipping several times into Jamaican street patois from his youth—a sure sign the old man was livid.

"*More* guilty?" Shawn had asked meekly.

"Yes. Then you are not only a rastagoo thief, *but* you have also helped to corrupt your friend."

The old man had pronounced he was ashamed of them and left them to stew for two days before he would even look them in the eye. Talk about walking on eggshells.

No, Shawn wouldn't be buying the freedom of these women. That would only encourage the abduction of more. What he would do was have Kinte send a team in to investigate and try to shut down the system.

"I have another suggestion I'm *sure* you'll like," Anthro-twit explained. "You could start a program, set up an intervention service in San José. I've had people back home research this, and they've found an excellent model in Houston. A place called FuturePlan."

Um, sure. Why didn't Shawn think of that?

EIGHT OR TEN OF THEM scurried about, all in labcoats behind shatterproof glass, some double-rechecking equipment, others making notes, one fidgeting nervously—the tech who'd first shot laser into the crystal shard brought in by Shawn and Marcie.

There it waited on the other side of the glass, mounted in some type of wand clamp, sensors and various devices arrayed proximately. It sparkled pale violet, another of the crystal shards, one of the few left.

"Clear."

"Clear," another announced.

"Clear."

"Let's do it," Tech ordered.

The light on the other side of the glass faded to black; then a beam appeared, perfectly calibrated, shining just across the top of the shard. Needles and LCD displays danced, a plotter spitting continuous feed, faces in labcoats watching in anticipation.

The beam started to move lower.

It kissed the shard.

Prisms of rainbow colors shot every direction; needles went wild, the plotter berserk.

"Gas spectrometer shows ballooning!" one of the labcoats warned.

Too late! A burst of color, readings off the chart, the crystal exploded.

The lights came up just in time to reveal a wisp of gaseous smoke where the shard had been, then nothing. They would be the rest of the day collecting micro-particles from inside the room, analyzing and studying, readying the next shard, their hopes growing dimmer with each burst of colored light.

Tech headed down the hallway and stabbed the phone with his finger. He had to go through several people, trying to reach Foster B. Garbus, but wound up with Kinte Bilal.

"Just too small," he complained, exasperation straining his voice.

"I trust you have been unable to adjust your experiment to collect sufficient readings before losing more crystals."

"*Too damned small!* The gasses heat and expand too much and the shard isn't big enough to conduct the heat away—outside temp regardless. We can't get a measurable increase in power at lower settings, yet as soon as we cross the line where we do, we lose the shard. The first one they brought in, the one we lost recklessly before we realized this paradox would dog us, that one was only slightly bigger, but it made a huge difference. That's still the best data we've got. I'd give my left nut for one the size of a baseball."

"Mr. Garbus is still negotiating to secure cases of larger stones for you to analyze, hopefully to acquire at least *one* that is substantially larger."

"Well, I'm ready to call it. We're down to less than three-hundred left, and we're not gaining any new data by continuing to try. I suggest we save them until *after* we learn more from larger samples, maybe use these for ancillary data collection."

"I will defer to your expertise."

"Hey, this could be the biggest thing since electricity, a discovery that changes global economics and politics, securing a place for *my* name in the history books. Trust me, I'd not shut down if there was *any* way to proceed. We've got enough data to spend the next week just crunching, see what we can find, any hints or clues, something maybe we've overlooked."

"Please keep Mr. Garbus or me informed of any new discoveries."

"Um, what about that other request?"

Kinte hesitated like maybe he hadn't even tried. "I still consider it very unlikely—"

"Good god, man. This could make somebody *filthy* rich. And he's the one uncontrolled factor I *know*—not suspect, *know* affects this unexplained phenomenon. I witnessed it myself, his effect at the site *and* his impact on the crystal's output."

"I will make your request at the appropriate time."

"I sure hope so. You give me a week to study a *big* crystal and that guy with the lizard *at the same time*, and we could very well change the world!"

"I'M GONNA SPEND THE NIGHT with the sexiest babe I can find," Shawn pronounced, "whomever catches my eye, especially if *she's* got the hots for *me*."

Scallywag perched on the bathroom counter watching Shawn lasershave. He looked as skeptical as Marcie, Shawn's friend sitting there on the bed.

"Then you better let me paint Sam's skin-protector on your thingie— and any other parts that might get some action." She sounded serious.

"You don't need to run those nineteen-fifties hygiene films for me; I know how to protect myself."

"But if you're wearin' your crystal, she just might wanna do more than blow in your ear."

"She gets even a *gander* at my lizard and she'll be following us home." Scallywag used the open drawer to skedaddle down and out of the bathroom. He'd heard enough.

"So you don't want me to play dress-up?" she asked with mock petulance.

He stuck his head out and grinned. "Maybe I need to find somebody who likes three-fers." As if she wouldn't.

She wagged her brows suggestively. "Can I help with the selection, then? I'm picky, you know."

"Yeah, right. I've long suspected your only criterion is *still breathing*—and even that I've wondered about."

"Lots of things are scary until you try 'em," she teased. He knew she was kidding. She wasn't *that* open to the wild side. She liked 'em both breathing *and* clean. Actually, based on what he'd seen through the years, he knew she was most intrigued by young and powerful guys who seemed on the edge—a wild look, tattoos or piercing or bizarre hair and clothes. Uninhibited. Experimental. Sense of humor about the whole thing. Very casual, not overly interpretive.

She probably wouldn't have been drawn into her friendship with Shawn back at Berkeley if not for the pique of his so-called rainbow aura. He'd been a bit shy, somewhat awkward until he relaxed and let his passions and vulnerability come through, but Shawn hadn't been the type who normally would excite her sense of adventure. They'd had some fantastic times together, though, until they became such good friends that it was clear he needed to remain open for that one true love who may or may not ever come along, while she wanted to dally and dabble and play until the day she draws her last breath.

Unless whoever she was with didn't care about that breathing thing—

Shawn left the bathroom, stopping to put some beetle grubs in a dish for Scallywag.

"Why the sudden urge to share your lizard?"

He smiled knowingly again. "Thou doest give overbreadth to my motives, wench. I figure if I act like a dick, any woman trying to bed me must be working for Bulagrét and trying to convince me the crystal is doing it. If I can get her alone for a while, test her a bit to be sure she's not just some tourist with low standards—"

"Who *likes* dicks—"

"Then find out her price," he continued, "get her to talk and reveal how this thing works so we can figure out how to shut it down."

"You mean the next morning, *after* you've had your nasty way with her."

He didn't, but it was a fun thought. He just smiled and shrugged, then picked up the phone and called Moolhuizen. "Activate the shoe, Sam, and do your test." He hung up, recited the alphabet, Marcie counting off from across the room. The phone rang, Moolhuizen confirming AOK. "Remember," Shawn reminded him, "if I say *Sam-Off*, that means shut it down and stop listening; I may want some privacy."

Marcie donned her blond wig, bypassing the outrageous outfit and make-up. "If you won't let me play, I'm at least gonna go watch the opening ceremonies," she pronounced.

"You just wanna laugh when I get snubbed by everyone I hit on."

"Shawn, even without your crystal, you've got a magnetic power that draws people in. Any babe not affected ain't worthy."

Ignoring the off-hand compliment, he wondered, "Think I should take Scallywag?"

"If you're trying to scare off the *normal* ones, then yes."

They stopped by Moolhuizen's room so he could paint skin-protector on Shawn's wrist.

Marcie and Moolhuizen left first, a lovey couple staking out a table at The Wet Orchid. The place was hopping and, except for karaoke coming from the next room, had a nice, relaxed atmosphere. A lot of young women nursed silly drinks with umbrellas and elaborate fruit constructions, most paired with girlfriends, all scanning the room.

Shawn walked to Tsala-Pu, went through the paste and crystal ritual, got the manager all hot and bothered, then left before she could lose control. He took the resort shuttle to The Orchid.

He presented quite a sight carrying that lizard on his shoulder, grinning like a goof, a bit loud and boisterous. He rather enjoyed playing the role. Demanding a certain table be cleared for him, he took the seat affording the best view of the room, ordered a beer, and placed his lizard beside his drink for all to see. Scallywag looked bored with the whole situation.

In no time, gals started eyeing him and winking, touching themselves suggestively, one even coming over to admire and pet his lizard. Rather provocatively, she petted.

Scallywag seemed to like it—a lot.

Two women came in. One he remembered seeing at The Pink Parrot, but the other one was—!

Long, beautiful chestnut hair, big gold-flecked hazel eyes, tight halter-top with fantasmanomical breasts—

His lizard snapped from its reverie, took one look, and stiffened. It was her! The sex worker from Houston, party-girl from The Gaseous Giant, new client of FuturePlan.

She froze, those beautiful eyes locked on Shawn and his lizard, lips slightly apart—

Still they stared, he tingling all over, she glowing radiant like an old movie with gauzy lens.

Lyla selected a table, but she looked surprised that her companion hadn't followed.

That's when Shawn made the mistake of trying to straighten his hair, rendering it a hopeless mess. Then he stood awkwardly, almost knocking over his chair. He pulled out the one next to his and gestured for her to join him.

Did he mean to do that? Seemed like he was on auto-pilot.

She looked shy, demure, but drawn in, unable to resist. She glided over, gave him the warmest smile of his life, and accepted the seat without speaking. Very different than her devil-may-care demeanor at The Giant, *she* seemed to be on auto-pilot, too.

He started having difficulty breathing—trying not to hyperventi-late—and noticed Marcie rolling her eyes, Moolhuizen no doubt watching intently from behind those shades, ready to spring at the sign of a mickey or hypo or anything that suggested his boss might be in danger.

But there was nothing to be afraid of. He knew it, felt it, embraced it. Only one thing bothered him.

"I don't buy," he whispered so only the two of them could hear.

"I don't sell."

They were both breathing hard.

"Cool!"

"May I touch?"

"Please."

She gently stroked his lizard, Scallywag responding amorously, rubbing against her hand, his eyes closed, rocking gently to the rhythm of karaoke permeating the Caribbean jungle.

Shawn touched her hand, her gentle stroke moving up his, to his arm, across his shoulder and chest.

"I don't like being watched," he whispered.

"Then let's go to *your* room rather than mine," she suggested.

He left some money on the table, held her chair while she stood, took her hand, and started to lead her out.

"Aren't you bringing your lizard?"

"My friends can take him."

"You might need him."

He looked into her eyes. She smiled mischievously.

"Maybe I will." He picked up Scallywag, placed him on his shoulders, all three disappearing into the tropical night.

They decided to walk down the road toward D'Shawn, an exotic evening, a cacophony of rainforest sound effects, salty breeze across breaking water.

"What's your name?"

"Can you keep a secret, Shawn?"

"You know *mine*? Yes, I'm good at secrets."

"Remember to call me Judy."

"Okay, Judy."

"It's Carly."

"Do I know you?"

"Not yet. Well, sorta. But you will."

Louder, Shawn ordered, "Sam-Off!"

Carly smiled, eyes glistening in the moonlight. "Todd! You shut yours off, too!"

FOSTER WATCHED FROM another console, Kinte in front of the main viewscreen. Moolhuizen's frantic face talked from the chopper, jungle foliage and walled resort as background in the shot.

"I know I should've called sooner, but—well—"

"Yes, and you should have taken greater precautions." Kinte looked angry, running a hand through his short, graying hair.

"Three hours with a babe in a resort," Foster interjected with a smile. "Leave him be. Sounds like he and his lizard are having a good time."

Ignoring the young tycoon, Kinte admonished, "He could be drugged or incapacitated by now. Why did you discontinue audio monitoring?"

"He *told* me to." Moolhuizen looked like he didn't like being caught in the middle. "I waited several hours, then defied his orders, assuming you would authorize me to override, but I can't hear anything. He's either disconnected or put his shoe somewhere else so I can't monitor."

"Or *she* has. Are you sure they are still in there?"

"Yes." The operative shuffled through a packet. "I've had two people on it since they went in. Nobody's come out. Here—" He found what he was after, a wafer about the size of a postage stamp. "I *did* get three digital shots of her so you can start running her down. She probably has a passport, likely came in on a recent Bulagrét charter or commercial flight from the States. Marcie says it's the same woman they saw at Houston's

FuturePlan and also charming the crowd at The Gaseous Giant. That oughta be enough for you to get an ID and some background."

"And count the freckles on her ass," Foster cut in, clearly an unwelcome intrusion in what *some* people understood was an urgent matter.

Moolhuizen inserted the wafer somewhere below-screen and keypunched some instructions. A triad of digital shots taken at The Pink Parrot scanned onto the monitor, two at the table with Shawn, the third as they were leaving. "That's all I have for now. I'm gonna go check in and stay on top of it."

"Leave him alone," Foster admonished. "Don't burst in and scare that lizard at an awkward time, or he'll start sending you on cold trails just so he can have some privacy. You know where he is; assume he's just havin' fun."

"Mr. Garbus's advice, surprisingly, is good," Kinte admitted. "Intercede only if you detect imminent danger."

"Yes, sir. Let me know when you find out something about her that might be helpful."

The screen blank, Foster expected to see Kinte's fingers blur on the console, sending search commands and accessing data systems. Instead, the old man sat back and stroked his chin.

Foster said nothing, just watching.

"Are you not late for your rendezvous with Miss Blanton?" the big Jamaican asked without turning.

"Oh! You're right. See you in the morning, old man." Foster headed toward the elevator that would take him to the level where he had his own private suite. He paused, turning to add, "Hey, leave him be. We've been trying to *encourage* more of this."

"I will take your suggestion under advisement," Kinte said, still without turning. "Good night, Mr. Garbus."

KINTE WAITED UNTIL FOSTER had been gone a full ten minutes before he even touched the console. When he did, it was to activate a single database, access a comm code, and touch the *open* command, audio channel only.

Immediately, a cheerful young woman's voice answered, "Mr. *Bilal!* It's been a long time!"

SHAWN HELD HER IN HIS ARMS, swaying gently to the music, leading her around the room, savoring her soft body and warm breath and silky chestnut hair. He'd avoided dancing as long as he could remember, never before summoning the confidence to learn how, but Carly proved to be a very good teacher.

And Shawn found himself to be a very eager student.

Even ol' Scallywag seemed to be having a good time, perched on the back of the couch, bobbing his head in perfect time with the song.

The music over, Shawn still held on, still swaying gently, but slowing until they stood there, cheek to cheek, and he kissed her . . .

And she him.

Then again.

Scallywag closed his eyes. Sheesh, like a couple of love-struck teens. Hose 'em down.

She looked into his eyes, hers glistening, reflecting the soft lights around the room, offering another hint of mischievous smile. "We made a deal," she whispered.

"I won't hold you to it. It was heat of the moment. After all," he added, smiling, "you were under the spell of my magic crystal."

She laughed. "That's the main thing we need to talk about."

"Well then, if *talk* is what we'll be up to, I get to ask my questions first."

"You know they teach girls not to talk about themselves on the first date," she sparred good-naturedly. They were moving to the couch, trying not to let go of each other. Scallywag scooted to the arm to make room, closing his eyes again. This might get too icky to watch.

"How did you know my name?"

She considered for a moment. "I admire your work, even try to do a small part myself sometimes. I was a child growing up in poverty, but then a benefactor gave me a chance to go to private school and university, even helped me invest in my first business, which I built into substantial hold-ings, though not in a league like yours."

"What kinda stuff you in?"

"You've heard of CG-Temps?"

"*Heard* of it? It's like the biggest temp-worker service in the world, isn't it?"

"Depends on how you measure. I'm CG, Carly Geiss."

Rich! Hey hey hey . . .

Shawn suddenly realized the irony in feeling pleased to find out the lady of his infatuations had her *own* mega-mound o' moolah.

"I saw you in Houston, at The Gaseous Giant."

"And I saw *you*. Nearly threw me off my stride, you did. Trying to work the crowd and you got me worryin' about how I look."

She settled in against his shoulder, his arm around her and lightly stroking her shiny chestnut hair. Scallywag wanted a piece of the action, easing over to get comfortable on the cushion, resting his head on her leg, closing his eyes. She giggled, gently petting the lizard's head, no objec-tions there.

"I saw you at FuturePlan."

"You and your friend sure get around, don't you?"

He smiled. "Marcie drags me *every* gosh-durn place, and then some. When she's not on some mystical quest, she's hell-bent and determined to make sure I go places and have fun."

"Sounds like my kinda friend. Methinks she been *good* for ya. I like her style."

"So . . . out with it. What were you doin' at The Giant, at FuturePlan . . . *here*? You're not tailing me, are you?"

"Silly man, no—"

"Whoa!" He jumped; she'd groped his hiney too quick to see.

"Not that I wouldn't like to foller your tail around a while—you know, see if you ever cut loose and shake it a little."

"Just did, didn't I?"

"Touché. For good or bad, I've corrupted you."

"Everybody I care about says I need a good corrupting or two. Ain't been that tempted too often, though. You must be quite the debaucheress."

"I'll take that as a compliment." She stroked Scallywag's belly, the lizard rolling sideways appreciatively. He was gonna have to put a stop to this pampering . . . *later.*

"I repeat my three queries, damsel with the chestnut locks. Why, why, and why?"

"I like to rescue people sometimes. I'd befriended a sex worker in Houston who was helping my cohorts change some things in the area."

Shawn had to interrupt. "Prostitutes? Um, did *you* used to—uh . . . ?"

"No no no, not me. My sister was, but I was still a girl when I got my chance to get ahead, *years* before I started growing my own little boobies."

"A project you accomplished quite well, I might add."

"Why *thank you!* I'm rather proud of them," she pronounced like a prodigy's mama. "Can't yet appraise *your* pubertal accomplishments . . . but, well, maybe someday."

She'd stopped stroking a moment, maybe distracted by greater thoughts. Scallywag turned his head and opened one eye, giving her that look—let's not forget the lizard.

"So you're buddies with a Houston hooker."

Looking sad, she didn't speak for a moment, finally taking a deep breath. "She was found murdered, in the park."

He held her tighter. Damn. "Was it solved?" he asked quietly.

She shook her head, her voice catching as she explained, "I suspect it mighta had to do with what I was trying to accomplish there. I'd stepped on a few toes."

Shawn remembered times *he'd* stepped on toes and had to be bailed out by Kinte or Foster or even Marcie. He'd never had somebody wind up dead, though, especially somebody he cared about. "So you were in Houston investigating?"

She shook her head again. "No, I have people working on it, but they say it's cold. I went there for her younger sister, a young black woman named Chaleeshia Poeky. The original plan had been to get them both on track for a better life. But then—then—"

He used the backs of his fingers to brush a tear from her cheek. *Please don't cry, Carly.*

"Chaleeshia has a little boy a few years old. I set her up in FuturePlan, kept an eye on her, tried to give the program some money, but Vivian Podrassky said she couldn't take any—"

"I hear that's because they don't want *any* other rules or regs and agendas—too many cooks and all that."

"A smart way to do things," she agreed. "They were already set up right there downtown, and Chaleeshia didn't want to leave her world until she could see a clear way out, so it was perfect for, you know."

"So that's why you were at FuturePlan?"

"Um, actually no. You see, she disappeared—she *and* her little boy. Recruited along with some of the other ladies for a mysterious opportunity to live in paradise and earn a hundred-thou for a year's work. I went down there to find out more about it, decided to play the part and try to get myself recruited, too." She sighed again. "Might not've been the smart way, but I was scared, afraid I'd be too late. I wanted to get inside fast."

Shawn nodded. He understood. Marcie certainly would, too, though such recklessness would drive Kinte nuts.

"I allied myself with another sex worker, Swallow Gagnon, and found out you had to have a young kid—no more than one—to be offered the chance. CG-Temps doesn't rent out kids, so I was lost. Then Swallow pressed me to pretend one of hers was mine so we could both go. She'd already agreed to do this with another woman, but thought I looked more like I could be her kid's mother, so she gave me first shot."

A glistening tear threaded down her soft cheek. Shawn stroked her hair.

"I convinced myself it was okay," she explained, her eyes closed now. "If she was going to risk her kids anyway, then it'd be safer to do it with me in case they needed help." She fell quiet, lost in thought.

"So what's the big opportunity?" He wanted to keep her focused. She was so sad.

"Come to Costa Rica, work for Joelle Bulagrét—"

"Damn! Um, I've been investigating her," he hastily explained. She looked at him, surprised for a brief moment, but he urged her to continue. Even Scallywag looked curious.

"They rent, then hopefully sell, magic crystals to rich dweebs—" She allowed a mischievous smile. "—Like *you*. We're her posse of prostitutes who watch these guys on a video-screen so we can recognize 'em before she deploys us to whatever place each mark has chosen to go sniffing. Our job is to act all hot and bothered so he thinks the crystal is working, then let him pick up however many of us he wants and go to his place or one we'd rented posing as tourists. We're supposed to slip him stimulants and boff him till he's ready to spend whatever it costs for a lifetime of encores."

"A nifty scam," he said quietly.

"Except that we're held prisoner here."

"How? I can see where it'd be hard for those with no money or resources, but what's stopping *you* from leaving?"

"They take our kids," she whispered, her face down, maybe ashamed she'd gotten herself into that bind, that she hadn't known better.

"*Take* 'em? Where? For what?"

"I don't know *where* yet, but they keep 'em at some kind of camp. We earn the right to visit and spend time with 'em on a regular basis—as long as we're playin' the scam. Then we get 'em back at the end of the year when we ship out. That way, nobody tries to escape or reveal the scam to outsiders for fear of losing access to her kid."

"You're *sure* nobody is in danger?"

She shook her head again. "I can't find Chaleeshia. I heard she was making noises about calling somebody to rescue her; then she *and* her boy disappeared. Story was, they sent her home. But I had somebody check. She never got off the plane. I'm afraid she mighta been killed."

He reached out gingerly, brushing more tears from her cheeks, both taking deep breaths. He didn't know what to say.

"The person she would've called for help—" Her voice broke as she tried to stem the flow of tears. "That would've been *me*. She had a private toll-free number to call if she ever needed help. I think— I wonder if giving her that safety net coulda—if that's what caused her—"

She buried her face in his chest. He held her tight, still trying to think of something to say, surprised to feel his own cheeks wet, his nose going runny.

He waited a moment, then asked, "How can we find those kids?"

She wiped her face with his handkerchief. "If you come out of here all smiles in the morning, return your crystal on time, and sign up for another night, then my reward is to see Swallow's kid, the one they think is mine."

"Can you play this out?"

"Doubt ye not, Shawn D'Fixx. I'm playing high-stakes—for people's lives."

"You don't think anybody else is in *serious* danger over the next few days?"

"Not unless somebody freaks and tries to run."

"Can you watch for signs, make sure you try to head it off if you see something like that coming?"

She nodded.

"Good. You go see, um, *your* kid tomorrow, keep your eyes open for potential problems, and we'll work out some kind of plan."

"What have you got in mind?"

He thought for a long time. "I don't know. But I'll figure something out."

She held him like he'd never been held before. "Oh, I hope so. I've not been sure what or how. I'm a wreck, haven't slept an hour since I got here. I'm too used to taking charge and making things happen. I'm discovering how easy it is to get lost when you're alone and near helpless."

"Not alone," he whispered.

"You, me, and the lizard," she whispered back, mustering a smile. Scallywag nodded agreement.

They held each other, shifting down lower, the tightness in her body finally relaxing, her face nuzzled against his neck, long chestnut hair tickling his chest.

He liked it.

They lay that way, losing track of time, trying not to worry. Soon she drifted off to sleep, her face serene.

Scallywag eased over gingerly, finding a narrow space between them, alongside her leg. He settled in and closed his eyes, instantly asleep.

Shawn had never felt this way, but he couldn't savor it. Too troubled, he would be awake for quite a while, reluctant to move, not wanting to disturb this adorable young jewel, beautiful and smart and caring.

He wanted to call Kinte and have him send in the cavalry, to become the grand general leading mercenary troops in to save the day, hero for the maidens in distress.

But it wouldn't work.

And could be dangerous, backfire, get people hurt.

No, he needed to figure out how to do this right, for all those women already here and more yet to come, for the desperate men falling victim to this crystal scam, for the children held hostage from their mothers.

For Carly Geiss.

Many times Kinte and Foster, even Marcie, had warned him he gets too close, cares too much, and risks getting hurt in his too-often-blind quest to help people who have no other way. But would he accomplish so much if he didn't wade in, self be damned, and discover what *really* matters?

Any rich dweeb can hand out money, but even Jeremy had known his little brother could never settle for that.

Shawn D'Fixx always played the ultimate gamble and put everything he had on the line.

Somehow having money helped, but what mattered is that he invested himself.

That's what made him Rich Mr. Fixx.

CHAPTER 10

"**N**O, MARCIE, I DID *NOT* slip her the lizard."

She looked at Scallywag perched on Shawn's shoulders, but he offered no confirmation—the lizard wouldn't tell any tales. "Whatever you say, Shawn," she teased. "You know Sam didn't get a wink of sleep, don't you?"

"Nor Kinte, I suspect. Good thing Costa Rica abolished its military—the old man would've rented the troops by now."

She opened the door, signaling all-clear to Moolhuizen. The operative peered inside, then entered awkwardly. He admitted watching the sex worker leaving a few minutes before, but had decided she looked too casual to have caused any harm. "Mr. D'Fixx," he greeted. "What did you do with your shoe—bury it?"

"What did *you* do—disregard my instructions to cease monitoring when I wanted privacy?"

Zing! "But—"

"But Mr. Bilal does *not* have authority to override my instructions." He put up a conciliatory hand. "Before we get into a pissing contest, let's just drop it. Suffice to say, I'm going to be more selective when and where I wear your listeners. And next time I say *Sam-Off*, I'll throw the bug out the window or flush it or set fire to it or something."

The operative chastened, Shawn still felt like he needed to take control, not be buffeted around by people coddling him and fussing over him. "I'm supposed to have this crystal over there by nine. Before I go, I need a few things done. It turns out Judy's not a sex worker—she's undercover, came down here to rescue a friend. She uncovered a bad situation that needs fixing—fast. I'm open to suggestions, but I have a few ideas already. First, contact Foster . . ."

"OOO—*SEÑOR!* I BELIEVE you had a *very* fun time last night," the manager cooed. She wanted Shawn bad, right then, right there—Oh! Oh! Take me! Okay, time to get down to business.

"Oh yeah—a *great* time!" Grin and leer; wag the ol' eyebrows. "When my friend set this up for me, I didn't realize it was the same as what another friend just bought. Back in the states I know a woman named Melinda who just got a bunch of these crystals. Only, we didn't know how to use 'em, like skin contact, mounted under the watchband—we should have thought of that. She wasn't gonna buy any more, but I called her last night and got her all excited. She's comin' down here today to check 'em out." He wondered where the camera hid. Surely by now Bulagrét had discovered her latest tourist dweeb was the guy she'd met at The Gaseous Giant.

Suddenly she appeared on cue; she just happened to be coming through a side door to speak with the manager. Surprise surprise!

"Excuse me, I am—" She recognized her guest. "Why, *Señor*—D'Fixx, it is? I am surprised to *see* you!"

Uh huh. "Hey, ain't it great? I came down with my buddy Carlysle for a few days and stumbled on a chance to try your crystals in action. Melinda wasn't that interested in any more, but I called last night—" He grinned suggestively. "After my date fell asleep—*finally*—and I told her get her butt down here and check this out. Bring a blank bank draft, I told her. These crystals work like there ain't no tomorrow."

"Well, I am *so* glad to hear this!"

"Yeah, I called Carlysle, too. You know, to thank him. He said he'd talked to somebody earlier who said if I had a good time, I should spend the money and go to the *next* level—whatever *that* is. Gawd, I can't *wait!*"

Bulagrét appeared to be thinking quickly. "Well, we charge one-half million U.S. to go to the cave where the crystals are, for the Tsala ritual, but if you can guarantee Ms. McNair will buy *muchos más* of the cases,

I would like not to charge you to be my guest today and to see the cave yourself—and to stay here at my resort."

"Wow! You'd do that for me? Great! Um, but I can't *stay* here—that would be an insult to Carlysle after treating me to the place next door. But I'll bet Melinda would. In fact, she's coming in this morning. If you wanna sell her more crystals, she should come to the cave, too."

"Yes!" Bulagrét looked very happy. "That is *very* good—if she can be here in two hours when we must leave."

"She's supposed to arrive next door any time now. How do we get to the cave?"

"I have a helio-copter. My assistant will go with us, and we will meet the ancient Tsala shaman who will take us to the cave. You should wear shoes good for hiking in the jungle."

"So what's gonna happen? Will this make me even sexier?"

"Oh yes!"

The manager nodded vigorously, agreeing whole-heartedly. Of course, she *still* wanted him right then, right there.

Bulagrét explained, "You will see the cave of the crystals and see the magic light making rainbows, and it will fill you with the power for always."

"Wow!" He was excited to no end. "I had the best time in my life last night. I've never had much luck with women—you know, *casual* sex and stuff—more than one night, anyway. She said she'd try to see me again before she goes back home to the U.S. If I do this crystal cave today and that same woman—Judy, I think her name was—if she wants to be with me *again* tonight, then it must work, and I'll guarantee Melinda takes more cases even if I have to buy 'em myself."

That chance meeting certainly proved a lucky coincidence. Uh huh.

He rushed back to D'Shawn to welcome Melinda McNair in from the states, and to prep for his jungle trek to get sexually charged by magical rainbow crystals. He figured Judy Morey would be receiving her next assignment at that very moment.

"Okay, I like it," Marcie agreed. "But why am I checking in over at her place?"

"Sam said he wanted to get some operatives in there to track her movements, gather data, be our eyes and ears when the rescue starts going down. Who better than you?—her special guest, doted on, getting her full attention."

Moolhuizen seemed torn between liking the advantage, not wanting Marcie at risk, and wondering how he'd explain it to Kinte. Shawn assured him he'd tell the old man—*later*, he thought to himself.

To Marcie he added, "*You* can be the one all wired up for him to spy on for a change. What do you think, Sam? A couple of microphone pasties for the red-haired wench? Camera in a chastity belt?"

They looked at each other a moment, considering the possibilities. Finally, Marcie grinned and wagged her eyebrows. "I'm on to you, Shawn D'Fixx. You're keeping Sam and me both busy tonight so you can get Carly off somewhere in private."

"*Moi?*"

"You're planning to slip her the lizard."

WHILE KINTE BILAL communicated with Moolhuizen and Brinkley, Foster B. Garbus assembled a team in the adjacent conference room. A half-dozen people including BJ arrived, along with one man whose fingers busily danced on a mainframe terminal.

"Beej will continue on oversight," Foster began. "I'm restless, feel like stirring up some muck in Costa Rica. We've acquired an established resort on the Caribbean coast for the D'Shawn International chain and have installed our own management." Nodding to BJ, he added, "Good job yankin' that together overnight. Anyway, I want to establish a nuisance presence in the area—"

Interrupted by a beep, he touched the panel in front of him. "Foster B. Garbus."

"Mr. Garbus!" came a Hispanic voice on the speakerphone. "I returned your call as *soon* as I heard. This is Torrez, president, and I'm here with Robert Simona, chairman of our commerce agency, as you requested."

"Hello, sir!" came another voice.

"Greetings, gentlemen. Thank you for responding so quickly. I'm on speaker with a team of my best managers. We're discussing how to expand our presence in your country."

"This *is* good. We are *very* anxious to help."

"I understand, Mr. Torrez, that several of your agricultural conglomerates have balloons and bond payouts coming due, and they might be looking for investors or financial backing?"

"Oh, yes! Yes, indeed. Some of our bank's largest and oldest associates."

"Good then. I would like to have my man BJ review your prospectuses over the next week, keeping an eye toward giving you significant consideration for the cooperation I'm hoping you'll provide today."

"How may we be of assistance?"

"I've taken the liberty to set up data links. I'd like your authorization to access commerce records, real-estate holdings and sales databases, anything related to the tourism and agriculture industries, communications, utilities, and transportation."

Foster knew the men calling from San José must be drooling by now. Foster B. Garbus could drop tens of millions like gum on a sidewalk, and here he was talking major development and expansion industries. A presence like his could help pull the small Latin American country out of international debt, give it more prestige and clout in world politics, make powerful men of these two very eager new "friends" who were about to bend over in a blind quest to give this man anything he wants.

The computer dude recited some access codes that would connect the San José systems to an encrypted satellite relay on FosCom.

"As soon as you gentlemen have that set up, please call me back and we'll start scanning. I'll have more questions for you then."

The link disconnected, Foster continued, "BJ, put one person on tourism and resorts. If we're gonna build up D'Shawn, I want existing properties and potential locations scouted for several more at Nicoya—" He touched his panel and made a map of Costa Rica appear on a monitor, regions highlighted, symbols denoting various landmarks. "The entire Nicoya Gulf, likewise Golfo Duke down near Panama, Cahuita near the national park on the Caribbean side; check out Tortuguero, also, since we're already up on that end. Hmmm . . . maybe between Santa Rosa and La Cruz near the park up there. Also, look into something in the highlands that might include lakes and volcano tours and neat jungle stuff for that rainforest kind of vacation. At the same time, have somebody scout all transportation, like bus lines and car rentals, plus other tourist support services for those areas. Right now, though, between San José and where we have D'Shawn up near Limón, I want *all* trans-support. Go ahead and buy *today* if reasonable. I want stuff in place by tonight."

BJ's eyes went wide. "Scattershot?"

"Everywhere but what I just said. Our two friends in San José will be up all night spreading rumors to all their cohorts, so our sniffing will become very public very fast. That's why I want thorough reports so we can pick and choose the best opportunities, speculators notwithstanding. It's also why I want trans for our current D'Shawn resort bought up today, before prices start going up."

BJ nodded to the woman Foster had assumed he would select for that job. She was furiously taking notes.

Foster continued, "Put other people each on the utilities, national trans, communications, agriculture, and—though I didn't mention it in front of our friends—medical, and political. There's a big biz in people from the U.S., Canada, and Europe traveling there for treatment, especially cosmetic surgery. I want political hooked up with some of our international attorneys to find out the best way to get things done down there, both above and below the table, and for getting 'em done quicker."

The man at the computer was punching and highlighting references he'd located, a list slowly building on another monitor. "How deep you want cross-ref and indexing?" he asked Foster without missing a beat.

"Deep as it gets."

"How about this? D'Fixx already owns controlling stock in Pacifica Power, which owns or floats bonds for three major Mexican utilities companies. Referencing Costa Rica, I see that one's subsidiary is the electric utility that feeds the whole eastern half of Costa Rica, fifty-fifty with the government, though the feds down there had to float bonds to cover their half and—wait . . ." He stabbed the machine some more, did a bit of rechecking. "Yes, *you* own the bank that backed most of those bonds. Between you and Mr. D'Fixx, you already control power to your resort *and* your competitors in the area."

Music to Foster's ears. "I want a whole team inside their operations by tonight. Use whatever muscle it takes, oversight, investigation, stir up some fear if need be—but muscle some micro-cooperation. I want to know where every relay is and be able to order maintenance shutdowns, or to access records, whatever. Squeeze it hard."

Tall order.

Another beep, different guy on speaker. "Barclay here. Winston's run down the people you want to speak with. They're awaiting your call, but I've got some background for you before you do. Also, you were right—in Costa Rica you can buy or sell vicarious liability for financial damages and punitive damages, just not criminal culpability."

Foster restated it back for him, mostly for the benefit of those in the room. "So if I know somebody who's been defrauded or conned within Costa Rica's jurisdiction, I can purchase his right to sue for damages. I just can't press charges on his behalf." Foster was smiling.

"As long as he'll ride along as party of the first-part. And I have an associate down there who, shall we say, *specializes* in that type of litigation."

With another bleep, the display identified Torrez and his cohort calling again. The man at the computer pointed at his screens, a signal to Foster that he was linked, streams of new data at his fingertips. "Listen, Barclay, set these guys up for a chat in thirty minutes. I'll finish what I'm doing and get back to you in fifteen so you can brief me."

Foster studied some of the streams of entries the computer guy was highlighting and pulling to separate screens. Interesting. "BJ, you got a trans person designated yet?"

Young Henderson looked *very* pleased to be named.

To the computer man, Foster instructed, "Let's start with car rentals and bus services, east coast, anything that covers north of Limón."

Several of the international car-rental franchise names appeared, then a handful of independents.

"Good. BJ, be sure Henderson makes it priority to buy one or two of these by tonight. I want at least two-dozen good vehicles for immediate service. Dig into the backgrounds, ownership, financing, debts; find at least *three* good marks if you can and open negotiations. Tap Barclay's connections down there for any legal help. Don't be afraid to bribe if need be; lots of deals are cut that way down there," he added with a smile. "Then any shuttling between San José and that area is next in line. You know what everybody else needs to get on. Any questions?"

Hearing none, he nodded, then left and headed for his office on an upper level. He paused at the sight of Kinte still sitting at his console and running his hands through his hair, Moolhuizen on a viewscreen.

"But he said *no*," the operative was arguing. "Absolutely not, just him and Marcie, trekking God-knows-where through the jungle to some magic cave. I figure it's probably just past those cliffs by the Tsala village, though."

"Okay, then here is how we will handle it," Kinte said.

Foster just smiled and entered the elevator. Good ol' Kinte, mother hen. Imagine, back in their early teens, he and Shawn had been naïve enough to think they could get around this extremely educated and very savvy Jamaican, a man who'd proven equally adept at surviving the streets of Kingston, playing academician at Cambridge, and partnering in some of the elder D'Fixx's international business enterprises.

In his office, he opened a channel to Barclay.

The lawyer explained, "It's two brothers. These guys *know* they got fleeced by Bulagrét, but they're small-time and, much as they hate to admit it, they were intimidated by her. They were about to lose everything they had, so when she came at them with the buyout offer, they decided to cut and run. They had no resources to go after her."

"Clear-cut?"

"Oh yeah. They even have a lot of it put together already. Especially proof of her double-dipping and diverting materials and labor costs to build the apartments. They bribed somebody who copied the actual occupancy records for three fiscal quarters. They'd been talking to an attorney who told them what to gather, but they couldn't afford the expense and risk of suing her."

"And though it may have left a burn scar, they're happy to have it behind 'em."

"You got it."

"They doing better now?"

"Some. Their families are comfortable. They'll never achieve well-to-do, though."

"So flipping 'em *anything* to dredge history will be better than nothing."

"They're ripe—especially for revenge. Funny thing, though—they're good, honest men with the right resources. If you're going to expand and develop down there, they're the kind you might want handling things for you."

"A good thought. A *very* good thought. Well, let's get 'em on. See if we can make some new friends."

THEY DROVE OUT TO Jersey Village, northeast edge of Houston, looking for an empty bus-stop shelter where Roux Tumowt, private investigator, could sit with local background noise.

One that wasn't out of order.

His secretary/assistant, an older woman with a soft face and hard voice, blocked the view of passersby while she phoned and started recording the 800-number Carly had given Chaleeshia Poeky.

"Hello? Becky here."

"Hello?" The secretary sounded tentative, hesitant.

"Who are *you?*"

"Can I talk to Carly?"

"Is there something you need?"

"She said don't trust nobody else."

"I'm the one you want. Who are you?"

"I don't think I should say."

"Can't do anything unless I know who you are."

"What can you do?"

"Why are you calling?"

"She said I should, if I ever—you know."

"No, can't say I *do* know. You've not told me anything. Start with who you are, then what you need."

"Can I just talk to Carly?"

"Not an option right now. Where did you get this number?"

"Um, *she* gave it to me."

"Who?"

"Carly."

"Carly who?"

"You don't know Carly?"

"Carly who?"

She hesitated. "Carly Geiss."

"Why do you wanna talk to her?"

"She said I could call."

"For what?"

"I'd rather talk to *her*."

"Gotta deal with *me*, hon, and who you are is where we start."

"Well . . . I don't feel safe."

"What are you afraid of?"

"I don't think I should say."

"Then there's nothing I can do."

"Um, is there a charge?"

"For what?"

"For what you do."

"What do I do?"

"Provide help."

Becky wasn't missing a beat. "What makes you think I provide help?"

"You said you did."

"No, you *asked* for help. I just wanna know who *you* are, and why you're calling, before we talk about me."

"Well . . . I don't think I should."

"Who did you get this number from again?"

"Carly. Carly Geiss."

"Where did you see her?"

"She said don't say."

"Oh she did, huh? What's she look like?"

"Long brown hair, young and pretty."

"Walks with a limp?"

"Um, yeah."

"I see." Dead silence.

"You're not gonna let me talk to her?"

"About what?"

"It's private."

"Not from *me*."

"She said I could call."

"Not the Carly *I* know."

"Why do you say that?"

"Mine's in a wheelchair—couldn't limp if she wanted to."

"That's what I meant. I thought the chair was because she had trouble walking."

"You've seen her in her wheelchair or walking with a limp?"

"Look, is there a better time to call her?"

"Not till after you've met her and she's *said* you could call."

Roux Tumowt made a slashing signal across his throat. Secretary/assistant disconnected the call. She drove as they headed back to the office.

"Well, it's a match," she said. "Phone line's held by CG-Temps and the woman who answered knew Carly Geiss's name. I think I blew it at the limp, though."

"You didn't blow it, honeybunch. They was *no* gettin' around her. I was surprised you held in long as you did. I'm right proud."

She blushed. He liked how she still got a kick out of this private-eye stuff.

"So you want me to send Ms. Bulagrét that picture?" she asked.

Tumowt studied the annual report from CG-Temps, a beautiful young woman with long chestnut hair smiling above the chairman's message.

"Naw, wait till tomorrow, first thing. I want to bill her for today *and* tomorrow."

WAS BULAGRÉT SUSPICIOUS? Hard to tell. She wasn't showing it. In fact, it looked like old-friends' week, gushing all over Melinda McNair, giving her a big hug, so thrilled to have her in Costa Rica where she could see the crystal cave for herself. Shawn could only wonder what to expect from this Joléa de Tsala.

Still, though, what a coincidence. Hook up a deal with the Herbs & Oils lady, sell her four boxes of crystal shards, then next thing you know her dweeb friend is right next door. Maybe Bulagrét *was* suspicious. Quite possibly *very* suspicious. So what would she do in a situation like that? Might as well get as close as possible, invite McNair into the viper's nest, keep an eye on her, and try to figure out her game.

And if it's all innocent, no harm done. Be the gracious hostess, get her all excited, show her that the crystals really are authentic, and forge the bonds of a long and profitable relationship. But always with one eye open, an ear to the ground, a dozen more clichés all of which suggest that human motives are usually *very* self-serving.

Bulagrét *insisted* Ms. McNair be her guest at Tsala-Pu, the finest suite, anything she could want for. Shawn grinned, pleased to have played a part in this wonderful surprise and—better yet!—a trip to the authentic crystal cavern, source of the magic channelers of psychic rainbow power, bits of sparkling geode that had contributed to the best night of his life.

"Cool!" Count Melinda in. Sounds like a hoot.

With an hour before the cave trek, Melinda settled in and freshened up while Shawn went next door to prep and fret over what-all he might encounter in the untamed rainforest of Costa Rica. Brinkley and Moolhuizen were waiting, ready to cocoon him in all sorts of micro-tracking and listening and panic-button devices. They repeated the same process they'd just gone through with Marcie, the difference being that Shawn kept squirming and resisting where Marcie no doubt turned it into an impromptu session of sexual innuendo and teasing.

Yes, Scallywag would go with them, but don't even *think* about trying to wire Shawn's lizard.

MOOLHUIZEN, BRINKLEY, and the young Tsala Indian boarded the Jet Ranger and lifted off to head for the volcanic mountains near Lago Amarillo so they could get set up. Moolhuizen hoped Tsoo-Ki's assertions proved correct, that the source of crystals must lie beyond the deeply cracked ridges where he'd fallen and hurt himself, where he believed Takú Litál had taken up residence. In either case, they would be ready for that likelihood even as they tracked Shawn and Marcie, ready to lift off and go another direction if their predictions turned out to be geographically off-base.

By the time the Ranger landed at Tsala Village, two large crates had already been dropped off. They contained sensors, electromagnetic and thermal-imaging and infrared and pressure and concussion—not to mention cameras and microwave feeds—all beyond comprehension for the curious but trying-to-be-helpful brown faces gathered around.

Everything preset and ready to go, they loaded the chopper. Brinkley sometimes landed it, other times lowering Moolhuizen by cable, at various locations to mount camouflaged cameras and sensors in the cliffs and surrounding jungle. If that's where Shawn and Marcie were going, Moolhuizen would be able to track them precisely. Their biggest concern was Tsoo-Ki's warning that Takú Litál, if he lived back in there somewhere, might be roused and even alarmed by the presence of this chopper flying around. Couldn't be helped, though. Moolhuizen kept it quick and efficient, hoping the Indian would think they were one of the numerous tourist copters that periodically invaded the tranquility of these volcanic slopes.

Bulagrét's chopper appeared, heading their way right on schedule, predicted and planned for. Moolhuizen and Brinkley both breathed a sigh of relief.

Tsoo-Ki acted excited but nervous. "You are sure Señor D'Fixx and Señorita McNaught only do things for the good?"

Moolhuizen gave him the get-real look. Brinkley just nodded. "Long as I've known 'em, son."

The young Indian seemed relieved. "If they find *las cristales*, the power must be for the good."

SHAWN NOTED THAT Big Man followed a route just north of the Tsala village, then swung south for his landing point three or four kilometers past the volcano, other side of the cracked ridges and deep crevices that separated the area from the village and its yellow lake to the south. He probably didn't want the Tsala to notice regular chopper flights coming so close to their homes.

Big Man landed them in a clear area of rocky ground among sparse patches of foliage. They stepped into the hot glare of sunlight, a wave of humidity washing over them. With the chopper powered down, the sounds of jungle came instantly to life.

Marcie watched Shawn, barely suppressing a smile. He knew he'd surprised her by enthusiastically agreeing to this trek, what with the heat and bugs and critters and no-telling what else lurking all around just waiting to pounce or sting or bite or suck blood or devour . . .

He still reveled in the passions so stirred by that woman with the long, chestnut hair—he'd still never even offered to tell Marcie her real name—by her plight, and the need to rescue those children and involuntary sex workers. The intensity of those feelings, his determination and resolve, that allowed him to override his customary reluctance to confront nature anywhere beyond his spectacular private beach at the compound south of Monterey.

But—damn!—there *were* an awful lot of monster bugs out here!

Shawn had insisted on wearing long pants with his hiking shoes, Marcie having settled for cooler shorts. He set Scallywag on the ground to avoid contaminating him with chemicals, then fished insect repellent from his backpack and applied the umpteenth layer to his face and arms.

The lizard seemed to realize where he was, eyes darting every which way, taking it all in. Shangri-la for iguanas!

Or a good place to find some lizard tail.

The group set out following a circuitous route, sometimes the trail obvious, sometimes crisscrossing others, sometimes their path indiscernible.

Shawn acted stoic about it all, scanning into the dense jungle, jumping when several boar-like animals scurried through the brush, constantly watching for bugs that might land on Marcie, grateful she'd been doing the same for him—without being asked.

Bulagrét separated from the group, doubling back to select a different path, leaving the silent Big Man to lead their guests for a while. By the time they worked their way down a zig-zag trail and approached the first of a series of very deep crevices, they found her and a berobed old Indian waiting for them.

"Takú Litál," she introduced him.

After the usual polite glad-to-meetchas, Shawn found himself increasingly uncomfortable with how the old man stared at him, studied him, and seemed almost vexed by some unseen mystery about this *tourista rica* come to see the magic crystal cave.

Shawn had been catching Marcie giving him that same look every now and then as long as he'd known her.

The first footbridge proved to be a crude wood-and-rope structure suspended at least forty or fifty meters over blue-white water flowing through the narrow crack far below. No way did Shawn intend to cross that thing. Not safe, too rickety, could sway unexpectedly, vertigo, you name it. Before he could rank his objections, though, the other three crossed and waited for him on the other side. As if to add insult to injury, Scallywag scampered down to the ground and caterpillared his way across, then waited expectantly with the others. Big Man looked impatient, Bulagrét urging Shawn like a small child afraid to taste his mush, Litál concerned about arriving at the cave too late, Marcie simply making eye contact and diverting her friend's gaze down toward his lizard. Scallywag winked, and before Shawn could stop, he found himself on the other side.

The second bridge proved not quite as difficult, the third even less so. Shawn kept mental tally, though. Every bridge crossed meant another for the return trip.

Both Shawn and Marcie kept stealing surreptitious glances at surrounding cliffs, into dark jungle, at the sky, wondering where and how Moolhuizen monitored their progress. Shawn suspected half-seriously that Litál worked for Kinte, that these trees had been bugged, that the occasional sounds of wild animals were really trained operatives.

When they finally reached the narrow crack ringed by sparkling, six-sided geode crystals, Shawn paused to study the location. The main crater of the volcano loomed off to the left. Straight ahead rose a series of stairstep ledges leading to the narrow plateau where Brinkley had landed the chopper during Tsoo-Ki's tour, more rises separating them from the sloping valley leading down toward Lago Amarillo and the Tsala village.

At least it looked that way.

Marcie seemed too much in awe to notice. She acted like a child at the altar of some grand cathedral, enveloped by the majesty.

This *was* the real deal.

Trekking deep into the mountainside, even Shawn had to be impressed. "It's like being inside one of those rocks you break open and find it's lined with crystals," he offered profoundly. Truth be told, he was fighting nausea, trying not to think about that queasy feeling he'd experienced around crystals several times before. Could be bats in there, too. Rabies or worse. Never know.

The great cavern with the waterfall opened before them, sunlight streaming through a crack above, all indescribably beautiful. It reminded Shawn of the makeshift chantry in the Tsala building with a hole in the ceiling, but on a grander scale.

Marcie seemed at a loss for words, Big Man echoing the sentiment, but minus her enthusiasm. Takú Litál set about making preparations, always keeping an obtrusive eye on Shawn. Bulagrét grew excited with anticipation, quickly stripping to the waist and donning her pendant before passing the others around. Marcie didn't hesitate to expose her own hooters and find just the right place for her sparkling stone to nestle.

No, Scallywag didn't get a pendant, but it was considerate of Shawn to ask.

Litál put some water into the chantry basin, then added some kind of herb-smelling concoction, motioning everybody to stand around it in a circle.

Shawn didn't like the idea of sharing soup out of a community crock, but he grew increasingly distracted by what else he saw. The angled sunlight shined crystals along the crevice where the waterfall disappeared deep underground, shooting tiny beams of rainbow-colored light every direction, sometimes striking other crystals to be splayed into many hues.

"What do we do?" Marcie asked. Shawn knew she wanted there to be some ancient, magical ritual, some profound words or chanting, a ceremony handed down through time immemorial. No, just wait. Let the sun strike the big crystal and channel all the power of the universe around and through these lucky people anointed to join the cosmic gobbledy-whatever.

"The water will rise to this high," Bulagrét warned. "Do not be scared or move and you will be safe."

As the sunlight inched closer, the colors grew brighter, more crystals firing, rainbows crisscrossing each other in a shimmering whorl. Marcie kept watching Shawn as if she expected something else to happen, but she grew disappointed.

Much to his relief.

The water in the chantry basin was heating up, starting to boil, steam rising. The roar of the waterfall grew louder, the rush increasing until spray started to billow through the cavern. The sunlight hit the biggest crystal nearly straight on. Beams shot six directions, cutting right through all five people standing there, fragmenting into a trillion rainbow arcs refracting through the mist.

The roar almost deafening, the crevice filled and then overflowed, the water steadily rising. The colors started moving, joining in a concerted swirl that encircled the group, faster and faster around. Marcie's face rapt, Bulagrét and Litál looked surprised, confused, possibly even panicked. The water at their feet also started to swirl with the light, a deepening whirlpool forming around them, rainbow lights now playing off a wall of rippling water roaring around and around like the eye of a giant water-spout reaching into the crystalline sky.

Shawn wanted to freak, to grab Marcie and run. But he could see no place to go. He snatched off his crystal pendant and threw it into the circling torrent, vaguely aware it had disappeared, too blinded by lights to see where. He reached for Marcie's but couldn't find it, grabbed for Bulagrét's and felt his hand slapped away.

"I don't believe this!" he shouted over the thunder.

Then it started to fade, the water swirling slower, its level dropping, rainbow beams winking out, colors retreating to the netherworld that spawned them. The mist billowed away, water now sloshing their ankles, their feet, draining off to leave tiny puddles between crystal shards, shiny sparkles winking good-bye.

The chantry basin was steaming, the last of its ritual waters misting away, empty except for one unexpected surprise: Shawn's pendant. The leather strap was missing, but its crystal stood upright in the center, refracting from the tiniest bit of lingering sunlight just passing beyond the crevice high above, rainbows reflecting in Shawn's eyes.

"You should have warned us about the whirlpool," Shawn complained.

Bulagrét seemed at a loss, stammering, "Never has it done this before. It is supposed to rise up *to* us, but this time something was holding it away from us."

Marcie removed her pendant and started buttoning her blouse, Bulagrét and Big Man reminded to do the same. Shawn put his shirt back on, noticing Litál left his pendant on as he pulled his robe back up.

"It's time to go," Shawn grumbled, reaching for Marcie's hand and turning to leave. His red-haired friend must have been too overwhelmed by what she'd seen to speak, but Shawn's anger was obvious. Bulagrét motioned for Big Man to go with them and power up the chopper; she would meet them there.

Time to head back for the real world, Shawn D'Fixx had something to do.

AS SOON AS THEY EXITED the cave, Bulagrét asked Takú Litál, "Was he—?"

The shaman seemed lost in thought. "Tsawa-Ki," he pronounced.

"So he is the reason why . . . ?" She gestured a swirling motion around herself, not sure how to describe what had happened.

He nodded.

"This is not good."

"He has the power. It is not good only if he will not share it with us. *Mañana está* Tsala-Pu, when we will give the life of many children so *we* may stay young always. You will bring him here the day *after mañana* so *we* may have his power for always."

"*Take* the power of Tsawa-Ki for ourselves?"

He shook his head. "We must ask it of *las almas joyas.*"

"How can the spirits of the crystals give us *his* powers?"

He regarded the long, pointy shard used to sacrifice children in a desperate quest to steal their youth. "We must first *give* his powers to *them.*"

CHAPTER 11

"LOOK, FOR YOUR *DAUGHTER'S* SAKE, you have to find a way to make this work!" she implored. Carly's Judy Morey was trying desperately to get Swallow Gagnon to calm down, play along, and not blow their cover this close to possibly solving their problem.

"*Please*, Swallow, don't mess this up," Lyla DeCivvio also pleaded, "I *swear* it'll work out okay if you just learn to play along."

Swallow wasn't buying it. "I want my girls. I want out of here."

Damn. *Shut up, Swallow!* "You'll get to see her," Carly cut in. "I'm going to see *my* daughter this afternoon, after working only one night. You'll get to see *your* daughter in a few days, soon as *you* get to work. But you have to *play along*."

The reference to two daughters hadn't gotten by Lyla, though. "If you take your *daughters* now and leave, you'll lose *all* the money and won't have nothin' to go back to."

"Your girl is safe," Carly assured, trying desperately to get her on track. *That's only one daughter, Swallow.* She couldn't trust her to correct her mistake; Swallow remained too distraught, too focused on running away. "Isn't there some way," Carly asked Lyla, "to let her see *her* little girl same time I see mine today?—you know, just to help calm her down some? She needs to confirm that her girl is *safe* wherever she is."

Swallow looked distracted, staring into Judy's bedroom, wringing her hands, shaking her head slowly side to side, tears brimming in her eyes. "This ain't what I signed up for. I want my girls and I want out of here."

Carly started to speak, but Lyla cut her off. "If you leave now, you only get *one* of your girls."

"No! No way! I'm not leavin' without *both* of 'em."

Damn! Damn! Damn!

"You mean the one Judy's pretending is hers, too?"

Swallow nodded as Carly frantically tried to figure out how to handle this. She'd seen it coming; she should've had a plan.

Carly got up and walked over to where she'd found the hidden recorder. It wasn't there. Hmmm . . . Her secret was still in this room. Incapacitate DeCivvio . . . Make her disappear for a day . . . Take her out completely . . .

"What's going on?" Lyla demanded. "Is Judy's daughter really yours?"

Carly eased into her bedroom, then walked around with a fake make-up compact checking for newly activated bugs.

DeCivvio stood defensively, confused by Carly's behavior.

"Yes. They're both mine," Swallow admitted. "Want 'em both, and I'll just get on out of here."

"All clear, Todd!"

"What's goin' on?" DeCivvio demanded. "Who's Todd?" She eased over and also checked for a recorder, tacit admission she knew where it might be hidden.

Swallow grew tearful, then seemed finally to realize what she'd done. Tension in the air, all three eyed each other, none sure of the next move.

Then Carly did what Carly does. She took a chance and gave some-body the benefit of the doubt.

"Don't tell Joelle."

Lyla exhaled, her shoulders relaxing slightly. "What makes you think—?"

Carly gave her the look, Lyla shaking her head. Okay, everybody's on to everybody.

"You've got a problem," Lyla pointed out, nodding toward Swallow.

"We've *all* got a problem."

"Yeah, but *I'm* turning it to my advantage. If she finds out you're scamming her, she'll send you *both* home without a cent."

"She ever done that before?"

"Just last week. We had a black girl talking about calling somebody to come get her. Joelle packed up her and her kid and shipped 'em straight back."

Carly's shoulders dropped, her head down. Damn. "Chaleeshia Poeky?" she asked quietly.

Lyla looked surprised. "Um, yeah. How'd you—?"

"She was a friend. And I know for a fact neither she nor her son got off the plane. She *wasn't* sent home."

Lyla looked suspicious, concerned . . . then alarmed—all in the space of a few seconds. "But . . . but I—they took her to get her kid when they made the weekly flight to San José to meet the jet."

"Lyla, *nobody* goes home. Not even the ones who put in a year." She shook her head forlornly. "She uses them as long as she can, then makes sure they can never reveal what's going on."

Swallow put her hand to her mouth, obviously surprised by this Judy Morey knowing as much as she did, growing even more scared about her daughters.

Carly pressed harder. "You've never heard from anyone who's left here. You've never seen 'em get on that charter plane in front of the other tourists. *You've never seen any of those children leave this country alive.*" She paused, moving closer—not threateningly, but in a comforting way. "And you're counting on leaving here someday with your *own* child safe in your arms."

Lyla stammered, lost for words.

Carly wondered, "If they'll slap down somebody like Swallow right in front of everybody, if they'll kidnap small children as soon as they arrive— what else do you think they're capable of, out of sight, when somebody's no use to them anymore? *When somebody's a danger to them?*"

They all looked at each other for the longest time. Finally, Swallow broke the silence. "Can you help me?"

Carly nodded, looking toward Lyla. "If I *have* some help."

"What can you do?" Lyla asked. She had swung over to Carly's side. Wringing her hands, scared for her child, she'd swung over in a *big* way.

"I have reason to distrust you," Carly pointed out.

Lyla, nearly in tears now, pleaded, "But you *can*. But—but—"

"It's going to end soon—and stopping it is a *lot* bigger than me," Carly warned. "Question is, who'll get out safe and who won't. Anybody crosses me now—" She spread her hands, a can't-help-it look on her face.

"Michael just turned three," Lyla stammered, choking back sobs. "He just turned three," she repeated quieter. It seemed to be all she could say.

It was enough.

"You going to see him this afternoon when I go?"

Lyla nodded, wiping her face.

Carly turned to Swallow, "Can you play it straight a few more days, weeks if necessary, to get in on a chance to get out of here with both your daughters safe?"

Swallow's features hardened. No longer distraught and lost, she'd become a woman with a mission. She nodded resolutely. "What do we do?"

"*You* act like you're ready to play the game. Lyla, you need to tell me everything you know, *now*—" Louder, she interjected, "Todd, make sure you get all this!" Then she continued over the puzzled but almost-relieved expressions, "When we go see the kids, we need to check out everything about the place, how we can get them out of there safe."

"You can get some help?"

"I already have."

FOSTER B. GARBUS SCROLLED through screens of inquiries, occasionally stabbing keys, answering questions, assigning responsibilities. He sat alone in his massive office, his chair half-turned so he could glance at the birds circling the cliffs above the crashing waves, glowing rays of sun piercing snow-white billows of cloud drifting by.

A buzz, then BJ appeared on the monitor off to the side. "Two car rentals, one bus-line; all three deals will close before end of business today."

"Good job. Any prospects?"

"You interested in a tour-copter? It's a Bell & Howell owned by the little place at the north end of the cove. Since converting to condos over the past year, their tour business has mostly dried up."

"Sure, *if* it's worth it. Not a major priority, though. Hook up with Daryl at the aviation division and have him assign you somebody to spec it out, technical and value appraisal. What else you got?"

"She's spent most of the day running down the right people at the Costa Rica switching plant and demonstrating you have the power to call shots. Had to use Barclay's connects and put some local political squeeze on. There's somebody *you* need to talk to, but I have to warn you, he'll ask *exactly* what you might want, twenty-four hours in advance."

Foster agreed, suggesting he set it up for ten minutes later and to come up to his office for a dual-speak. He was about to contact Barclay when a buzz alerted him the Costa Rica law-firm senior partner already waited on the line.

"They signed off," the lawyer reported. "Fifty-thousand dollars U.S.—then any damages, compensatory or punitive, will go to the corporation you designated. There's a strict clause that all liability for costs will be on you. Also, the brothers get nine-fifty a day each for their time beyond five days."

"Good. No problem."

Barclay's smile could almost be heard over the phone. "Those are the *terms*. Fact is, they're grateful—hell, they're fifty-grand ahead—and ready to do anything they can to help you stick her. When your other people requested a capabilities package, and they realized you could become a very *big* customer, they were ready to *give* you the rights. But I stayed with your directions regarding compensation."

"Yes, I can't yet make promises to give them work. Much as it's a common tactic to dangle bait—real or not—to squeeze a deal, it's not something I want to do with small-timers like these. I like a good game of chess, but not with checkers players. Besides, if I *do* decide to do business with them later, they'll see how tight my people are and accept more because *this* will have started us out on equal footing, the image of being straight and fair and generous."

"An image you cultivate well," Barclay confirmed. "I can't stress enough how much your name is being whispered in certain circles around San José, and your reputation is not only sterling, but envied. If you ever get lonely, a lot of people down here want to be your friends."

"Just don't let the speculation get out of hand," Foster cautioned. "I *do* understand your firm is posturing as if you have the inside track, and that's fine—ride it for what it's worth, you deserve it—just be careful not to mislead anybody. Protect my image and it'll pay off for your people in the long run."

"I like your style, sir. So, we prepared the initial complaint against Bulagrét as you requested. Have you decided when?"

"Be ready as early as tonight or sometime in the next few days. I know you're limited to court hours for the actual filing, but I want to control the time Bulagrét has the papers actually served to her. I want to create a distraction, muddle her up, send her running to the phone—so have somebody with a package stay out at D'Shawn Costa Rica north of Limón, next door to Bulagrét's place, and be ready to trot over on a moment's notice."

BJ arrived, so Foster hurried Barclay off the phone.

"He's the maintenance manager," the aide explained about their next contact, "for the relays covering Limón, Tortuguero, Colorádo, and four towns along Guapiles Highway. If he knows what you might want shut down or rerouted far enough in advance, he can check back-ups and breakers to avoid damage. We've convinced him you've got the say-so—had to put the squeeze on his bosses until they capitulated—so all we need now is for you to establish a relationship and let him know what to expect."

"¡*Hola!* Señor Garbus?"

"Greetings, sir! I'm here with BJ."

"How may I be of help?"

"I understand you're *the* man on the switch down there . . ."

DURING THE CHOPPER FLIGHT BACK to the resorts, Bulagrét and Melinda McNair still acted both excited and confused. Shawn ignored them, gazing out the window with a fixed stare, watching the jungle and peaks and rivers and patchwork orchards and tracts of cleared farmland.

Marcie jabbered about what-all she'd seen. "And the rainbows—and when the sun hit that big one—and it got so hot it started to boil—"

Bulagrét kept pitching the crystals' retail potential, obviously careful not to ascribe too much to any extra capabilities somebody in particular might have exhibited. Somebody like Shawn. "Yes! You see? The crystals *are* powerful! They are doing *fantastic* things and that is just *part* of what they can do!"

Big Man landed the chopper directly behind the resort. "You will take the peoples without me this afternoon," Bulagrét instructed him cryptically. His passengers out, he lifted off and headed northwest.

Melinda and Bulagrét gushed for a moment, Shawn politely thankful for the trip and rather unique experience. Bulagrét reminded that they had an appointment to do it again day after tomorrow, promising they would see and learn even more, apologizing that prior commitments would have her tied up until then.

Shawn followed Marcie to her suite to pick up a few things—and to verify by secret markers that nobody had searched—then they courtesy-shuttled over to D'Shawn.

Rich Mr. Fixx never said a word.

BULAGRÉT WENT STRAIGHT to her office, stopping to remind the manager to make Shawn D'Fixx a prime target for *all* of the girls that night, wherever he went, even though he wouldn't be coming by for the shard-under-watch treatment. She went into her office, closed the door, and called an associate of hers just arriving at his home.

"Adaló. It is me, Joelle Bulagrét. Are you working *imigración por la mañana*? That is good then. I need for you to check some records. Melinda McNair—" She spelled it for him. "She arrived early today. Her employee in the U.S. say yesterday that she was *already* away, so I need to know where she came from—what country and airport—and how she came here, if it was commercial flight or private, and *with whom* she came here. Yes, was today, *madrugada*—morning. *Gracías*, Adaló. I will call you in your office *por la mañana* to learn what you know."

She hung up, then thought for a minute and remembered something. Going back to the manager's office, she instructed, "That Shawn D'Fixx, he say he wants to see if the same girl is still attracted to him after *la caverna*. Be sure the driver is watching when he leaves his resort to see where he is going; then be sure the new girl *Judy* is there for him."

MARCIE HAD TO HURRY to keep up. Shawn was tearing through the resort looking for something, not saying a word, but clearly growing angrier by the second. She'd tried several times without success to find out what was on his mind. He didn't object to her following, so all she could do was wait and see. And try to keep up.

Standing at the rail scanning the beach, Shawn found him. He spotted Tsoo-Ki in his fluorescent-orange tee and D'Fixx shorts and rubber sandals, way down at the southern end, just before the rocks, away from tourists trying to overdose on rays. He was standing at water's edge where gentle waves lapped his feet, staring into the mist over the water, gazing at the rainbow cast by late-afternoon sunbeams refracting through gathering clouds.

Shawn jumped *over* the rail, dropping several meters to the reed-grassy sand, then marched purposefully toward his quarry. Marcie had to climb over.

Shawn stopped a dozen meters short, balled fists on his hips. "I *see* you!"

No reaction from the Indian, his gaze unwavering.

"I *said*, I *see* you now!"

"And I have been seeing *you!*" came the response. Without turning, he added, "So?"

Shawn couldn't be still. Not quite pacing, he turned like he might leave, whirling back, staring into the sky, toward the resort, avoiding

Marcie's face, slowly moving closer to the Indian at water's edge. "You lied," he accused.

Tsoo-Ki finally turned and faced him, resolute. "So? You are a liar to yourself."

"About what?"

"What am *I* lying about?"

"The cave," Shawn pronounced. "You've *been* there."

"Only one time. But I made a mistake, and now it is too late for me. I was trying to go back and make it right, but I am not strong enough. I had my legs hurt, until you helped fix me, but I was not able to fix my own mistake."

"What mistake? What were you trying to fix?"

"Takú Litál. He is using crystals for the bad. I do not even know for what, but it is bad."

"Does *he* have the power?"

"No."

"Do you?"

"No."

Shawn hesitated. "Do the *crystals* have power?"

Tsoo-Ki snorted like gringo didn't get it. "No."

Shawn paused. Don't ask . . . "Do *I*?"

Tsoo-Ki regarded him, then seemed to be amused. "The answer does not matter. *You* are the liar."

"I am not!" Still angry, he hadn't calmed down since the cave. "I don't lie to people," he said quieter.

"I have said, the lie is to yourself. Why is the cave making you so mad?"

That was a poser. Shawn had been avoiding explaining his rage to Marcie because . . . well, he couldn't. A lie? Something he wouldn't admit? He took a deep breath. "Okay, I'll admit it. I saw something in that cave I've never seen before. Some unexplainable . . ." He shook his head. "Some kind of power."

Tsoo-Ki looked surprised, then pleased with the revelation. "Ha! It was the first time you ever saw the *other* power."

"Of the crystals—"

"No! The crystals have no power—"

"But—"

"But you cannot understand if you keep lying. You miss the truth by making everything be what you want. You have all the monies. You have the best friends helping. You are doing much goodness, but you cannot do more because you will not touch the powers bigger than your own. You have love for your friends, yet there is a greater love for you that will give you power and grow from what you give."

"I *believe* in love. I can admit that. It's just these *other* powers—what people like Marcie think I have—well, that doesn't make sense. It's all superstition."

Tsoo-Ki shrugged, looking to Marcie. She stood close to Shawn, watching, not daring to speak. The young Indian offered a disarming smile. "It will be okay. You do not need to believe in the bigger power, not even to believe in your own. You can still use what you have, like for healing my legs. But be careful, Shawn D'Fixx, for when you face the bigger power, if it is being used by someone else for the badness, then it will defeat you. That is why it almost defeated you in the cave when Takú Litál was using for the bad. You were not defeated this time only because he was *showing* you, without so much badness *this* time. Even then, I can see it was almost too much. How did you save your friend and yourself?"

Shawn rubbed his eyes. He didn't want to go down this road. Still, he was determined not to let this little brown nuisance call him a liar again. "By holding back the waters?"

"That is but one part of your—" He had to search for the word. "Destiny? Yes, I believe the word is destiny."

"So the crystals could have *killed* us."

"No!" Tsoo-Ki looked disgusted. Duh! "They are just crystals which are able to *channel* the power." He took *el cristal de la aldea*—the village crystal—from his pocket and tossed it to Shawn. "It is just crystal. You have the power of the rainbow *inside* you. But the same power of the rainbow is bigger *in the world*—" He gestured to the sky, out to sea, back across the landscape. "It is not good *or* bad. How you use it, that is what matters most. When my village was using for the bad, it defeated us. When the Spaniards used for the bad, Tsawa-Ki came to help save us from them. When Takú Litál and Tsoo-Ki used for the bad . . ." He lowered his head in shame. "Shawn D'Fixx came to save the peoples." He looked up intently at Shawn, tears brimming in his eyes. "It does not matter if you believe, but what you are doing *must* be for the good. If you take the power of the rainbow away from Takú Litál, you will, um," stumbling over the word, "*restore* the good. Then *I* will be restored."

"You'll become what I see?" Shawn asked quietly. "What I see *now*, I mean?"

He nodded, wiping tears from his eyes. "And *you* will become all things others see in you."

Shawn was perplexed. "See what?"

The young Indian wiped his face again, a smile of hope, eyes glistening in the late-afternoon sun, a clear rainbow undeniably gracing the sky behind him. "Many peoples see Shawn D'Fixx doing the good things. Marcie, she is seeing the rainbow. I am seeing Tsawa-Ki." He hesitated over the words. "And, even if you are never to believe, as long as you are not lying, you will see it when you can see yourself."

Shawn finally knew the answer, but he had to ask. "What will *I* see?"

"What you have always wanted. You will look inside yourself and see Rich Mr. Fixx."

CHAPTER 12

"DROP HER IN A VOLCANO!" Shawn insisted.

Marcie was giving him that look.

"I'm serious—we *know* what she's doing. Let's drop her in a volcano. That'll put her out of business."

They were seated in the chopper, still parked on the ground, conducting a vid-conference. It was the only place with the right equipment for linking with the Monterey Compound. Shawn had Scallywag a-shoulder, Marcie beside him, Brinkley and Moolhuizen in front, Kinte's face on the screen with Foster and a woman working on a computer in the background.

"I hardly think that is a practical—" Kinte started.

"Naw, that's too quick," Shawn decided. "She believes in crystal magic—let's grind some up and load a shell with crystal buckshot, shoot her ass full of mysterious powers—"

"This instead of dropping her in a volcano?" Marcie asked, humoring him.

"No, *then* we drop her in the volcano. We'll see if the crystals help save her."

"If you are quite finished, Mr. D'Fixx," Kinte said evenly, "we now have sufficient information to intervene. I recommend you and Ms. McNaught bring the jet home and allow Misters Moolhuizen and—"

"Let *them* drop her in the volcano? No way, old man. I'm at least sticking around to watch her fall. I'll need Marcie, too, so she can tell me what my rainbow aura does when the bitch gets swallowed into the ground."

"And this is the plan you spoke of?" Kinte asked.

Shawn took a deep breath. "Actually, no, but it's a fun thought. This woman needs to be brought down, but I want her to hurt where it counts. And where's that, you ask?" He didn't wait for an answer. "Where her *greed* lives."

"Now you're talking," Marcie allowed. "—But that volcano idea sounds good, too."

"This woman is defined by greed," Shawn continued. "She gave up her family for it; she's *killed* for it, sold out her cultural heritage and her peoples, now preys on lonely men and desperate mothers and innocent children for it—" He stopped for a breath.

"And that's just the stuff we *know*," Marcie pointed out.

"And to burn a greedy bitch, I've got the ultimate weapon."

"And that is?" Kinte asked.

"I've got me a Foster B. Garbus."

Foster looked up at hearing his name, then wandered over to join the conversation. "Hey, guys and girlie!"

"Hey!"

"Hey!"

"Hey!"

"Hey!"

"Whoa!" He grabbed his head and faked being dizzed out by the swaying camera.

Kinte rolled his eyes. No, old man, your boys will probably *never* grow up. He quickly pointed out, "I believe we have started to assemble a very credible package that could lead to her arrest for kidnapping, running a prostitution ring, possibly even for murder."

"Yeah yeah yeah." Shawn waved him off. "We'll do all that, but first let's make her twist in the wind. Foster, how goes plans to take her goodies away from her?"

"We've been building a fraud case against her that's bigger than I expected. I bought—*you* bought the rights to settlement or judgment from the brothers she conned, so our holding company will get anything that comes of that. Under Costa Rica law, we can get triple losses *plus* punitive damages. I'm sure we can get the apartments and her resort; plus I'll do a supplemental in the U.S. to grab anything she has hidden here. But the beauty of it is, I've got a solid Costa Rica tax-fraud case against her, too. Means she'd probably rather settle and give up everything she has than face tax charges and lose it all anyway—assuming she doesn't catch on that you're going to seek criminal charges against her later."

"What if she skips out?" Marcie wondered.

"Or gets killed?" Shawn asked. Everybody looked at him, such an odd question for Shawn.

"We'll file right away. That'll preserve our claim, even in absentia, or against her estate if you, um, get impatient and drop her in the volcano."

"What about taking all the crystals?" Shawn asked. Marcie's face brightened at the thought.

"Well, there's good news and bad. The bad news is that they're not hers to take away." Shawn was disappointed. "The good news is that they're not hers to take away." Foster grinned.

"Out with it, shark."

"The land where the cave is was designated for indigenous peoples— whichever ones occupy the area for a demonstrated period of time. In that sense, it belongs to the Tsala peoples and, since she has the birthright heritage, ostensibly Bulagrét may reside there. *But*—and here's the big but—the government retained all *mineral* rights. Who's to know that maybe someday down the line oil or gold or something might be discovered in the region."

"Or psychic-channeling crystals," Marcie supplied.

"I'm making steady progress," Foster boasted, "toward having the government in my back pocket. I'm sure we could work out some kind of deal to assume some of the financing of their national debt, using the crystal cave as security, maybe a portion of the interest to be paid in exclusive extraction rights for Marcie's mystical magical moo-goo stones."

Now Shawn was grinning. "I remember, back when we were ten years old, I lent you four bucks out of my allowance and you parlayed it into a vast real-estate empire by the end of the week. I knew right then I better keep an eye on you and harness this power for good."

"For Mr. Garbus to effect this plan," Kinte pointed out, "there is no reason you and Ms. McNaught need to stay—"

"We got a higher priority, old man," Shawn interrupted. "We need to rescue the children and their mothers. If we turn over the rock and expose Bulagrét to the light of day, there's no telling what she might do—or *who* she might do—trying to cover her tracks. No, we need to lead a full-scale rescue, and I think Foster having the legal papers served on her would be a good way to distract her while we pull it off."

"We've got operatives and the chopper," Moolhuizen interjected. He and Brinkley had that look, like they might have some fun after all.

"I've already got you a fleet," Foster pointed out. "—Three busses with drivers and a dozen or more rental cars already in the area."

"And your jet should be sufficient to fly them all back to the U.S.," Kinte agreed reluctantly. "I will make arrangements with immigration in Houston. Be aware, though, that the mothers will need to be with them. Any children not accompanied by a parent may be taken into custody by Family Services pending hearings."

"Have Podrassky and FuturePlan ready to handle a big influx of people needing help," Shawn instructed.

"That might be imprudent," Kinte pointed out. "We still do not know how these women were recruited or referred. You might be alerting somebody who is in contact with Bulagrét."

Shawn nodded, lost for a moment in thought. High-stakes games carried inherent risk. "Okay, here's the plan. Foster has the papers served on Bulagrét in her office. I'll have my liaison here, the woman playing Judy Morey, scare the daylights out of the mothers. Sam, you send a handful of your operatives to bus in there and load them up, then high-tail it to the airport. Carly—um, Judy can handle the people part of it, I'm sure."

"What if some don't want to leave?" Marcie asked.

"That's their prerogative. Either way, the kids will be rescued. We'll send operatives back to give any stragglers a second chance after Bula-grét's operation has collapsed. They'll fall in line."

"And the children?" Kinte asked.

"I'll lead the rescue, Les handling air cover, Sam on the ground, our nurturing-babe Marcie handling the children—"

"Diaper duty, nose-wiping, *Did everybody pee before we go?* kinda stuff? I'm your gal," she boasted.

"Our spiritual Mother of Earth—" Shawn teased.

"*My Fixx-man!*" she returned like a damsel just saved from the rail-road tracks.

"And I'll be the big kahuna," Shawn pronounced gallantly, "who just stands around and makes sure all is okay—*no risk*, Kinte—just ready to think fast if anything goes wrong."

Kinte ran his hand through his hair, resigned but ever-worried.

"Shawn," Foster interjected to break the obvious tension, "you want I should find a job or some kind of biz opportunity for your *liaison* Judy when she gets back to the U.S.?"

"No, she'll have the same chances as everyone else."

Kinte betrayed no reaction. Foster looked surprised, Marcie disappointed.

"I'd hoped there was more there," she whispered, causing Shawn to blush.

"We'll do this in the morning," Shawn said by way of changing the subject.

Foster gestured toward Scallywag still on Shawn's shoulder. "Don't get your lizard shot off. Or them li'l boobies, Marcie—though *that* would take quite a marksman."

"Had to see a doctor last time you made fun of my pouters, remember?"

"Touché."

Kinte rubbed his hand across his hair again. "Please be careful, Shawn. Innocent people's lives are at stake."

There was an awkward silence, Shawn noticing the old man's rare use of *Shawn*.

"It'll work okay, Kinte," Shawn said quietly. "And if something goes wrong, I have a Plan B."

"Oh?"

"Yeah, we shoot the bitch full of crystal buckshot and drop her in a volcano."

"WHAT I *WANT* IS TO TEST and see if the crystal cave made *me* irresistible, too," Marcie pouted. They were walking down the road toward Tsala-Pu.

Moolhuizen started to speak, but Shawn held up his hand, then eased over next to Marcie, wagging his eyebrows suggestively, rubbing up against her, putting his arms around her, nuzzling her neck. He used a lame French accent, but he had fun with it. "Ah, *mon ami*, but theese eez zee mos' bee-yootiful—"

Catching him by surprise, she swung him around into an unexpected dip and planted a big wet one on his mouth, going for it, still going for it . . . threatening to swallow him whole. Then she swung him back up to stand there beet-red and stammering.

"Don't play with matches next to a cherry bomb—"

"I wouldn't call it a *cherry* bom—"

Marcie's deft crotch-hold was highly persuasive. Enough of this silliness. Ha ha. Okay, that's enough.

Please!

"He's right, Marcie," Moolhuizen cut in, wincing at Shawn's, um . . . "With plans to implement in the morning, it's important we have you accessible and able to communicate in case anything changes, and to have you there keeping an eye on Bulagrét, not being, um, *distracted*."

"Yeah yeah yeah. Oh well," she said with mock resignation. "I already *know* I'm the sexiest thing on the coast. I guess I'll just have to deprive a few tourists from the thrill of their lives."

Shawn started to crack on her, but thought the better of it. That *did* hurt.

"Actually, Miss *McNair*," Moolhuizen said gallantly, "I would be proud to escort you for a tropical evening of mystery and enchantment."

She smiled and batted her eyes demurely. "Can the chivalry, Sam. You just wanna have a cover while watching Shawn dangle his lizard in front of that chickie with the chestnut hair. If you go with Brinkley, you'll have women hittin' on you all night. With me, you'll be free to watch Shawn."

"And if *you* go without *me*, you'll be hounded by all the handsome *men*."

Truce, impasse. Decided.

"Where we going?" she asked.

"Let's try The Wet Orchid," Shawn suggested. "Use their shuttle, make it clear that's where I'm hoping to find that same woman. They'll arrange to have her show up soon after we get there."

He hoped.

"Sam, I admit," Shawn continued, "that we have some planning to do, but we can't risk detection by bringing you into the room—looks suspicious, or like something *Marcie* would do. So you *can* use the listener." He shifted Scallywag up behind his neck. "*But—*" He lapsed into a sing-song kiddie-show-host patter. "Have we learned what *Sam-Off* means, boys and girls?"

"Yes, sir," Moolhuizen said contritely—the "sir" being the politest of jabs back.

'Nuff said.

Bulagrét came out of her office to greet them, glad to meet Shawn's friend Carlysle, good to see his lizard again—Scallywag, is it?—insisting she'd run a tab wherever they wanted to go—oh, The Wet Orchid, a good choice. "The *touristas* like to sing karaoke."

Marcie giggled, whispering to Shawn, "I want to hear you sing 'Muskrat Love' to a room full of strangers."

The "couple" took a table at The Wet Orchid, Shawn grabbing a seat at the bamboo bar, lizard on the stool beside him. Marcie wasn't having much luck convincing Moolhuizen to sing karaoke, but she seemed to enjoy scanning the crowd, sipping something exotic, and watching Shawn have to practically beat women off with a stick.

He was *very* popular—and in a quandary over why. He didn't consider himself all that attractive or desirable, bank accounts notwithstanding, nor did he believe the crystals had any effect on his sex appeal, either. What could account for all this attention?

Bulagrét is what he figured. Too bad he couldn't just enjoy it.

Then a vision appeared: big, gold-flecked hazel eyes, sharp and intelligent, belying deep passion; long chestnut hair shimmering in the flickering lights, stirred by evening breeze; silk halter-top tied midriff, last defense against imminent escape by a pair of the naughtiest young pouting hooligans . . .

She smiled shyly as several tourist gringos stared in awe, already calculating their moves. But she looked only at Shawn. He stood, offering her the stool next to his, suddenly self-conscious he might be drooling, tongue hanging out.

The lizard raised his head; he'd spotted her, too. Good, he liked her. He started flicking his tail back and forth.

They had a drink, didn't say much, stealing glances at each other, a gentle touch, then holding hands on the bar. Going for a walk would be a nice idea, maybe wind up over at D'Shawn.

The night felt warm, but breezier this time. The full moon glowed, a golden corona reaching across the sky.

"We're not private," they both said simultaneously, laughing at the coincidence.

"But we *will* be after we talk about, you know, once we're inside my room and have our talk."

They walked along, holding hands, Scallywag trying to climb from Shawn's shoulders over onto hers. They paused so she could lift him off, arraying the lizard around her neck and petting his head, smiling at the little greenish cutie.

"How'd you come up with that name?"

"Kinda stupid, really. Marcie got him for me, said he had a rainbow on him." He indicated the colored markings on the lizard's neck and shoulder. "I told her get that scaley thing away from me, so she set him on the table. He looked like I'd hurt his feelings, sitting there wagging his tail back and forth, until I finally picked him up. I was calling him Scaley-wagger at first—even though his skin is actually smooth and clean—then I wound up with *Scallywag*, like pirates used to say."

She liked his story. "And he rides your shoulder like a pirate's parrot."

They entered the resort, walking past the gift shop toward the building of beachfront suites, his temporary home.

Inside, door closed, she went over to the bar and proceeded to pour two clear sodas with slices of fresh fruit, Scallywag watching from *her* shoulder.

"Did it go okay?" Shawn asked. He waited awkwardly, not sure if he should help or take over, be the host, let her be gracious, offer to take the lizard, and put out some snacks. That's it, cheeses and more fruit, some crackers. He gathered the wrappers and deposited them in the trash.

"I got Lyla DeCivvio, Joelle's main mole, to swing over. Are you admitting FuturePlan is yours?"

"Huh?" He was surprised by the frank question. "Um, I guess. To *you*, I mean."

"Then I'll leave it to *you* to clean house. It's that fat director, Mr. Suggly, the one who works for Podrassky. He recruits for Bulagrét."

"Him?"

"Yep. Who better? He's got access to their personal data, knows which ones have a young kid, learns who would likely jump at the opportunity—then has Bulagrét make the approach so they never know it was him. Lyla found out when Suggly came down here for a week's vacation and they talked about new prospects in front of her. I didn't suspect it was him, either, because my first contact was with Bulagrét at the airport since I was getting in on the two-fer with Swallow."

They moved to the couch, a tray and two glasses on the low table in front of them. She started toward the in-room sound system, but stopped when Shawn pointed to his ears. Wait until the listeners are shut off. They weren't alone yet.

"I'll have his testicles fried and fed to the pigeons."

"Shouldn't do that," she cautioned, slipping in beside him. Scallywag climbed up on the back of the couch to preside over the festivities. "Lyla couldn't be sure he really knew this was a scam. He could've been duped into thinking he was doing favors, helping the right people take advantage of extraordinary opportunities."

"Well, he needs to be shut down."

"I agree, and if you do it right, you'll be able to find out how much he knew, how guilty he is."

Shawn thought for a minute. "He'll have records."

"Yes!"

"We'll make sure we get them, try to track down everybody Bulagrét's hurt." He looked off into unseen distance. "We'll find out, even if . . . And if not, I'll do what I can . . ."

She bit her lip, a single tear spilling onto her cheek. "I was—Chaleeshia Poeky was—I owed her sister. I got here fast as I could, but I'm afraid it was too late."

He held her in his arms, shifting down, closer. She lay her head against his chest. He stroked her hair.

Scallywag eased over, a sad expression, his head down.

"We may find her," Shawn whispered, but he couldn't sound hopeful. Not when he didn't believe it. He wouldn't try to convince her. No lies.

"As much as I tried to do for her . . ."

"She led you here, so now you can save scores of children, and help so many women who have nobody else, nobody who cares."

"*We* do, huh, Shawn?"

"Yeah."

They fell quiet a moment before she asked, "So what's the plan?"

"What did you find out?"

"It's a fenced camp with forty or more infants and young kids."

"So we'll need child carriers, containers or *something*. Where is it?"

"You go about two miles up the coast road, head inland at the split about a half-mile, then look for the rutted road north. If you stay to the left when it branches off, it'll lead you straight in. There's a local guy who watches the gate, not too bright, usually not very awake. Two other guys move around inside; plus there are local women, usually about three or four at a time, who look after the kids. Several sleep there, according to Lyla, and some come and go. Ironically, they live in the apartments alongside the women whose kids they watch."

"Any defenses, surveillance, sensors, anything to complicate this?"

"The men carry rifles. That's all Lyla knows of."

"My people can handle that. In fact, Moolhuizen's itching right now—" he announced, getting louder and lifting his foot, "wondering what he's gonna do for excitement!"

"So how do we do it?"

"Marcie's staying at Tsala-Pu. She'll keep an eye on things and let us know if and when Bulagrét and her goon cousin leave. Bulagrét's supposed to take some tourists to the cave; a little after ten o'clock is when *we* left. She's going to be served with some papers in the morning, which'll freak her out and probably tie her up on the phone with lawyers, so *you'll* have time to get the women together best you can without worrying about her showing up. If goon cousin gets in the way, somebody'll be there to take him out. There'll be a bus ready—and extra cars down the road if you need 'em—to take all of you to San José where I have a jet standing by. I'll be with the team getting the kids. Marcie'll join us there; we'll meet you at the airport; then everybody back to Houston. FuturePlan'll be ready to help out. If you have problems getting anybody to go along, they're free to stay if they want. We'll have Bulagrét completely wrapped up by the next day; plus there'll be a team left behind to get any stragglers."

"Sounds like a good plan," she allowed. "I can't think of anything else that might help."

"Then it's time to relax and quit thinking about it for now."

She turned her face up toward his, radiant, more serene than before. He wiped her cheek with his fingers.

"Sam—Off!"

"Yeah," she agreed, "no more listening."

They shifted down even lower, closer together.

"Yow!" Shawn the romantic, yelping in pain.

"What is that? You must *really* be glad to see me."

"It's not *that*—don't get me wrong." He shifted around to get his hand down there. Scallywag scowled at him, Carly barely suppressing a laugh.

It was the crystal in his pocket, *el cristal de la aldea*, given to him by Tsoo-Ki. It had migrated to a rather uncomfortable spot. He held it up, letting it sparkle in the light.

"It's so pretty," she said. "You think it really does have power?"

"Naw. Marcie and that Indian think *I* do, though." He chuckled, but without conviction.

"Do *you* think so?"

"Naw."

"Don't rule out the possibility, Shawn D'Fixx. When I can't be sure of something, I try to leave it as a *maybe*."

"Okay, *maybe* I have special powers."

She nuzzled closer, then reached down and caressed his hand holding the crystal.

They both started to tingle, drawn together, swept up in the power of a maybe.

But it felt very real, very much bigger than they were.

And the room filled with light.

With all the magic in the world . . .

And rainbows.

BULAGRÉT SAT IN HER OFFICE early the next morning, trying to get things squared away so she could be gone most of the day—this one time a year when the sun would be aligned perfectly with the cavern's great crystal.

Tsala-Pu.

Big Man came in and nodded.

"Remember, we must leave at least one hour earlier today," she reminded needlessly, "for the extra time of hiking three childrens to the cavern, one for each of us.

A rap on the door. "A man is here with some important papers for you," the receptionist informed.

She didn't recognize him. He laid a packet on the desk and asked Bulagrét to sign his receipt; then he hurried out.

She opened it and found a summons for civil action naming her and her Tsala-Pu company as co-defendants, those damned brothers as plaintiffs of the first-part, big San José law firm, blah blah blah.

She slammed the papers on her desk, jerked them up and flipped through them, then slammed them down again. She picked up the phone, stabbed out a number, then jabbered in Spanish to somebody, leaving off with, "You are sure we have two weeks?" She paused, then relaxed a bit, satisfied. "Okay, then. I will fax you a copy in a few *momentos.*"

Big Man looked angry, flexing his fists, shifting from one foot to the other.

She studied him, then allowed a sinister smile to creep across her face. "These brothers, they must be killed—but we will have time for that later."

She picked up the phone and stabbed another number, asking to be transferred to Immigration. "Adaló, *por favor.*"

She waited several minutes for him to come on the line.

"Señora Bulagrét, it has taken me some time to find what you wanted. Melinda McNair did not arrive when you said. She has been here all week. She arrived with—" He paused to refer to his list. "With Shawn D'Fixx and six others." He read the names.

Bulagrét recognized the manager from just having met her. "There is no Carlysle Hizen with Shawn D'Fixx?"

"No, Señora. Not in the past month has a Hizen arrived. Just *Mool*huizen."

"¡*Gracías*, Adaló!"

Hanging up, she kicked the desk and stood up, then kicked it again for good measure. "Lies. All of it is lies! They have come here to steal the crystals. We are taking Shawn D'Fixx to the cavern tomorrow to give his life and his powers to *las almas joyas* so they may give his powers back to us. Now I have decided we will kill *her*, too. She is not going to be a crystal customer."

She swore in Spanish for several minutes, pacing around the room before starting to calm a little. She looked at the clock and decided to get back on track, then took the packet of lawsuit papers over to the fax machine in the corner and started to load the feeder. The machine beeped, an incoming transmittal.

From Roux Tumowt, Private Investigator, Houston.

Chaleeshia's Poeky's benefactor and would-be rescuer's 800-number did, indeed, belong to a company owned by a woman named Carly Geiss. As the woman's photo started to come out of the printer, it was looking *very* familiar.

"Judy Morey! She is *here!* She has come for Chaleeshia Poeky, not knowing she is dead, and to get the Poeky child, one who we plan to sacrifice to the crystals *today!*"

Big Man punched the wood-paneled wall several times, the sound reverberating through the office and the outer lobby.

"We will still sacrifice the child today," she decided, "and dispose of Miss Carly Geiss when we come back." She thought for a moment, then realized, "That means Swallow Gagnon is part of this, too. We will also take both children from Carly and Swallow today. Lyla DeCivvio is close with those two, so I no longer trust her, either. I think she is planning something. We will take *her* child, too. Then there will be six children for the crystals, and each of us will take the living youth from *two*. This is good after all. Then when we come back, Lyla and Swallow and Judy—I mean Carly Geiss—all three will join Chaleeshia in the crater of the volcano."

She glared at Big Man. "If they are lucky, we will kill them first. If they are not lucky, we will drop them alive . . . and they will see their graves as they are falling."

MARCIE TALKED ON THE RADIO with Moolhuizen. "Yeah yeah, I'm up. Bulagrét was in her office fifteen minutes ago. The gift shop'll be open in a few minutes, so I'll go for a walk around the place and wind up there. If I don't get on too big a spending jag, I'll be back and check in with you in a while."

She fussed with her hair a minute, put her Tsoo-Ki hand-crafted rainbow pendant around her neck, slipped out of her sandals in favor of some footies and deck shoes, then locked the door as she headed into the bright morning sunlight.

"Miss McNair!" Bulagrét was coming her way. "Good morning to you! Please, I want to show you something."

She led her red-haired guest past the pool and along the beach rail, around the lounge deck, to a path in the trees.

"I have some *very* big crystals on the helio-copter. You may choose the one you like and have it as my gift." She urged her on, Marcie not suspicious at all.

Emerging from the trees into the clearing where the chopper sat idle, Marcie didn't see anybody else around. They walked up to peer inside. Just then, out the corner of her eye, she caught a glimpse of Big Man holding a blanket.

Grabbed, wrapped and held, the breath squeezed from her lungs. Couldn't see, her struggling futile.

Somebody, must have been Bulagrét, wrapped her wrists, tying them together behind her back. Same to her ankles. The blanket pulled back, brown plastic shipping tape across her mouth.

Panting to regain her breath.

Lifted into the chopper, squirming.

Face down, ankles tied to the equipment console.

"Relax, Miss McNair." Bulagrét's face appeared so close that Marcie could feel her hot breath. "We are leaving soon to show you our beautiful Costa Rica jungle!"

CHAPTER 13

"YOUR CHILDREN ARE IN DANGER!" Carly didn't need to talk about the $100,000—or lack thereof. Backed by Swallow and Lyla—who carried a *lot* of weight with the others—Carly's message proved simple and effective.

Your children are in danger.

"When your year is up—or sooner if you make Joelle angry—your children will disappear forever. *You* will disappear so you can never tell what is really happening here. You are not safe; your children are in danger!"

"What? What do we do?"

Two armed men guarded the perimeter, a third staying close to Carly. He reported by radio to Shawn that it was going well here, a bit panicky, but that's what they wanted.

"Your children are being rescued *right now* to be flown back to the U.S. When the bus arrives here, any of you who go with us will be reunited with your children in San José for the flight home. If you stay, you'll get another chance to leave tomorrow, but you risk having your child taken into state custody."

"What about our money?" one finally had presence of mind to ask.

"There *is* no money," Carly shouted over the din. They filled the court-yard area between apartment buildings, everybody outside now.

"Nobody has ever received the money!" Lyla shouted. "Many of you know my time is almost over. I would not give up my own money if I still believed there was any!"

"But our children are most important!" Carly wanted to keep them focused on the kids.

"What will we do?"

"Those of you who stay in Houston will have all the free services of FuturePlan—education and housing and child care and help finding good jobs. If you want to go elsewhere, we will make similar arrangements for you anywhere in the U.S. We will make sure you're *all* okay!"

"*Who* will?"

"My friends and I! We came down here to investigate after some of the children and their mothers disappeared—when they never made it back home. We have learned the worst and are giving you a chance to save your lives, to save your children!"

"*I'm* taking their help!" Lyla yelled.

"Me too!" Swallow concurred.

"Are you with us?" Carly shouted.

The crowd's fear and outrage competed with unfulfilled greed.

"Anybody rather stay and take their chances?"

Several hesitated. "But if we stay, what about our kids?"

"We are taking them, whether *you* want to leave or not. We can't risk *their* lives for *your* mistake," Carly declared. "They're already kidnapped and held hostage from you. We are saving *all* the children and as many mothers who accept our help!"

The declarations in the crowd quickly became unanimous.

"The bus will be here soon. Go and pack your most important things, no more than one small bag, and be ready to load up as soon as it arrives. We must move fast before Bulagrét finds out and people get hurt!"

Lyla and Swallow and Carly were already packed, ready to go. They waited in the courtyard, watching and worrying.

"This was easy," Lyla remarked.

Carly felt distracted, though, hoping the other parts of the plan were running smoothly. "As long as they get all the children out safely," she said absently. "If they run into unforeseen problems, it could be *very* dangerous."

"What if we get all these women to San José and their kids aren't there?" Swallow asked.

"Then *we* got problems," Lyla fretted. "What then?"

"Then we improvise," Carly assured her. She tried to project an air of confidence.

If only she could feel it.

TSOO-KI WATCHED THE SKY, Shawn on his radio, Moolhuizen pacing nervously and growing angrier by the minute.

"Come *on*, Marcie." Shawn was worried. She'd been out of her room more than thirty minutes, way too long without checking in.

"Look," Tsoo-Ki said quietly, pointing to the sky.

Both followed his gaze, but couldn't tell what he saw.

"There is blackness in the rainbow. The power is being used for the badness. The *very* bad."

"Let's go check on her," Shawn decided.

"Les," Moolhuizen said into his radio.

"Not the chopper," Shawn cut him off. "Not yet. Leave him close to the kid-camp." Brinkley had made a dawn reconnaissance of the compound, verifying only one ground route in, feeding info to Moolhuizen to plan the assault. He'd landed nearby, now waiting with three operatives to scramble at the last moment. Taking off now would alert the people guarding the camp and possibly make the chopper cross paths with Bulagrét's.

"We'll drive," Moolhuizen agreed.

They began to climb into the rental car, Tsoo-Ki getting into the back. Moolhuizen tried to stop him, but Shawn intervened.

"We don't need him," the operative argued.

"We don't know," Shawn disagreed. "Let's cover our maybes."

They drove to Tsala-Pu and trotted through, failing to find Marcie. Her room remained undisturbed. Bulagrét's chopper was gone!

Damn! They'd been scanning for the past twenty minutes and detected no aerial activity. That meant she had quite a lead on them.

Brinkley's voice came over the radio. "Bulagrét's chopper just passed over me from the direction of the camp. She must've got by you."

"Let's take the kid-camp *now!*" Shawn decided. "We may have been compromised. Getting the kids out safely is our first priority."

Moolhuizen responded, "Les, stick with the plan. Be ready to hit the kid-camp in five minutes. We're on our way. Marcie McNaught is missing and presumed in danger. Bulagrét *and* her cousin are gone. Mike, send the bus for the women now!" He turned to run to the car, Shawn on his heels.

"Tsoo-Ki! Let's go!"

But the young Indian had fallen to his knees beside Bulagrét's landing site. He was holding something.

Shawn stopped Moolhuizen, both running back to see it.

Tsoo-Ki held up the petite ankle bracelet with crystal-shard inlays. "This belonged to Marcie?"

Moolhuizen looked questioningly to his boss. Shawn nodded confirmation.

"They took her in the chopper," Moolhuizen pronounced.

"By force," Shawn surmised.

"Without her crystal," Tsoo-Ki lamented. "This is not good."

THE FIVE-YEAR-OLD CAUCASIAN GIRL and slightly younger Hispanic boy sat up front next to Big Man while he piloted. Between them, Chaleeshia Poeky's two-year-old son, fastened into a canvas papoose and strapped down, slept quietly.

Bulagrét presided over the rear seats, Swallow's youngest daughter fastened into a similar canvas carrier on one side, her three-year-old sister and Lyla's three-year old son on the other, both sharing a seat belt. A regular kiddie copter.

Bulagrét turned to look over the back where Marcie lay tied up, ankled to an equipment rack in the cargo area of the helicopter. Mouth still taped, Melinda McNair looked none-too-happy sprawled on the floor like a beef flank waiting for the butcher.

"You own thousands of the real crystals," Bulagrét remarked, tugging on Marcie's Tsoo-Ki-crafted pendant for a better look, "yet you are wearing *ésta basura*—this garbage."

Marcie remained quiet.

Bulagrét let the pendant drop, turned to shush Lyla's fussy son, then regarded the prone figure behind her again. "I do not care what becomes of you. You will not be my customer now, because you were coming here to steal the crystals from me!" she accused. "The reason I did not invite you and your friend to the cavern today is because it is Tsala-Pu, when we give the lifes of these children so the spirits may give *us* long lifes."

The chopper climbed higher as they traveled, the terrain below graduating from farmland to tracts of jungle broken by ever-steeper ridges of stone and volcanic formations. They banked northward, following a necklace of tiny lakes strung through crevices and tied by stairstep waterfalls.

"It does not matter to me if you live or die. We will bring Shawn D'Fixx to the cavern tomorrow, and he will come because we have you. Takú Litál wants to steal his powers. He calls him *The Man Who Shatters Light*. He say your friend can give us the power to control the crystals. Me?—I am not so sure, but we will find out."

She had to calm the kiddies; Big Man had made several quick maneuvers, the resulting belly-butterflies a bit unsettling.

"So you must listen carefully, Señorita McNair. When we arrive, if you do not cooperate, then you will die. Your only hope is for Shawn D'Fixx to have the power to defeat what the crystals ask of him—or you *both* will die."

She grabbed Marcie's shock of red hair and turned her face to look into her eyes. "Are *you* believing in the powers of your rainbow friend? You must hope so, because he is the only chance you have!"

"LET'S GO! LET'S GO!" The bus was pulling in, Carly hustling the women to load up.

It looked like an old commercial model in good condition, painted blue, the words *Costa Rica Fletero* along both sides advertising charter service. It parked where the drive dead-ended at the opening to the court-yard between buildings. Two operatives guarded access from the main road, their rental car parked off to the side. A third operative helped super-vise passenger boarding, the rag-tag group hurrying from their units, some with nice bags, some carrying sacks, none fully prepared.

Except Carly, Swallow, and Lyla. Carly put a small carry-on in the luggage compartment and placed a similar, partially open bag beside the driver's seat, the old Costa Rican gentleman promising in broken English to watch it personally.

As Lyla and Swallow boarded, Carly circulated, calling out for strag-glers, hurrying those who still lingered around the bus, helping them stuff clothing and miscellany into whatever they'd grabbed.

Already falling behind schedule, they had no time to spare.

TWO WOMEN LOITERED ALONG the driver's side of the bus, fuss-ing over their bags, kneeling to rearrange their belongings.

When nobody was looking, one flipped open the fuel compartment and twisted off the cap while the other grabbed handfuls of sand from the ground and dumped them into the tube.

As Carly came around their side, one slipped the lid closed while the other dropped the cap into her bag.

"LET'S GO! HURRY! GET ABOARD!" Carly shouted.

"*¿A donde estámos?*"

Carly understood she'd asked where they were going. "*A Los Estados Unidos.*" To The United States. She recognized these two as locals, prob-ably working the kid-camp rather than seducing crystal renters.

"Yes!" one agreed. "I want to go." She jabbered something to the other, who was shaking her head no.

"She has family, must be staying."

One loaded onto the bus, the other walked back to her apartment, pausing to wave good-bye.

Carly and the operative boarded last. The bus pulled out and headed south, followed by the two men in the rental car. When they picked up the main road west, the rental turned around and headed back to provide back-up for Moolhuizen's group.

THE LOCAL WOMAN WHO DECLINED to leave waited until the bus passed out of sight, then emerged from her apartment with a bicycle and rode quickly down a path in the jungle. She followed a direct route to Tsala-Pu. She pedaled right into the lobby, then dropped the bike and rushed in to jabber to the manager, the woman who distributed crystals every evening and collected them every morning, processor of cash and credit-card transactions.

Manager grabbed one of the burly bellmen, thrusting a satchel into his hands. The local woman showed them she had a .38 in her sack. Manager grabbed a box of ammo from her bottom drawer, placing it and a .45 in a third sack for herself. All three sped off in Bulagrét's old Caddy, full of praise for the fast thinking of their cohort.

When the blue bus came into sight, the local woman confirmed their target climbing a slow rise in the distance.

"Not too fast," Manager instructed the burly bellman at the wheel. "We must be ready when the motor stops running." It would only be a matter of time until the bumpy road sloshed enough sand into the intake to clog the fuel filter and choke the bus's engine. "I am hoping it will be next to the jungle when the bus stops."

"Bringing anybody back?" the bellman asked.

Manager shrugged. "I hope so. But not Lyla or Swallow or Judy Morey. They will have to die."

MOOLHUIZEN, SHAWN, AND TSOO-KI waited on the road, just around the bend from the kid-camp gate. The other operatives fanned into the jungle around the perimeter, linked by radio. Their only barriers appeared to be an electric cattle fence, chain-link, and several armed men patrolling lazily in the hot midday sun. The sound of recorded music could be heard from somewhere inside.

"You're *sure* it'll cut phones, too?" Moolhuizen asked unnecessarily.

"When we get back, I'm gonna tell him you doubted his thoroughness," Shawn said quietly. It was a tease—sort of.

They waited several more minutes. Hot as hell, it was.

"Any time now, Foster," Shawn mumbled to himself. As if on cue, the power went out, the radio died, and the fence stopped buzzing.

Ninety seconds to power up the chopper.

They could hear it, then saw it appear over the trees, coming from behind the camp. All three patrolling men rushed toward it, leaving the gate unguarded.

Quietly, they cut the fence in six places, operatives slipping through, crossing the compound, working around the ramshackle bunkhouses.

The chopper hovered curiously, then eased closer, then slightly closer.

The men raised their weapons.

Pfoom! Pfoom! Pfoom! Poofs of dust erupted from the ground around them.

Chickens! One dropped his gun, all three turning to run. Didn't get very far, though. They found themselves surrounded by armed men, weapons trained. The chopper came in to land, but they dared not turn to look. Scared they were, their weapons out of reach, hands in the air. Hey, we just *work* here.

Several men emerged from the chopper and covered the patrollers while four operatives penetrated the buildings. Two women surrendered without incident. By then, the children had streamed out into the hot sunshine, surrounding the armed men, hands out, jabbering for treats. Inside, several infants began to cry.

Shawn and Tsoo-Ki walked up. "Good, nobody hurt," Shawn said.

The adults gathered together, Shawn demanding to know who spoke English. One woman held up her hand.

"Bulagrét landed here in the last hour?"

"Yes."

"Did she take anyone?"

"She and her cousin were taking six childrens." It had obviously upset her.

"Why? Why take the kids?"

The woman shook her head. "We are not told. But—but—" She lowered her head, speaking quietly. "When she takes them, they never come back. This is the only time she is taking so many."

"These are just workers," Shawn said to Moolhuizen. "Keep 'em detained until the operation's over. You need to get the bus in and take all these kids to the airport. I'm going with Brinkley before it's too late."

Moolhuizen started to protest, but Shawn held up his hand. No time to argue. Explain it to Kinte later, hopefully after all has gone well.

Shawn hurried to the chopper, Tsoo-Ki on his heels. He turned to tell the young Indian no, but Tsoo-Ki insisted.

"You need me. I know the way."

Shawn climbed in, telling Brinkley, "We're heading toward the cave, gotta rescue Marcie and six kids."

Tsoo-Ki stood in the open door, fingering the home-made pendant around his neck.

"Okay," Shawn said.

Brinkley looked inquiringly at Shawn as the young Indian climbed in.

Shawn shrugged, busy trying desperately to anticipate what might go wrong.

"Rich Mr. Fixx is Tsawa-Ki," the Indian explained to Brinkley as they lifted into the vivid blue sky and headed west, "to make the badness into good."

TWO-THIRDS OF THE WAY to San José, the bus full of women climbed over a high set of ridges, having to switch back several times. The engine was laboring, missing sometimes, not sounding good. Bouncing over a rough stretch, it sputtered and finally died. The driver coasted it off to the side adjacent to dense jungle.

He couldn't start it again.

Just as the operative began to climb out and provide cover for the driver to look at the engine, the local woman seated several rows back came forward, volunteering something in her bag that might help.

Boom!

A single bullet exploded the operative's head, blood spraying on the windshield, the dead man slumping in the doorway.

First one scream, then another, then sobbing and rising panic.

The woman pointed her pistol at the driver, gesturing toward the door. He reached to the handle and opened it for her. She stepped over the operative's body and down to the ground, waving her gun menacingly toward the scared women. "Do not move!"

An old Caddy pulled up. Three people got out and approached cautiously, each with a bag in hand.

Waiting until a lone car passed, Bellman pulled the operative's body out, then rolled it under the bus, out of sight. All four had pistols showing now.

Manager stepped inside the bus, the others waiting just outside the door. She surveyed the group, some cowering, most in tears, several barely containing their rage.

"You will do what we say," she pronounced. "Now—where is Judy Morey?"

CHAPTER 14

HOT.

Blinding sunshine. Stifling humidity. Hot.

Really hot.

Marcie hadn't been this wet without a hug and a kiss in a long time.

Or tied up, either.

The children disembarked, the older two each assigned to lead one of the middle two, the youngest two papoosed on Big Man's and Bulagrét's backs. Big Man untied Marcie's ankles from the equipment rack.

"We are untying your feet so you will be able to walk," Bulagrét explained. Big Man fastened a six-meter rope around her neck—in a noose. "You will walk in front," she continued. "If you try to run away, my cousin will pull you until you pass out. Then he will tie you again and drag you."

Marcie knew how to play that. Like going over a cliff—ain't much choice but to fall.

She was burning up.

Hot as hell out there.

It proved a slow trip, three-year-old legs and all. Big Man carried a canteen, kept everybody's sweat-makers going at full tilt.

Marcie tried to formulate a plan. She couldn't let these kids be killed, whatever happened to her. She couldn't come up with ideas, though, except to keep stalling, slowing them down. Big Man undid the tape on her mouth for a drink. She took advantage to remark how hot and tired those kids must be. Suggestivity and all. Get 'em cranky; delay as long as possible. If they missed the sunlight hitting the big crystal, they'd probably have to wait another day. Or maybe she could at least buy enough time for a rescue.

And just where the hell was Shawn, anyway? And Moolhuizen and Brinkley and the chopper and the four-thousand or so Costa Ricans who must work for Kinte by now? Where were the sensors and lasers and techno-wooga antidisestablishmentarianisms? Where's the damned cavalry?

Old Bulagrét had no idea who she was messing with, certainly not some space-head Herbs & Oils chickie and her leisure-dude friend. Bitch had no idea Foster probably owned her *and* her cousin by now, that Kinte probably had a team tunneling under them this very minute. Mother-hen Kinte . . . sure could be a nuisance with all his worrying and all . . . but still . . .

Hot.

Kids getting fussy, Bulagrét promised they could rest in shade in a few minutes.

Sure would be a good time for Rich Mr. Fixx to show up.

The route looked different than the way she'd come the day before. They followed a path through the jungle, enveloped by sounds and odors and cooler humid air, relief from that interminable glare of sun.

To a small log-and-stone house they walked, met by Takú Litál. He looked surprised at Marcie all hog-tied and leashed, but delighted to see six—count 'em, *six niños*—for Tsala-Pu. They agreed the weather was perfect, the sky a cloudless blue.

Hot, though.

After some quiet conversation, drinks for the kids, lots of looking at Marcie and debating, they finally decided. She would remain in the cabin while the others went to participate in Tsala-Pu. Shawn hadn't been to the cabin. He didn't even know it existed. Even if he discovered she'd been taken, he wouldn't know how to find her. If he showed up at the cave, the secret of Marcie's location—with her inability to survive more than a day or two tied up in a cabin in the hot jungle—would be an excellent bargaining tool. And if he *didn't* show up, she'd make great bait.

To catch a Tsawa-Ki and give his power to the crystals.

Then neither Shawn nor Marcie would ever leave the jungle alive.

So they tied her ankles, then tethered her to a notch in the wall and left her face-down on a floor of rough-hewn wooden planks. Don't squirm, Marcie—you'll get splinters in your boobies.

She wished she'd made a pit-stop, but now she was alone. Everybody had left, inexorably drawn toward the cave, through the jungle, over the footbridges, on a hot and humid day called Tsala-Pu.

To kill six children.

And for Marcie there would be no cavalry, no worrisome Jamaican, no magical powers, no best friend.

And no rainbows.

Hot.

BRINKLEY APPROACHED the Tsala village, flying toward the cave from the south. Tsoo-Ki got all excited, insisting Shawn show him the jawbreaker crystal he'd lent him. Shawn pulled it from his pocket, and the young Indian cupped it reverently in his hands.

"Please, you must land. Hurry!"

Brinkley showed no intention of making a village pit-stop, but Shawn told him to hold up. They hovered for a moment, the chopper casting a shadow across the opening in the roof of the big building where the Tsala had gathered for ceremony.

"You are breaking the village light," Tsoo-Ki pronounced portent-ously. He assured Shawn the stop would prove brief but worthwhile. Brin-kley landed and waited with the chopper.

The crowd streamed from the building to meet them at the village center. Tsoo-Ki jabbered something to the old woman and shaman, all three nodding their heads. When the old man barked orders to the group, everybody drew closer, packing into a tight circle with Shawn in the mid-dle. Tsoo-Ki had him hold the crystal up so the sunlight could strike it. He cupped Shawn's hands in his own, the shaman wrapping his around them, the old lady adding hers, several others adding theirs. Children were lifted to participate, people packing in tighter, some who couldn't reach center touching and holding the arms of those closer.

Shawn could feel pressure from the hands holding his. They seemed to be easing the crystal around until it was aligned perfectly, letting it catch the sun where it faceted out to six sides. Suddenly, the light blinded Shawn, bright colors beaming every direction.

Colors.

Colors and three sets of very old eyes watching him and waiting.

For what, dammit? Sheesh, give him the orientation if he's supposed to lead this congregation.

The crystal felt hot. Hotter. *Really* hot!

He wanted to let go, not get burnt, but he couldn't. His hands were wrapped too tightly, too many people holding on.

But the heat proved bearable, as if so many hands were drawing it off, sharing the burden, all doing their part.

Taking of the power.

Or contributing to it.

The very air began buzzing, electric, vibrant. Goosebumps, hair standing on end, sparks in the colors, and tiny static charges grew into bolts of lightning reaching into the sky.

The sound of water crashing down from cracks in the ridge faded away. Shawn strained to see, watching as the stairstep waterfalls slowed to a trickle and dried up, leaving tiny pools scattered along steaming rock ledges.

The buzzing died, the colors shimmering into nothing, hands dropping away, Tsala people easing back, nodding, satisfied.

Shawn examined his hands: no burns, no blisters, just faint lines from where sharp edges had pressed into his flesh.

The people turned and filed into the big building, not even looking back. The old shaman gazed at Shawn, at Tsoo-Ki, then back at Shawn. "Tsawa-Ki," he said before turning to leave.

The old woman regarded Shawn, seemed satisfied, then looked at Tsoo-Ki, her time-grooved face softening, eyes glistening. She reached up and touched the young Indian's cheek with the backs of her fingers, he caressing her hand, a deep and profound love in his face.

"*Por la bondad,*" she said. For the goodness.

He nodded. She took her hand away, then warned Shawn. "You will bring back my Tsoo-Ki to me."

Then she turned and hurried away.

BELLMAN AND THE TWO WOMEN who'd betrayed the prostitutes stood just outside the bus. Manager hovered just inside, brandishing her weapon, explaining what to expect.

"Judy and Swallow and Lyla will come with me first. We are going into the jungle to talk. If you try to escape, you will die."

Carly didn't need a written rundown; the plan was to kill all three miscreants, then detain the others until a ride back could be arranged.

"Then the rest of you will follow to a safe place in the jungle until a ride comes for us."

An old school bus coming from the other direction, empty except for the driver, slowed to investigate the problem. He pulled over across the road.

"Hush!" Manager ordered. "If you say anything, I will *kill* him *and* you for speaking."

Carly fidgeted in the front seat, distraught, clutching her bag, wringing her hands, mumbling to herself.

A young man emerged, standing beside his bus, surveying the situation. He went around back and opened the door, pulling out some kind of tool kit or something, maybe a jacking system, probably to volunteer his assistance. He crossed the road, walked around behind the bus and along the side.

Bellman held up his hand, assuring him all was okay. "We do not need help. We are just stopped for a rest."

"Good," he said, but kept coming. "Now," he said.

Carly kicked and jabbed simultaneously, Manager caught off guard, falling out the door and into one of the women.

Pfft! Pfft! Pfft! Pfft! Pfft!

The young guy was shooting! Concussion bursts of air strong enough to knock a big man off his feet and . . . sticky nets? Guns went flying, all four captors sprawling, spider-webbed together, a gluey mess made worse the more they squirmed.

Until they couldn't squirm anymore.

"Todd! It's about time."

"*Told* you a spare bus in the back pocket never hurts!"

"We're okay, Beckster," she said into her bag.

"I'm going to the airport." Todd grinned. "Anybody need a lift?"

MARCIE WAS DOING PLENTY of her own squirming, a regular eel out of water.

She actually did get a splinter in her boobie. Yow. Paybacks are gonna be a bitch.

Rub rub rub rub rub. Aha!

She rolled over, her hands free. The pendant with the broken glass lay face up where she'd been squirming. She had rubbed her binding on it until it cut through, and she didn't even have a scratch on her.

Faced with a choice of first untying her tether, her ankles, or getting that tape off her mouth, she went for the mouth.

Yow! That hurt. Mental note: when telling Foster the story later, describe undoing the tether and ankles first. She could hear the litany of smart remarks: "Tie her up, drop her in a hole, feed her to the sharks— just don't try to shut her up—*Oooof!*"

Didn't feel so hot anymore—not outside anyway. But she simmered a slow boil on the inside. If she didn't get there in time to save those kids, she would be capable of the most heinous, the most violent revenge. Don't even *think* about getting in her way.

She traced the path back the way they'd brought her on the leash. She noticed orchids hanging in the trees—had those been there before?— beautiful and vivid, dozens of varieties, some tiny, several bigger than she'd ever seen. And hummingbirds! Everywhere! Most boasted plumage shimmering ruby with iridescent markings every color of the rainbow, flitting here and there. An iguana, watching her from the branch. Another scurrying out of her way. Several more watching from atop a hot rock.

One winked at her.

She kept moving, finally picking up the trail she recognized from the day before, the one leading to the crystal cavern. She trotted off, keeping a good pace without exhausting herself, careful not to trip on rocks or twist her ankle.

She had already crossed the first two footbridges when something stopped her dead.

An iguana—with odd, colored markings on his shoulder, just like the one she'd given Shawn. But this one had to be more than a meter long, right in the middle of the path, looking at her. She started around him, but he moved. The other direction, moved again. Smaller ones began appearing, sauntering from among the rocks, gathering in a semi-circle, just looking at her.

And insisting she go no farther.

Hmmm . . . Or at least not *that* way. Where? Up? Up there? Up over that ridge?

Gawd, she'd lost her mind. Talking to the lizards. Thinking they wanted her to turn around, climb up and over the ridge off to her right, not cross the bridge, not continue toward the cavern.

A dozen walked toward the ridge, then paused to wait, watching her, the big one with the rainbow colors steadfastly blocking the path to the footbridge.

What the hell. She took a dozen steps. The group waddled ahead, the big one coming up to stop behind her. She moved; they moved. Moved again, right with her. Always that big one right behind her.

"Don't goose me," she warned. "Looking for some tail, are ya?"

The route steeper now, she picked her way up among the cracks and broken rocks. Some of the smaller iguanas wandered away, the biggest sticking with her, up the ridge, always right behind. Once when she whirled and glared at him, he glanced off in every direction, a regular cherub, innocent, nothing going on here.

All the way over the top, nothing remarkable to see. The big iguana climbed over behind her, turned around, and positioned himself where he could watch, one eye still on Marcie.

"Now what?"

The other iguanas were finding spots, settling in—let's hang out with our pal Marcie, the babe with the red hair and pretty tail.

"I'll give it a minute," she said, finding a flat rock to sit on. She couldn't see over the ridge she'd just climbed, but the big feller seemed satisfied with her choice.

"So what are we waiting for?"

Then she saw it, in the distance, from the direction of the Tsala village. Refractions of rainbow light reaching into the sky.

The lizards were all watching, too.

"Shawn," she whispered to herself.

Big feller winked.

"THERE'S NO PLACE TO LAND by the cave!" Brinkley shouted over the sound of the rotors. "Only up on that highest ridge where Tsoo-Ki said he fell and got hurt."

"That's too far!" Shawn shouted back. "They're gonna hear the helicopter, even from deep in the cave. By the time we get down there, they could have an ambush waiting for us!"

"There's no other way—"

But Shawn was rooting through a gear cabinet, pulling out a harness.

"No way! Mr. Bilal would—!"

"Gotta do it!" Shawn argued, already strapping it on. "Get down within fifty feet and lower me on the cable."

"Need some distance from the cave—or you'd be a hanging duck if they came out shooting. And the chopper'd be vulnerable, too!"

"Then the flat area other side of the first footbridge."

"Lower *me*, too!" Tsoo-Ki shouted.

Shawn looked at him. "You said there's only one way down from the high ridge. You need to come down with Les—show him the way!"

The young Indian couldn't argue.

"You wait," Brinkley argued—probably knowing it would be ignored even as he said it, "until we can get down close to the cave before you move in!"

They ascended over the highest ridge, the place Brinkley would return with Tsoo-Ki to land and hike down, Shawn fastening his harness to the cable. He tried not to think about being scared of heights and subject to sudden vertigo.

Gotta focus on the goal.

"Have to save those kids!" he shouted to nobody in particular.

"And Marcie!" Brinkley reminded.

"I have a feeling she can take care of herself. Unless they've taped her mouth shut, she's probably *talking* 'em into submission!"

No arguments there.

Take it easy, Shawn. Getting closer.

Tsoo-Ki rubbed something on his fluorescent-orange Costa Rica t-shirt.

It was *el cristal de la aldea*—the village crystal. He pressed it into Shawn's hand, a solemn, earnest expression on his face.

A look of confidence.

Shawn took a deep breath. He sure didn't need to be carrying some *rock*, but what the hey. What could it hurt?

Maybe, just maybe, the crystal could help.

Naw!

Well . . . maybe.

"OOOO! IT'S SO *PRETTY*," reacted the five-year-old girl.

"*¡Muy bonita!*" agreed the Hispanic boy, four.

Swallow's and Lyla's three-year olds concurred. They gushed another round of *Ooos!* when Takú Litál used his crystal-encrusted lighter to fire up the lantern, a glow creating myriad rainbow prisms and twinkling sparkles deep into the cave tunnel.

It felt much cooler than outside, a mild, misty breeze blowing toward them from the great cavern. With plenty of time to spare, they relaxed and let the kids take it easy, slowly working their way down through the levels and deep into the volcanic formation. Bulagrét's back ached from the long trek with papoose, but all this effort would be worth it.

Very much worth it.

Litál estimated at least thirty minutes before Tsala-Pu would begin, so Bulagrét gave each of the children a crystal pendant to wear, removing their shirts, cautioning them to leave the strap around their necks, but showing how they could hold them up toward the lantern light and cause rainbow refractions and kaleidoscope designs. It worked, fascinating them to no end. Chaleeshia's young son kept putting it in his mouth, not that it tasted good, but, well, it seemed the thing to do.

The sound of a chopper! Getting closer, almost directly overhead, passing by, but pausing somewhere close at low altitude. It was difficult to tell from the way sound reverberated through the cave.

"There is no place to land here!" Bulagrét hissed. "But maybe it is lowering somebody down!"

Takú Litál leapt to his feet, fury in his face, glaring his rage at this damned woman and her machinations. He had warned her he would let *nothing* interfere with Tsala-Pu, the one day a year the sun would strike the big crystal in perfect symmetry, his best hope of transferring the youth of these children to himself, to live a very long time.

Or to live forever!

Big Man checked the clip in his Glock 19, looking at Bulagrét for instructions.

"Quick! You go see what is happening. If someone is coming, kill them all. And hurry back before Tsala-Pu!"

BIG MAN SPRINTED ACROSS the planks and up the incline, heading into the tunnel that would take him to the narrow crack in the side of the formation, out into the bright sunlight.

Racing toward the first footbridge, he could see the chopper lifting higher in the sky, banking toward the high ridge behind the similar crack at the top of the cavern. He spotted Shawn D'Fixx almost immediately, the dweeb crystal customer still on the other side of the first footbridge, a good hundred meters up along the edge of the crevice where the rock was smooth with no loose gravel.

D'Fixx was running, too, a race to the bridge.

It would be close.

SHAWN RAN AS FAST as he could. Unarmed, he could see Big Man clutching a pistol.

When it became obvious Shawn would barely win the foot race, he had to make a choice. Being stopped cold in the face of this man with a gun wouldn't be smart strategy. Not that Shawn had a strategy.

Instead of crossing the bridge, Shawn passed it and kept running along the crevice. Big Man bounded across and went after him, gaining quickly. Shawn had covered more than a hundred meters when the ground began sloping downward, steep and rugged. A high, loose-rock ridge rose to his right—no way to climb it quickly, plus it would make him an obvious target. But climbing down would risk a deadly fall. Over the cliff to his left, the crevice opened to its widest, its stream flowing into a sulphur-hued tarn at least twenty-some meters below.

Shawn stopped and faced him, panting from the exertion, perspiring in the heat, squinting into the glare of sun almost directly overhead.

Rats. Now what?

He slipped his hand into his pocket, feeling the jawbreaker crystal, and caught himself thinking, *Now would be a good time!*

But nothing happened.

Just Big Man walking closer, the Glock aimed at Shawn's chest.

Ten meters, now eight, seven, six.

Big Man stopped.

Shawn could see him tensing and knew he was about to fire.

"Kinte!" Shawn shouted, but his voice echoed pathetically, fading to nothing. There was no response, nobody to help, the faint sound of a helicopter landing off in the distance, not much good right here right now.

What the hell was he thinking? This hadn't worked out at all.

And the damned crystal wasn't helping, either, not that he believed in it.

But a man staring down the barrel of a Glock can find some remarkable things to believe in.

Shawn looked down at the yellow-green water below, wondering how deep it was.

Big Man took another step forward, aiming. An iguana scurried between his feet. He stumbled.

Shawn jumped, arms flailing like a baby bird.

Boom! Boom!

Splash!

BIG MAN'S ADVERSARY DISAPPEARED below the surface, sulphur bubbles rising.

Boom-ptuh! Boom-ptuh! Shooting into the water, he emptied the last fifteen shots from the clip, then reloaded.

No body.

If the gringo's wind was knocked out on impact, his lungs sucking in water, he might stay down, struggling and gasping desperately until he drowned. If his lungs were pierced, his lifeless body would take on water, and he might not come up for days, bloated and gassy, decomposing.

Big Man swapped out clips, watched and waited. A few bubbles. No place to climb up sheer cliff, even if he'd managed to swim underwater. Nowhere to come up without being seen, a clear target.

Aimed and waiting.

A few more bubbles, the rippled surface gradually smoothing. A full minute, maybe more.

No sign.

Minute and a half—two minutes—and a half—three.

Big Man allowed a slight smile, nodding his head.

Four minutes. Five. No way humanly possible to stay down that long.

Drowned or shot to death, Shawn D'Fixx would be a threat no more.

The iguana rested his head on the edge of the precipice, a sad expression on his face, and closed his eyes.

And the water stopped rippling, the surface smoothing to glass.

And Shawn never came up.

CHAPTER 15

NOW WITH SHAWN DEAD, Big Man needed to get back to the cave quickly. He didn't want to miss Tsala-Pu, not after all he'd been through, the least of which was putting up with his domineering cousin's crap.

A problem he'd have to solve someday.

He scanned the water one last time, half wishing he could see the corpse to know if sharp shooting or simple drowning had eliminated this nuisance, half glad he'd left no signs of foul play to risk attracting attention from those damnable tour copters getting to be like gnats on a sweltering evening.

Iguanas began scurrying about, attracted to the edge for some reason. Like pesky rats, they were. He heard one behind him as he shoved the gun into his waistband and turned to head back.

Conk!

That was no lizard. It was Melinda McNair!

With a jagged rock the size of a softball. It had blood on it. So did the back of his head, seeping into his hair, running down the back of his neck.

His gun fell to the ground.

Woozy.

He swayed for a moment, had to sit down . . . fell hard.

Where did the gun go? Melinda was picking it up. He needed to get away. Hands and knees, crawling, a piece of loose rock at the edge—

And over he went.

MARCIE WATCHED HIM GO OVER.

His head smacked a sharp, broken ledge about halfway down, a tangle of arms and legs hitting the water hard. One big splash and he bobbed back up to the surface. Very still, face down. Floating. A hint of orange blood coloring the water around his head.

"Shawn!" she shouted. It echoed without answer.

She dropped to her knees, tears glistening on her cheeks. More feebly, "Shawn!" But it was no use. "Shawn!"

Crying now, she buried her face in her hands. The big iguana eased over beside her, placing his head on her leg in sympathy. She wiped her eyes and looked down again.

Just Big Man, floating dead. Scanning the far set of high ridges glaring in the sunlight, she could see two specks pausing to watch, Les Brinkley and Tsoo-Ki. It looked treacherous, almost impassable. They had a long way to go.

She took a deep breath, then climbed to her feet. She felt dizzy, hot, overcome with a sense of loss.

She studied the Glock, a weapon she knew from dating that survivalist years before. It was fully loaded.

Time to go save those kids.

She looked around, down to the water, high into the sky, as far into the distance as she could see.

But there were no rainbows.

Just two very evil people to stop, no more using the crystals for the badness.

Time to finish Shawn's last job.

For the late Rich Mr. Fixx.

WATCHING WITH MINI-BINOCULARS, Brinkley saw Shawn jump off the cliff. He knew there was no way to climb out, that the only possible escape would be to swim to the far end of the tarn and down through the stream until it opened into the next steep canyon. If he could tread water that long, Shawn would need to be lifted out.

If he survived all that shooting.

"Keep going. Help Marcie!" he shouted to Tsoo-Ki. "I'm going after Shawn."

He hurried back up the ridge to the chopper, fast as he could, working hard in the searing midday heat. No way Shawn could've swum that far underwater. Had to hope Big Man had missed, that Shawn had got out of range, now waiting somewhere for rescue.

Had to try.

And if not, Brinkley still had a job to do.

Try to recover the body.

"*HEWWWWWWWW!*" AIR SUCKING into desperate lungs.

"Ow!" Both sounds hollow, eerie. Shawn rubbed his head. That hurt. Conked it on something hard.

Total darkness. And it stunk of sulphur and stale air.

Shawn treaded the cold water, reached up to feel solid rock just above. No wonder he'd conked it; he'd come up fast and hard after kicking desperately underwater as long as his breath would hold. He could feel stone wall to his left, an opening. His eyes adjusting now, he looked down into the eerily lit water, faint green-washed sunshine filtering in through doors and windows. He must have swum into some kind of ancient house, apparently built under a ledge in the cliff—now submerged. He gazed around the dark, gloomy air pocket, detecting some kind of horizontal crack in the rock, silhouettes of pottery standing in a row. The crack looked too small to climb into, so he would have to stay in the water.

Pfoom! Pfoom! Shots out there. He decided to stay right where he was for a while.

Pfoom! Pfoom! Pfoom!

Stone ledges and air pockets—highly recommended for any similar predicament.

More shooting, a long pause.

Splash!

Say what? Throwing big rocks?

Shawn propped his feet in the window, then wrapped an arm inside the opening. Rest a bit. Pants pocket felt twisted, that jawbreaker crystal digging into his leg. He fished it out and held it underwater.

Catching the green sunlight streaming through the window, it lit up, glowing a spectrum of colors and filling the underwater refuge with light. Shawn could see he'd entered a long building, thirty or forty meters at least, the length of the cliff overhang. He saw broken pottery, remnants of stone furniture, the wood long since rotted away.

The crystal felt warm in his hand, the water not so chilly anymore.

Didn't smell so bad now, either.

No more shots.

Wait a few more minutes before checking it out. But then what? Climb a sheer cliff? He looked at the bottom of the crystal. No, there was no little 8-ball window with answers—like how to get out of the crevice, how to save those kids, how to rescue his friend.

Marcie was probably counting on him this very minute, confident he would come save her life.

He looked at the mysterious crystal.

Wait just one more minute.

Then what?

STILL NO SIGN OF HER COUSIN, Bulagrét knew they were out of time.

"We have a *big* surprise for you all!" she announced to the children gleefully, removing a small sack from the bottom of the papoose, purposefully letting a few pieces of candy fall out before mischievously scooping them up.

Takú Litál fumbled under his robe, but she held a hand up for him to wait. He shrugged and walked over to scoop several handfuls of water and trickle it into the chantry basin.

"You must have your eyes closed to get a surprise!" Then to Litál, she instructed, "We will be starting from the eldest."

The old shaman studied the crack high above, the sunlight streaming in at an angle, working its way down the wall of crystals, beams of colored light shooting every direction. All six children were fascinated by the vision.

"I will cover your eyes now," she explained just as friendly as could be. "You must not peek, or you will not get the surprise treats," she warned.

She set the two youngest on the crystal floor next to the chantry, motioning the other four to move closer. She carefully tied small strips of cloth around their heads, makeshift blindfolds to keep them from panicking before they could be sacrificed and bled in quick succession.

The light moved slowly down the wall; one whole side of the cavern filled with refracting prisms, a hint of buzz filling the air. Just a few more minutes and the edge would strike one side of the giant crystal, the start of Tsala-Pu.

Litál took the hewn-crystal dagger from under his robe and laid it on the edge.

Bulagrét whispered, "Okay, you get your treat first," to the oldest girl. "Up you go," she said, lifting her onto the chantry, her back to the long, piercing shard jutting out from the base.

She could hear Big Man approaching. Good, he'd made it back just in time.

It was that Melinda McNair! And she had his gun, aiming it at Bulagrét!

The light moved closer, almost blinding now, filling one end of the cave.

Bulagrét put the girl between herself and Marcie. Litál ducked behind the giant crystal.

Marcie crossed the last set of planks.

Bulagrét snatched up the crystal dagger, holding it against the girl. "Stop! If you move, what happens will be *your* fault!"

MARCIE HAD TROUBLE SEEING, the lights behind her adversaries shooting beams everywhere, colors glowing steadily brighter.

The younger kids pulled their blindfolds up, all now confused about what they saw. The three year-olds began creeping away. Marcie stepped forward, but Bulagrét warned her again. The oldest girl squealed from pain, bursting into tears.

Marcie couldn't shoot, kids moving around, two bright to see, that crystal dagger at the girl's throat.

More movement, then a flying glint of light. Litál had flung a crystal! It hit Marcie's hand, knocking the gun loose to skitter into the crack and fall to invisible depths. Marcie grabbed for it, lost her footing, started to slip over, and barely managed to grab the plank, now dangling over the void, holding on for life.

THE SUNLIGHT KISSED THE EDGE of the giant crystal.

"Now!" Bulagrét announced. "Hush!" she hissed to the little girl, turning her back to the spike again. "Hush!" she shouted at the other children when several started to cry.

Takú Litál hurried back into position, his dagger poised.

The waterfall began to roar.

"Ready?" she shouted.

"Tsala-Pu!"

SHAWN SURFACED CAUTIOUSLY, scanning the cliff above. No sign of anybody up there. That could be good *or* bad.

Then he saw Big Man floating not too far away, face-down in the water, arms and legs askew, slowly drifting toward Shawn.

Then moving faster.

Shawn felt himself being pulled, a current tugging at him. He looked around frantically, but he couldn't discern what had brought the water to life, he and the dead man caught in its inexorable liquid grip. Both were crossing toward the far cliff, now moving the other direction, crossing back again, the current increasingly stronger.

Shawn kicked and tried to swim toward the lower end, but got swept there faster than he expected, then yanked back across and pulled the other direction.

The tarn became a giant whirlpool! Moving faster and stronger, a vee-shape or cone formed its swirling dip in the center.

Around again, then again.

The water level began dropping, the ledge roof of the ancient building exposed, then some of the stone wall.

Pulled toward the center, Shawn kicked wildly, trying to keep from being sucked down.

Big Man's body swirled in, faster and faster, into the center where it disappeared from sight.

Damn!

Faster!

Faster!

Dizzy, Shawn fought against being tugged down, hacking from a sudden mouthful of water.

Now a loud sucking sound.

Drawn into the center, around and around, pulling him under.

One last gasp, holding his breath.

Disappearing beneath the surface.

Swallowed into the bowels of the Earth!

SUNLIGHT CROSSED THE TOP of the giant crystal, blinding prism beams bursting around two sides, three, four. The waterfall roared, water starting to rise, covering the crystalline floor, mist billowing through the lights to create shimmering rainbows.

"Now!" Takú Litál ordered.

Joelle Bulagrét held the oldest girl by the shoulders, the tiny child's back almost touching the piercing shard.

Water rose from below Marcie, submerging her legs, making her buoyant, lifting her up the crevice.

"Now!" Litál insisted.

The waterfall burst forth, the body of a dead man gushing from above, disappearing into the crack. Then a second man, this one flailing and gasping.

Splash!

Down and back up, washed in a wave across to the chantry, he grabbed the giant crystal. The little girl jumped down and fled in fear.

Marcie hurried through ankle-deep, now calf-deep water, grabbing kids, shouting over the din. "Run over there! Quick! Over there!" A toddler under each arm.

Shawn rose to full height, stood on the chantry, the village crystal held high in the sunlight, swirling rainbows surrounding him, enveloped in the mist, now only a pair of eyes piercing the light.

"Tsawa-Ki!" shouted Litál.

"*¡Maldita sea!*" swore Bulagrét. Dammit!

Litál backed away, scared. Bulagrét grabbed for his crystal knife.

The water was still rising, Marcie ushering, carrying, pushing and lifting kids onto an outcropping of flat crystals.

Bulagrét slashed at Shawn, Rich Mr. Fixx having to grab the giant, hot crystal, dropping his jawbreaker into the water. Steam swirled around him, but didn't scald.

The sunlight hit the giant crystal dead on, perfect symmetry, beacons of prism light shooting six directions and splay into a trillion tiny beams along the walls and ceiling, arced rainbows glowing in the billowing mist.

And the buzz and the waterfall roared.

And electricity bolted up through the crystal, through Shawn, up through the crevice and into the sky.

The water grew deeper, swirling faster, Marcie barely able to hang on, the children about to be swept away . . .

Tsoo-Ki rushed into the cave, but the water gushed at him in waves, knocking him down, blocking his way, bursts of rainbow light blinding him between surges . . .

A busload of former sex workers crossing the highest ridge paused so they could watch the giant rainbow climbing into the sky . . .

The Tsala people poured from their chantry building to gaze at lightning bolts piercing clear sky, a giant rainbow ascending in the smoky volcanic mist, now arcing in their direction . . .

And the animals watched, the monkeys and boars and hummingbirds ...

And the iguanas ...

The water swirled into a torrent, sweeping around faster, grabbing Marcie and several children, circling Shawn and the source of the rainbow.

The water grabbed Tsoo-Ki, pulling him into the cave.

A great rumbling sound filled the air, the ground beginning to shake.

Earthquake!

Eruption!

Brinkley lifted off, the chopper flying blindly into rainbow mist and belching tephra clouds, steam gushing from crevices, the ground shifting and cracking below, the waters flowing one way, then back, then back again.

And the world began coming apart ...

"MARCIE!" SHAWN SCREAMED, but no one could hear.

"Tsawa-Ki!" Tsoo-Ki yelled.

"Shawn! The kids!" Marcie squealed.

Then Shawn could see, two children, no—three!

He jumped into the raging waters, grabbed hold, had two of them, no—lost one. Then he saw Tsoo-Ki snagging one, then another. A shock of red hair, Marcie with two more.

"Help!" It was the little girl.

Litál and Bulagrét clung to the chantry at the epicenter of the torrent. She had the girl, struggling to hold her with one hand, the crystal shard with the other.

The girl fell to her knees. Bulagrét lifted the crystal dagger high for the kill.

"No!" Shawn screamed, and a nimbus of shimmering colors swirled around him, shooting tendrils of lightning every direction..

The giant crystal exploded, a trillion shards bursting every direction, Litál's and Bulagrét's bodies riddled by deadly shrapnel.

The little girl tried to crawl, but got sucked into the torrent.

Then Shawn had her, holding on tight.

The water still rising, crystals began exploding all around them.

Boom! Boom! Boom!

The rainbows were swirling and bending into undulating shapes, electric sparkles shooting from one crystal to the next.

Boom! Boom!

The ground shook harder.

Higher and higher, the water kept rising. Ten meters, fifteen, twenty.

Tsoo-Ki had hold of Shawn, still gripping two kids.

Then Marcie joined them, all linked together, three adults and six kids clinging to one another for dear life.

Higher they swirled, the whirlpool tightening as the ceiling narrowed, all blinded by the rainbow through the crack above, closer and closer.

Touching the rainbow, becoming part of it, embracing it.

Up higher, a surge of water right to the crack, then pulled back down.

A bigger surge, a wave of water bursting out to wash down the side of the mountain and disappear into cracks in the valley.

Another surge, another wave.

"Try to grab something!" Shawn yelled.

Another surge, and Shawn burst out through the crack, scrabbling to hold on, a leg wedged, clinging with one arm, the other with a girl held under it, a boy's shirt clutched in his hand's vice.

Another surge, water washing over them, pulling almost harder than he could grip, now with Marcie and two more kids wedged in, desperately trying to hold on.

"You sure know how to party!" she shouted at him.

Another surge, each getting stronger.

Tsoo-Ki nearly slipped by, but Shawn hooked him with a leg, the young Tsala clutching two kids by shirt collars. Shawn struggled to pull him behind the broken ledge before the next surge could take him down.

Pulling, pulling, one kid slipping. There!

Another surge, harder yet. No place to go, no way to hold out against all this water.

Another surge, this time not ebbing entirely, a steady flow forming a torrent down the side of the mountain.

Another surge, white-water city.

Brinkley roared on the scene with the chopper. Better hurry, dude—

The chopper skid lowered to within a meter, Brinkley holding the stick steady, reaching down to grab, lift and deposit the little ones. A kid by the shirt collar, a second by the waistband.

Another surge, water pushing against the skid, Brinkley trying to hold steady.

Shawn had to admire the man's skill.

Tsoo-Ki passed his kids up, barely able to hold on. Number three. Number four.

Another surge, an almost solid wall of water now bursting out the crack, pounding down the rock face, disappearing into mist rising from the valley.

Now the older boy, shirt tearing, slipping, got his arm, Brinkley had him. The oldest girl was climbing over, another surge; Shawn lost his grip on her! But she held on to the skid. Brinkley steadied, pulled her up.

Another surge, Marcie slipping!

"Shawn!"

He reached, *and she was gone!*—disappearing in a rush.

"Marcie!" Another surge, and he let go. "Marcie—!"

BRINKLEY WATCHED HELPLESSLY as Shawn and Marcie disappeared into the torrent. He reached out his hand for Tsoo-Ki. The young Indian looked up at him, then down at the roiling stream cascading into the valley, then back again. He shrugged, forced a smile, and let go.

Brinkley's last view of the young Tsala was a final good-bye wave as he disappeared into the depths.

Brinkley lifted off, swooped down, circled around, and searched. Then searched some more.

And kept searching.

Kinte's face appeared on the chopper console's view-screen, Foster behind him with a balled fist at his mouth, head bowed.

"Mr. *Brinkley!* What is *happening?*"

Brinkley checked his fuel gauge, already knowing he would barely make it back to San José. He banked toward the Tsala Village. He needed to set down and tell the villagers what had happened, to steady his nerves.

"Mr. *Brinkley!*"

"We managed to save all six kids," Brinkley answered sadly.

Foster looked up, helpless fear in his eyes.

Kinte lowered his head and ran both hands through his hair.

All Brinkley could say was, "At least we saved the kids."

CHAPTER 16

BRINKLEY SET THE CHOPPER DOWN in the usual spot by the Tsala village. Many of the locals gathered around, reaching for the rescued children, comforting, bringing—of all things—water to drink, fresh fruit. But the shaman and old woman didn't come. They stood at the shore of Lago Amarillo, watching the sky, the rising mist, the rainbow.

He walked up behind them, to tell them Tsoo-Ki had been lost. But no words would come. And he knew they didn't need to hear them.

They understood.

Without even turning to look at him, the old man said, "It is for the goodness."

Brinkley stood there a moment, feeling the ground vibrate again, a rumbling in the distance from the high ridges, the long dormant volcano yawning after long sleep. He thought maybe he should start evacuating these people, but he stood there transfixed, watching the sky, watching the lake.

More rumbling, gusts of steam and soot and tephra ash, the ground shaking intermittently. Water still flowed from the cracked dome where Shawn and Marcie and Tsoo-Ki had swept to their deaths, but the whole ridge was vibrating now, geysers spewing out to join the torrent. Then the water slowed to a trickle and stopped, the crack widening with a groan. Brinkley stood there awestruck, torn between fleeing and watching this natural wonder.

Gusts of steam burst sideways from the rift, farts from some great gaseous giant.

The shimmering cloud made the rainbow shine even more vividly. The steam billowed toward the village like a great cloud, arcing the rainbow with it, bringing it toward them.

The villagers watched. The old man watched. The old woman nodded.

The rainbow reached Lago Amarillo, curving down to touch the surface of the water. The lake started to fizz and steam, boiling under the kiss of magic light.

The water began to move, a slow current around the shoreline, counter-clockwise, another whirlpool on grander scale. The rainbow stretching from the volcano to the lake formed a perfect axis around which the water flowed, now faster, now furious. The center dropped away, a cone forming in the whirling surface, the eye of a liquid tornado. Then came the sucking sound, the water draining from the lake, swirling to the center and disappearing into the ground at the base of a rainbow.

Lower the water dropped, exposing the remnants of ancient buildings, the ancestral Tsala village, caked with mud and debris, but gloriously steeped in history and tradition.

The last of the water swirled into the center, draining away. It disappeared with a reverberating burp, drawn into the ground next to a chantry thousands of years old, its centerpiece a giant six-sided crystal identical to the one in the cave, standing proud again, conduit for the rainbow, beams of prismed light shining from all sides and reaching to kiss the sky.

Then the rumbling turned to a deafening roar, the ground shaking until everybody fell, the ridges at the other end of the rainbow breaking and falling away, the giant cracked dome opening to expose its crystal cavern to the powers of Earth and sky.

And then buzzing, electric lightning bolts, more steam billowing—
Ka-Boom!

The entire volcano exploded, a sparkling cloud of disintegrated crystals filling the sky, glitter sparkling every color of the rainbow as it rained across the countryside, no shard bigger than a grain of sand.

The children laughed and danced, scooping handfuls to throw toward the sky, more sparkles to float and drift with the wind.

The old shaman sat on the ground and buried his face in his hands, but the old woman stood unmoving, watching, waiting.

Boom!

The crystal at the center of the lake bed exploded, more glitter to rain on the village and the fields and the mountains, and to float to other villages and towns, for the wonder and awe of all.

Then came the water, a thundering wall rushing from the collapsed volcano, down through the crevice where the stair steps ran alongside the village.

Brinkley backed away, pulling the old shaman and reaching for the old woman, but she batted his hand away.

The torrent began refilling the lake, washing down broken trees and brush and rolling boulders. A shimmering cloud rose above where the ridges and dome and crystal cavern had once towered, now a vacant space in the landscape, only the iridescent mushroom and rainbow as monument to where it once stood. The lake nearly full, the sudden river slowed, shallowing out.

A single log floated out from the crevice, three soaked people clinging to it.

Shawn and Marcie and Tsoo-Ki.

The old woman raised her arms and wept. The villagers cheered, the old man standing now, one hand held to the sky as if reaching for the rainbow.

The log floated out to bob lazily in the lake. Brinkley raced for the chopper, time to launch a surface rescue.

But the water in the lake started turning again, a whirlpool whirling faster and faster. The log and the trio clinging to it were caught in the current, passing by the people, around to the south, the other side, the north, pulled inexorably toward the center. The water formed a vee again, the lake belching as it began to drain. All of the mud and muck and debris stirred up, the water brown and muddy, spinning around that rainbow axis, its level dropping steadily, the log twirling faster, nearing center.

Brinkley lifted off, the chopper hovering close.

Then the log passed under the rainbow as the last of the water drained. It wedged in the crack at the bottom, leaving three dizzy people standing there in a shiny rock lake bed scoured clean, its sediment washed away.

MARCIE AND TSOO-KI TOOK several awkward steps, then had to steady themselves. Shawn reached to help them, but he could barely keep his own balance.

And then he saw it.

The rainbow from the sky seemed tethered to a wet rock several paces in front of him. He took one step, then another, dropped to his knees, and reached out . . .

His hand passed through and severed the rainbow.

The sky rumbled, the ground shuddered, and the crack behind him snapped shut, splintering the log in a shower of toothpicks.

Then Shawn picked up the jawbreaker, *el cristal de la aldea*. He held it up in the light and grinned. "You guys all right?"

"Like the log ride at Six Flags," Marcie allowed.

They both turned to look at Tsoo-Ki, but he was gone. In his place stood a very old man, with old and wise eyes, one for whom the quest of youth had been the badness, but saving the children had been for the good.

"I am all right if now you see me as I really am," he answered quietly.

Marcie gaped, dumbstruck.

Shawn nodded solemnly.

Water sloshed over their feet, the lake slowly refilling, fed by crystal-clear water from the stairstep waterfall stream.

"We better get out of here," Shawn said, waving Brinkley off, signaling okay. "I can't hold back this water *all* day."

He reached out to help the old man walk, but Tsoo-Ki batted his hand away, drawing himself up proudly. "I have *two good legs*, you know." Then he smiled, adding, "Thanks to Tsawa-Ki." Still, he walked slightly stooped, slowly and carefully.

The villagers rushed out into the lake bed, meeting the heroes halfway, the little girl and several children doting on Tsoo-Ki.

"Whale-tico! Whale-tico!"

"What is Whale-tico?" Marcie asked.

Smiling proudly, the old Indian corrected her, "Abueltico—grandpa."

"Look!" Shawn exclaimed. The crystal-clear water brought schools of fish, turtles, frogs—the Tsala lake teeming with life for the first time in millennia.

As the crowd reached the shore where the old woman waited, everybody parted, a clear path between her and Tsoo-Ki.

She shook her head. "My husband and his cousin were being foolish men."

Having landed, Brinkley trotted over. "Where's Tsoo-Ki?"

Shawn pointed at the old man now hugging the old woman. Brinkley looked puzzled.

Marcie wondered, "The crystals had made him young?"

Shawn shrugged. "I guess he just *thought* he was young, and so did we—at first." He didn't offer to explain.

Ka-Boom!

The volcano exploded again, a fine shower of glitter blanketing the sky. And the rainbow disappeared.

Everybody moved toward the village center, birds darting among the glitters, an iguana scurrying out of the way. Having trouble walking, Tsoo-Ki had to stop, sit on a rock, and rest a minute. He looked exhausted, weak and fragile.

Shawn tried to hand him the village crystal, but he wouldn't even touch it, gesturing toward the old shaman standing solemnly off to the side. "It is for all the Tsala peoples, for the goodness."

The shaman accepted it reverently, turning to walk toward the building, toward the chantry, the place of honor for the ancient symbol of a people who always believed, even when they made mistakes, in doing what was right.

"We'll come visit you again soon," Shawn promised the exhausted old man on the rock being cradled by his elderly wife, surrounded by generations of children and grandchildren.

Tsoo-Ki looked up, tears in his eyes, and shook his head. "My time is to be very short. I am grateful you have made me whole again, and that you have saved the children. If you come back, I will not be here. And this is not your place. You must go on, to find and help others."

Shawn was at a loss for words.

Tsoo-Ki smiled through his tears. "You must go and be the Rich Mr. Fixx."

REUNION TIME! MOTHERS AND THEIR KIDS, laughing and hugging, raiding the private aircraft's buffet, excited about the trip to Houston, planning for a better future.

Brinkley would stay behind to oversee shipping the Jet Ranger back to the U.S. Moolhuizen would travel with him after debriefing his operatives, securing the apartments, and mopping up miscellaneous details. Shawn lingered with them in the hanger, awkwardly trying to find a way to express his thanks for, um, you know.

Yeah, they knew.

He walked across the tarmac and boarded the FBG 757, smiled at all the mayhem, gave Marcie a hug . . . but he felt distracted, looking around like he'd lost something.

"Where's Judy Morey?"

"Said she had her *own* ride," Marcie answered, watching Shawn carefully for his reaction. "She took the little Poeky boy."

"Her *own* ride? What? Where?"

Marcie pointed out the window. He rushed over in time to see a Gulfstream jet taxi to the end of the runway, turn, then take off into the late-afternoon sky.

Marcie was still watching him. "I gather there's—shall we say—more than meets the eye here?"

Shawn waved her off. "Isn't there always?"

"Hmmm . . ."

John Guyton announced they'd been cleared for take-off, that everybody needed to find a seat and strap in.

Anthro-twit spotted Shawn and tried to commandeer him. "I say, did you learn anything more about the Tsala?"

"Yeah. It was a hoax. We checked out the lake where Milo drowned and found an old man who remembered it. He said some locals had concocted that Tsala hokum just to lure tourists."

"Just as I suspected."

Yeah, right.

During take-off, the five-year-old girl who'd been in the crystal cavern regaled the group with fantastic stories about magic rainbows. Everybody enjoyed her fantasy—didn't believe it, but it was fun to imagine that maybe it *could* have happened.

Just maybe.

Once they achieved altitude, Shawn and Marcie migrated back to his private suite and positioned themselves in front of the view screen. Time to check in with the big Jamaican mother hen.

"Reports of volcanic activity *have* been confirmed," Kinte verified. "Not considered an actual eruption, early indications are that it was an expansion of gasses in pockets and caves beneath the surface. The layers of rock buckled in the explosion, then collapsed on themselves and left behind a series of deep, clear lakes. I trust you consider your adventure a success?"

"We shut down Bulagrét permanently and saved a lot of people's lives," Shawn allowed.

"And we proved that Shawn's Mr. Fixx powers channel rainbows and stuff," Marcie added.

Shawn shook his head no.

"Whatta you mean *no?*"

"Come on, Marcie. You heard him. It was volcanic gasses building up and exploding. And *of course* you get rainbows when mist fills the sky on a sunny day."

"Yeah, what about curing Tsoo-Ki?"

"Actually, Ms. McNaught," Kinte cut in, "further analysis of the tests have led to the conclusion that his paralysis was temporary, caused by inflammation of a pre-existing condition pressing against the sciatic nerves in his lower spine."

"What condition?" Shawn wondered.

"Severe arthritis. Not uncommon for somebody his age—"

"But he was barely out of his *teens!*" she argued.

Kinte looked puzzled. "I am referring to the elderly native fellow I spoke to via satellite in the chopper, the man sitting between you, wearing an orange shirt, the one we had tested for paralysis at the hospital."

Foster appeared in the shot. "What's goin' on, Marcie? You seein' things like rainbow auras again—things that nobody else can see?"

She growled at him, at Shawn, at Kinte—then sat back and sighed in resignation.

This issue would come up again someday.

"If you will excuse me," Kinte begged off, "I have some important communications coming in."

Good-byes all around, the big Jamaican headed toward his private quarters.

Foster grinned at Shawn and Marcie from the view-screen. "I understand Bulagrét was a casualty. Well, our claim has been preserved. By the time it's settled, we'll own her resort and apartments and anything else we can find."

"I want to funnel a chunk of it toward solving some problems down there," Shawn pointed out.

"Wouldn't expect anything less, Shawn."

"Foster," Marcie announced, "I wanna start an orchid business down there, too."

"I'll put somebody right on it. May need *you* to be a consultant."

She was grinning.

"You mind letting me talk privvy to Shawn for a minute?" Foster ventured.

She kissed Shawn on the top of his head and mussed his unruly hair on her way out.

"Don't suppose you came up with any big crystals for the energy research," Foster wondered.

Shawn shook his head. "No, and the cavern is gone now. Besides, the big ones exploded, too. This I *know*."

"That's what I was afraid of. Oh well. One more thing . . ." He lifted a small case onto the console, looking around to make sure nobody else could see. "I was walking the beach this morning—don't tell Marcie this—when I saw a huge rainbow. I was standing there admiring it, and something washed up on the sand right at my feet. What should I do with it?"

He pulled out the jawbreaker pendant, the stone given to them by Bulagrét and mounted on a gold chain by Marcie.

Shawn snorted, rubbed his face, looked at it like he didn't believe his eyes, then shook his head.

"Foster, do me a *big* favor. Get *rid* of it!"

KINTE ENTERED HIS PRIVATE SUITE and sat at the communications console. A beautiful young face with hazel, gold-flecked eyes and long chestnut hair filled his screen.

"Mr. Bilál!"

"Greetings, Miss Geissánte. I trust you are well?"

"It's legally *Geiss* now on both continents," she corrected. "And Carlicíta is now just plain Carly."

He nodded acknowledgment. "I appreciate the impromptu assistance you provided in Costa Rica."

She waved him off. "I was there to look out for Poeky. At least I managed to help save her son. I've already contacted his grandmother. She's looking forward to taking him. Of course, I'll provide some assistance, try to keep an eye on things."

"I understand." He *did*, too. "My investigation has determined that the bus you were on was sabotaged, sand in the fuel tank. Tell me, how did you arrange another bus at the last moment?"

She grinned and shrugged her shoulders. "One just came along. Musta been my lucky day."

He studied her for a moment, then allowed the slightest smile. "I see. So, what are your plans now?"

"Drop the kid, take care of some business in Houston, then I'm off to France on a new enterprise I've fallen behind on. By the way, my sister's son just graduated high school—"

"He is to be commended."

"But then you know that, I'm sure. Just like you know about the college trust fund he just found out he's had for nearly sixteen years."

"Well, that is fortunate for him. I hope he makes good use of it."

"Maricíta said to thank you."

"I am sure I do not know for what." Quickly side-stepping the subject, he asked, "Is your sister still successful with her dress-shop in Torrémoliños?"

"Oh yes. She's *very* happy." Carly hesitated. "Mr. Bilal? I've always been a little reluctant to ask, but now I have to know. Why, so long ago, did you come back to Málaga and do so much for my sister, a common prostitute, a woman who'd been—you know—*with* young Jeremy? I mean, I would think you'd be angry."

Kinte regarded her for a moment, then sighed. It was hard for him sometimes, thinking back to those last years of Jeremy's life. "But she had *not* what you call 'been with' him," he explained. "Young Jeremy confessed to me some weeks later what he had been up to, that he *had* kissed her, but that she had refused to go any further. It had hurt his feelings. I went back and talked with her, and she explained to me why. She understood he could easily be taken advantage of, that he was wealthy, innocent, and eager. She told me he still needed to learn that physical pleasure and love can be two very different experiences, that you can enjoy either without the other, but that together they can be—well, you know."

Carly smiled, her big hazel eyes glistening. "Yes, I know."

"I offered to help her move someplace with greater opportunities, but she was more concerned that you and her son have that chance. I vowed to make sure all three of you would. You see," he said, leaning closer to the screen, "she cared enough for my adopted son, Shawn's brother, to teach him one of the most important lessons in his tragically short life. I will always be grateful."

A single tear crept down Carly's cheek. "You know, I was only ten back then. I used to watch from the window in the shop across the street. I was fascinated with that eleven-year-old brother of Jeremy's. My sister told me to keep my eye on him, because Jeremy had told her that someday little Shawn would grow up to be Rich Mr. Fixx."

Kinte stroked his goatee, allowing just a bit more smile. "She was right."

"Yeah." Carly smiled, too. "I didn't understand what she meant, but *now* I do. Now it's crystal clear."

PFFFFFFFFFFFFFF-BOOM!

The crowd queuing outside The Gaseous Giant went wild.

A nondescript van pulled up, goons surrounding them when Shawn and Marcie stepped out, the special guests ushered past all the hopefuls and whisked straight inside. No, no private room—what fun is that?—but Marcie'll let you know who-all she wants killed later.

They wound up standing at a high-table, a buxom waitress in elfin costume with Saturn rings around her head serving Belgian beer and clear soda with chunks of fruit.

Marcie spotted some old friends across the room. She waved, signaled she'd be over in a few to say hi and, well, we'll see.

"You run off and have the time of your life tonight," Shawn offered. "I'll flop at the Galveston house, relax, take it easy, catch up on episodes of the original *Family Affair* and that madcap Mr. French."

"Such a gallant Fixx-dude. But I don't mind hangin' out with you and Mr. French—"

"They're calling you." He gestured toward her friends. "Go see what's shakin'—and who's shakin' it."

"I'll be right back," she promised, taking her drink and starting to work her way through the crowd.

A big fat guy got in her way, drunkenly trying to flirt with her, his skinny friend urging him to leave and head back to the hotel.

"I got powers'll make you *moan*, babe!" the drunk declared, spilling beer on his shirt.

"Leave her alone, Wally. C'mon, let's—"

"Whassa matter? Can't you feel it? You're gonna lose control—"

Marcie pushing past, he grabbed her arm. She held up a hand, stopping goons from coming every direction to teach Wally how to fly. She pulled his hand free and smiled up at him. "Touch me again and *I'll* show you power."

Shawn watched him throw the oddest tantrum, ripping his watch off, slamming it on the floor and stomping it to smithereens, then getting on his hands and knees to pick desperately through the debris apparently looking for something.

Marcie talked to her friends, then returned a few minutes later. "They want me to go to Seattle with 'em—some kinda big gathering tomorrow."

Shawn grinned and put his arm around her. "Have fun."

"You're sure?"

He gave her the look.

"Okay, no more arguments—*if* you'll answer my question."

"What question is that?" he wondered innocently—like he didn't know. She'd been asking it since they boarded in Costa Rica. "Then you're gonna miss your party because I'm *not* telling you what happened with me and her in the suite that night."

She grinned. He enjoyed being so mysterious. Then she remembered something else. "Hey! Whatever happened to Scallywag?"

"Oh, he probably found some pretty tail he liked more than me."

She started to wise-crack, but he was looking across the room, holding his crystal-inlaid money-clip, fingering it absently. She turned to see what fascinated him.

It was a beautiful young woman, big gold-flecked hazel eyes, long silky chestnut hair—with a very familiar rainbow-hued iguana perched on her shoulders.

Scallywag winked, and so did she.

Shawn kissed Marcie on top of her head. "See you back in Monterey."

"Shawn D'Fixx, *now* I know what happened that night." Marcie wagged her eyebrows mischievously.

"Oh?"

"You slipped her the lizard!"

ABOUT BRAY ZEPHENS

B ray Zephens grew up in the Detroit suburbs and earned his degrees at the University of Michigan. He designed and ran special programs, corporate training, then television production. He has composed and produced 1,000+ pieces of TV music while establishing pizzerias. As a publisher with his own company serving 100+ authors, he's written novels, short fiction, essays, how-to, and scripts under various names while editing the best work of others. A longtime scuba diver and film buff, Bray is mostly retired but always itchy.

As Stephen Geez

Novels

What Sara Saw
Fantasy Patch
Dance of the Lights
Papala Skies
Zhasou Pure
Invigilator

Short Story Collection

Comes This Time to Float

Essays

Been There, Noted That

GeezWriter How-To Series

GeezWriter How-To: Outlining
GeezWriter How-To: Indie Publishing
GeezWriter How-To: Dialogue
GeezWriter How-To: Point of View
GeezWriter How-To: Narrative

Fresh Ink Group
Independent Multi-media Publisher

Fresh Ink Group / Push Pull Press
Voice of Indie / GeezWriter

❧

Hardcovers
Softcovers
All Ebook Platforms
Audiobooks
Worldwide Distribution

❧

Indie Author Services
Book Development, Editing, Proofing
Graphic/Cover Design
Video/Trailer Production
Website Creation
Social Media Management
Writing Contests
Writers' Blogs
Podcasts

❧

Authors
Editors
Artists
Experts
Professionals

❧

FreshInkGroup.com
info@FreshInkGroup.com
X: @FreshInkGroup
Facebook.com/FreshInkGroup
LinkedIn: Fresh Ink Group
Instagram: @FreshInkGroup and @FIGPublishing

Fresh Ink Group
FreshInkGroup.com